LAST OF THE

TEXAS

CAMP

There are six books in this series
FORTUNES OF THE BLACK HILLS
by *STEPHEN BLY*

Book #1
Beneath a Dakota Cross

Book #2
Shadow of Legends

Book #3
The Long Trail Home

Book #4
Friends and Enemies

Book #5
Last of the Texas Camp

Book #6
The Next Roundup

For information on other books by this author, write:
Stephen Bly
P.O. Box 157
Winchester, Idaho 83555
or check out his Web site at:
www.blybooks.com

Fortunes of the Black Hills

LAST OF THE
TEXAS
CAMP

STEPHEN BLY

Authors Choice Press
New York Lincoln Shanghai

LAST OF THE TEXAS CAMP

Authors Choice Press
an imprint of iUniverse, Inc.

iUniverse books may be ordered through booksellers or by contacting:

iUniverse
2021 Pine Lake Road, Suite 100
Lincoln, NE 68512
www.iuniverse.com
1-800-Authors (1-800-288-4677)

Originally published by Broadman & Holman Publishers

Certain characters in this work are historical figures, and certain events portrayed
did take place. However, this is a work of fiction. All of the other characters,
names, and events as well as all places, incidents, organizations, and dialogue in this
novel are either the products of the author's imagination or are used fictitiously.

All Scripture citation is from the King James Version.

ISBN: 978-0-595-45143-2

Printed in the United States of America

For

Len & Carolyn

---

*It is vain for you to rise up early,
to sit up late,
to eat the bread of sorrows:
for so he giveth his beloved sleep.*

Psalm 127:2 (KJV)

The Fortunes of the Black Hills - 1895

Henry "Brazos" Fortune (70) - Sarah Ruth Fortune (d. 1872)
children
Todd
Samuel
Robert
Patricia & Veronica (indentical twins, d. 1869)
Dacee June

Todd Fortune (44) - Rebekah (Jacobson) Fortune (40)
children
Hank (14)
Camilla (13)
Nettie (12)
Stuart (11)
Casey (9)

Samuel Fortune (43) - Abigail (O'Neill Gordon) Fortune (40)
children
Amber (Gordon) (21)
Garrett (8)

Robert Fortune (41) - Jamie Sue (Milan) Fortune (41)
children
(Little) Frank (19)
Patricia & Veronica (identical twins, 17)

Dacee June (Fortune) Toluca (31) - Carty Toluca (31)
children
Elita (8)
Jehane (7)
Ninete (6)

AUTHOR'S NOTES

For many in America, 1895 was the middle of a great depression. Two years before, the silver producers of Colorado had shut down all mines and smelters to force the government to take steps to assist the industry. But the plan backfired; not only did the all-time-low silver prices of seventy-seven cents an ounce remain, but in addition, the entire stock market collapsed, leaving the country in economic chaos.

In February of '95, drought-stricken Nebraska farmers asked for a bailout of one-and-one-half million dollars. They were selling their horses for as little as twenty-five cents each, and hay was going for two dollars a ton.

Across the Pacific, Hawaiian Queen Liliuokalani was forced to sign papers abdicating and abolishing her monarchy. Also in that year, the Japanese defeated the Chinese at Wei-hai-Wei, the Abyssinians triumphed over the Italians at Amba Alagi, and the Cubans fought Spain for their independence.

People were reading H. G. Wells's *The Time Machine*, W. B. Yeats's *Poems*, or Henry James's *The Middle Years*. In St. Petersberg, Russian audiences heard for the first time Tchaikovsky's *Swan Lake*. That was the year Marconi invented radio telegraphy, the Lumieres developed a motion picture camera, and a man with vision named King C. Gillette came up with an idea for a safety razor.

TEXAS CAMP

Out West, Utah was making its sixth attempt at statehood. Bannock Indians in Wyoming had surrounded 250 white settlers in Jackson Hole. And anti-immigrant rioting occurred in Colorado coal mines where six Italians were lynched by masked mobs. Most all of that had little effect on the northern Black Hills town of Deadwood, South Dakota. With an economy based on gold, not silver, Deadwood enjoyed a hardrock boom and employed more miners than any year in the past decade.

But even economic boom had little consolation for the families on Forest Hill at the top of the Main Street stairs. For them it was a season of drastic change. And that meant a world turned upside down. In *Richard III*, Shakespeare said, "Sorrow breaks seasons and reposing hours, Makes the night morning, and the noontide night."

The world stands still for those in grief and faith hovers around us just waiting to be asked to assist. The Fortune family couldn't care less what was happening in Hawaii, China, or Abyssinia. Sorrow hung in the air and filled the lungs of every member of this pioneer family.

Such grief is the raw building block of the future. With trust in the Lord Jesus Christ and the help of the Holy Spirit, it can be a foundation of decades of spiritual growth . . . or it can topple and crush those who are closest to it.

Like a barbell, the heavy weight of grief can strengthen or crush.

Dacee June was not sure which would happen to her.

But she did know the sorrow would come, and there was no way she could stop it.

Stephen Bly
Broken Arrow Crossing, Idaho
Fall of '01

CHAPTER ONE

Deadwood, South Dakota . . .
Wednesday, July 3, 1895

We know the day a memory begins, but we have no idea how long it will last. It may fade within moments. Or we shoulder it to our grave. Some memories lie dormant, like seeds that wait for their time in the sun.

"Mama, these must be the sweetest-smelling bluebonnets in all of Coryell County." Dacee June Fortune pulled her long dress above her stocking-covered ankles and ran up the gentle slope of the green Texas hillside.

The lady with a long white cotton dress and brown hair stacked perfectly on her head flashed a wide easy smile. "Baby, you wait for your sisters."

TEXAS CAMP

Five-year-old Dacee June skipped back and clutched her mother's calloused hand. "Mama, I'm not a baby."

"Sweetheart, you will always be my baby."

"Sammy says that some day you and Daddy might make another baby and then I wouldn't be the youngest."

"Oh, he said that, did he?"

"Is it true?" Dacee June asked.

"I'm afraid not. Your daddy looked at you on the day you were born and said, 'Sarah Ruth, looks like this one is perfect. We might as well stop because it can't get any better than Dacee June.'"

They walked hand in hand up the gentle slope toward a short live oak tree.

Dacee June let out a deep sigh. "Mama, isn't this the best day in the whole world?"

"You just might be right." Sarah Ruth Fortune stopped and waited for her identical twin nine-year-old daughters to catch up. "What did you two do with your shoes?" she challenged them.

Patricia glanced over her shoulder toward the now-empty, narrow dirt road. "We left them in the wagon, Mama." She pulled off her round straw hat and fanned herself.

"Daddy said it was all right to go barefoot," Veronica added, her identical straw hat now also in her hand.

"I suppose your father would give you girls the moon if he could figure out how to lasso and dally it to a Texas saddle." Sarah Ruth stared down at the dry dark brown dirt squished between the twins' toes.

Dacee June tugged on her earlobe. "Mama, can I take off my shoes?"

Mrs. Fortune hugged each twin as they hiked the hillside. "You see what you two have started?"

Veronica ran her fingers across her mother's dangled hand. "Let her go barefoot, Mama; it feels so good."

Patricia had a spring in her step. "You ought to go barefoot, too, Mama!" she sang out.

"I just might!" Sarah Ruth laughed. "It is good to get back into the hill country. I'm tired of the hot land around Brownsville."

The twins pranced into the middle of the huge wildflower patch while Mrs. Fortune removed her lace-up shoes and white cotton stockings, then helped Dacee June out of hers.

"Can I lie in the bluebonnets? Oh, please Mama, please. . . . I won't get my dress dirty . . . I love lyin' in the bluebonnets and staring up at the clear sky," Veronica called out.

"It's just like being on a cloud in heaven," Patricia added.

"We'll all lie in the bluebonnets," Sarah Ruth announced.

"Oh, yes!" Dacee June clapped her hands and sprinted up to her sisters. She spun around and flopped down as if on a feather mattress.

Above her spread a pale blue sky without a cloud in sight. The bright yellow ball just past dead center blasted all the soft soil with heat and eye-closing brightness. Her head pressed on the dirt, the bluebonnets seemed to tower above her like beautiful wicks of perfume, flooding the hillside with the most wonderful aroma. The wildflower-perfumed air tasted almost like dessert.

Her mother collapsed beside Dacee June. She unpinned her hat, tossed it on the wildflowers, and eased herself back. The five-year-old felt her mother's hand reach for hers. On her left, Veronica grabbed her other hand. All four Fortunes sprawled out in the field of flowers.

"Mama, can we stay here forever?" Patricia asked.

"Oh, yes, Mama," Veronica added. "Do you think heaven will smell this good?"

Sarah Ruth laughed and laughed.

Dacee June thought it was the nicest laugh in the world. It meant Mama was having a good day. It meant the world was right and life was fun and dangers were past and no one was hurt and there was nothing ugly or scary for miles and miles. It was a good day to hug and giggle.

"But, Mama," Dacee June blurted out, "we can't stay here forever without Daddy and Todd and Sammy and Bobby!"

"You're right, punkin'. We might just miss those boys."

"I wouldn't miss Sammy," Veronica pouted. "He told me my embroidery looked like sawdust on the dance floor after a Saturday night in Matamoros."

"Well, it does!" Patricia added. "I don't know what the dance floor looks like, but your sewing is rather unkempt."

"I'm not sure how Sammy knows what that dance floor looks like either," Sarah Ruth said.

"Mama, what's a mattress-more?" Dacee June asked.

"Matamoros is a town in Mexico across the river from Brownsville . . ." Patricia explained, but the drifting sound from downhill caused her to stop.

At the clear sound of hoofbeats, Veronica sat straight up. "It must be Daddy and the boys!"

Patricia leaped to her feet. "They had the wagon, not saddle horses."

Sarah Ruth sat up and shaded her eyes.

Dacee June struggled to rise, but her mother's hand on her chest kept her down in the tall bluebonnets. "Stay there, baby, and don't move," she whispered. "Don't say a word."

Several horses approached from the low side of the hill. Her mother stood and brushed down her skirt as Patricia and Veronica clung on both sides. The three acted as a shield between the horsemen and the reclining Dacee June.

She tried to peer between the flowers but could only see a half-dozen blurry mounted men. She squinted her eyes but still couldn't see the men. From her prone position, her mother looked as tall as her daddy. She held her breath and chewed on her lower lip.

"Are they Indians?" Patricia whispered.

4

"I don't think so," Sarah Ruth replied.

"That one looks like an Indian," Veronica mumbled.

"What are you doin' up here?" Dacee June heard a man shout.

She covered her mouth with her hand, tasted Texas dirt, and clamped her lips together.

"We are enjoying the beautiful Texas spring and the field of bluebonnets," her mother answered, her voice very loud.

"All by yourselves?" the same voice asked.

Sarah Ruth folded her arms and Dacee June gritted her teeth.

"What difference does that make?" Mrs. Fortune demanded.

"There ain't no house around."

Dacee June couldn't tell who was talking but knew it was someone different.

"There's a house just a few miles up that draw," Sarah Ruth snapped back.

One of the dust-covered men stood in his stirrups and gazed around. "Where's your rig or your horses?"

Mrs. Fortune slipped her arms around the twins' shoulders and clutched them close to her. "Why do you ask?"

"It's dangerous for women to be out on the prairie all alone." The man sat back down in his saddle. "The Comanches could come along and steal your horses."

"Or your daughters!" another of the men laughed. It was a guttural, ugly laugh.

Her mother's voice was now flat, without emotion. "Thank you for your concern, but we're fine."

Dacee June heard a horse ride closer. "Don't seem right to leave women out on the prairie all alone. We can give you a ride. Just climb up here and we'll ride double."

"I get the mama," the man with the very ugly deep voice rasped.

"And I get one of them girls," another man mumbled.

"Which one?" a third man challenged.

Dacee June spied her sisters hiding behind their mother.

"Don't matter which one, they look exactly the same after a bottle of whiskey."

"They are the same," the lead man explained.

"I'll be. Twins. Ain't that handy?"

Dacee June didn't know if it was the blazing Texas sun or the fire inside that turned her mother's neck bright red.

"I do not like the tone and implication of your voices. This is not a fit conversation for women or children. I will have to insist that you ride on out of here immediately!" she snapped.

"You don't like our tone? You better get used to it, lady, because we've been on the run ever' since we left the Indian Territory," the man with the deepest voice growled.

"We're goin' to hole up down in Mexico, and we don't intend to hole up alone, if you catch my drift." A man chuckled in the same way that some people laugh at a chicken running around the yard with its head chopped off.

Patricia laid her head against her mother's side and began to cry.

"I'm scared, Mama," Veronica muttered.

"You are frightening my daughters with this crude talk. That's enough. Have you men no ounce of decency?" Sarah Ruth demanded.

"Decency?" one of the men shouted. "Decency? Woman, I got the decency shot plum out of me at Vicksburg when I woke up on the battlefield and the dogs was lickin' my blood. They stole my shirt, my britches, my hat, and my boots. I had to throw rocks at the dogs and drag myself for three miles to a creek and some shade."

Dacee June felt the sweat stream down her forehead as she watched her mother clutch the twins.

"I am truly sorry for your war experiences, but that gives you no excuse for improper behavior." Sarah Ruth's voice was a blend of anger and fear.

"We ain't lookin' for your sympathy."

"Yeah, what we're lookin' for is . . ."

6

"It's perfectly obvious what you are lookin' for," Sarah Ruth hollered as if signaling a person a hundred yards away. "Just ride on out of here before my husband and sons return. They are all well-armed, excellent marksmen, and not at all tolerant of those who would harass us."

"We ain't seen nobody for miles. I reckon that's a bluff. I'm tired of you talkin'. Y'all can come with us peaceful, or we'll hog-tie you."

"My daddy is Brazos Fortune, and he'll shoot you all dead!" Veronica called out.

"Fortune? You mean that traitor?"

"Our daddy is not a traitor!" Patricia shouted.

"I heard he wouldn't fight for the Confederacy."

"He spent the war running the blockade with Captain King down at Brownsville," Sarah Ruth asserted.

"But he wasn't at Vicksburg!" the man growled.

"Nor was he at Port Gibson, Champion's Hill, or the Big Black River, but that has little to do with the present situation. I want you all to leave right now!" Mrs. Fortune demanded.

Dacee June noticed her mother's hands quiver as she spoke.

"You're goin' to do what we say, and you're goin' to do it right now . . ." a deep voice demanded.

The bullet exploded from somewhere up the hill beyond the live oak tree. Dacee June heard the report and peeked through the bluebonnets. Dust flew and horses reared in panic. Mrs. Fortune shoved Veronica and Patricia to the ground. "Stay down, girls," she demanded, then stood tall.

A wonderful voice with the authority of Moses or Elijah filtered down the hill. "Back away, boys, or the next shot goes through that gray shirt!"

"It's daddy!" Veronica whispered.

The three girls continued to lie in the wildflowers. The twins on their stomach, Dacee on her back.

"I don't see you, Fortune!" a man screamed.

7

"He's got that fifty-caliber Sharps," another murmured. "We don't have to see him for him to reach us."

"We got you surrounded!" Brazos Fortune shouted. "Throw down!"

"I don't see any . . ."

Like at a pond at early morning during a duck hunt, Dacee June heard three loud shotgun explosions in succession.

Whump.

Whump.

Whump.

"They're all around us!" one of the men shouted.

"I ain't never been surrounded by no one I cain't see! Show yourself, Fortune!" another hollered.

Veronica pushed herself up on one elbow. "There's daddy at the top of the hill," she shouted.

Dacee tried to turn and watch the hillside, still lying in the blue-bonnets.

"We cain't reach him with the pistols."

"The next bullet goes through the gray shirt," Brazos yelled again as he ambled down the hill, the big-bore carbine at his shoulder. "Ride on out, boys!"

"We ain't backin' away from here. There's six of us and only one of you."

"Four of us, you heard the shots," Brazos called out.

"And there's six of us!" one of them shouted.

"But we've got position," Brazos said. "The worse we can do is lay four of you dead."

"I don't see 'em."

"You can see me," Brazos shouted. "You should be worried, boys. You heard shotguns and don't know where they are. They could have snuck around behind you by now." Brazos stomped closer. "No telling which one of you will be the first to die today."

One man twisted in the saddle and stared down the hill. "There ain't no one behind us."

A shotgun blast sounded from down the mountain. The horses danced and whinnied. Dacee June chewed on her tongue as she stared through the bluebonnets.

"Someone's behind us now!" one of the men shouted. "Come on, Tracy, let's ride."

"I ain't backin' down!" the man screamed.

"Then make your move," Brazos replied as he stepped up next to the girls. He towered above them. Dacee June figured at that moment he was probably a hundred feet tall. "I'm willin' to die for my family. You got to ask if you're willin' to die tryin' to take them from me. I can guarantee the man in the gray shirt is dead the instant I pull this trigger."

Dacee June watched his set jaw, frozen glare, and the thick mustache dropping like a frown across the sun-baked face.

"Come on, Tracy, ain't no reason to get anyone shot."

"I ain't goin' to take a .50 caliber slug for this," another hollered.

"We ain't through with you, Fortune! We'll be comin' back!" the one called Tracy growled.

"Why?" The word flew out of her father's mouth like a dart.

"I will be back. You can bank on it!"

The horses and riders retreated, and Veronica and Patricia crawled up on their knees to watch. Her mother's long dress caught the breeze. When it drifted back Dacee June could see her mother's bare toes buried in the dark Texas dirt.

"Todd! Sammy! Bobby! Come on in, boys," Brazos called out, "but keep your guns to your shoulder."

The twins jumped up and rushed out to meet their teenage brothers. Sarah Ruth threw her arms around Brazos, and he hugged her tight.

TEXAS CAMP

All Dacee June could see was a blue Texas sky, the sun-blinded outline of her mother and father's embrace, and tall bluebonnets springing out of the ground beside her.

Then he spied her lying there.

"Howdy, young lady," Brazos smiled, still holding Sarah Ruth. "Are you playin' hide-and-seek?"

Dacee June nodded.

"I found you first. Does that mean I get a hug and kiss?" Dacee June nodded again.

She was scooped off her bed of flowers by her daddy's right arm. His thick mustache tickled her nose. His lips felt chapped, but Dacee June thought it was a wonderful kiss, perhaps the best in her entire life.

Brazos pulled away. "How's my little darlin'? You aren't scared, are you?"

She shook her head.

One of her brothers tapped on her shoulder, but she couldn't tell which one.

"Lil' Sis . . . hey, it's my turn."

She turned and blinked her eyes. "Huh?" she murmured.

This time the voice was a deep baritone. "I said, it's my turn!"

She looked for a teenager but saw a tall, thin, gray-headed man. "Bobby?"

"It's Sammy . . ." He rubbed her shoulders, then the back of her neck. "Come on Lil' Sis, wake up."

The clean air of Texas faded to a stuffy room above a Main Street hardware store in Deadwood, South Dakota. The bluebonnets were no more than a patchwork quilt. The bright sun was only a bare electric bulb in the hall that reflected into the curtain-drawn bedroom. The sweet smell of bluebonnets dissipated into the aroma of a menthyl-soaked towel and suspended dust that was a permanent feature of every room in the gulch. The gray-headed brother tapping on her shoulder was forty-three years old.

10

"Wake up, Sis. It's my turn," Sam Fortune insisted.

She sat up in the hard oak rocking chair, and the quilt dropped to the floor. Perspiration beaded her forehead and wet the band of her high-necked collar. She rubbed her eyes and studied the frail, sleeping man in the bed beside her.

Sam took her by the hand and led her to the hall. She brushed her hair back over her shoulders. "I don't know how he hangs on," she whispered.

"I don't know why," Sammy countered. "He's been pinin' for Mama for almost twenty-five years. You'd think he'd just let go."

"Maybe it's me." Dacee June walked to the head of the stairs. "I just can't let go, Sammy. It's different for you boys. You've been out on your own. You know how to take care of yourself. He's always been here to help me. I've been his little girl my whole life. Sammy, I don't know if I can survive without being his little girl. It sounds horrible, doesn't it? I'm thirty-one years old, married, and have three wonderful daughters. But I don't know what I'm goin' to do without him. I really don't."

"I reckon the Lord can take care of that. Now Rebekah has breakfast cooked up at the house," Sam reported. "I think the whole gang is meetin' there this mornin'. That was the plan."

Dacee June dabbed tears with her dress sleeve and took a deep breath. "I was dreamin' about him and Mama when you woke me up."

"Were you in the field of bluebonnets again?"

"Yes, Sammy, it's the only image of Mama I have left."

He hugged her shoulder. "It's a good one, darlin'. No reason to remember how she looked after she took sick."

"What image will we have of Daddy?" she probed. "Will we remember him all weak and shriveled up like this?"

"Nope, I'll always remember the time he mounted that big sorrel stallion and bucked him right through the barn wall without losing even a stirrup. There were boards and splinters all over the place; but he rode him to a standstill, climbed down, handed me the rein, and said, 'That's the way you break a stubborn one, son.'"

"How old were you?"

"That was the year you were born, Lil' Sis, so I must have been about twelve."

"I suppose I'll always picture him riding through the blizzard out on the prairie to rescue me. He's always been there to rescue me." She leaned over and kissed her brother's cheek. "I guess you and Todd and Bobby will have to rescue me now."

"I reckon your husband can do that, Lil' Sis. Carty's a good man."

"Yes, and I'd better go rescue him from the girls, so he can come to work."

"Nettie and Camilla are with them, last I saw. Carty is downstairs opening up the store. He's the hardest-workin' one in the tribe. I think he's still trying to prove he's worthy of Brazos Fortune's daughter," Sam said. "Go on. I'm going to talk to daddy about cattle prices and tall grass and a mild gulf breeze." Sam disappeared into the bedroom apartment.

Even the air in the hardware store felt fresher than in the upstairs apartment. From the top of the stairs, Dacee June could see her husband's thinning hair as he instructed his clerks about some shipment that was going to the mines. She stared at her nephew, Little Frank. At nineteen, he stood taller than his father. Next to him, Quint Trooper rocked back on his heels and flashed the heart-stopping, dimpled grin that had captured the eye of every girl twelve to twenty-four in Deadwood. The store was still closed, and only a few of the electric lights were turned on.

There was a musty smell racked with steel, iron, tools, leather, ready-mixed paints, and assorted mining parts. Some items had been on the shelves only a day or two. Some of the others had been displayed for years. Some, Dacee was sure, had been stacked in boxes when the store first opened in the spring of '76.

One lone man stretched out in a well-worn wheelchair by the cast-iron woodstove in the far corner of the room. His bald head was perfectly proportioned to his thin face and pointed chin. He held a dark blue mug in his hand and seemed to be staring at its contents.

Dacee June dabbed the corner of her eyes with her handkerchief, then stuffed it back in the sleeve of her long dress.

"Good mornin', Quiet Jim," she called out.

An instant smile brightened the old man's face. "Good mornin', Dacee June, darlin'." Then the smile faded. "How is he?"

She scooted a chair over and plopped down. She reached out for his free hand. "He's the same, Quiet Jim. He keeps hanging on and none of us know why."

"The Lord knows," Quiet Jim murmured.

"That's what Sammy said too. It's just so hard. He doesn't talk. He doesn't respond. He just sleeps and sleeps or opens his eyes and stares up at the ceiling." She took a big sigh and let it out slowly. "I'm sorry, I thought I could visit without tearing up."

"It's OK, Dacee June. You know how I feel. Never has been a finer man or a more loyal friend than your daddy. It wasn't supposed to be this way, you know." He gawked at the empty chairs and benches around the wood stove, sitting as lonely as ghost-town buildings after the boom has passed.

Dacee June stroked the top of his age-spotted hand. "What do you mean?"

"I was supposed to go next. The Texas Camp wasn't supposed to end this way. I listened to your daddy say words over Big River Frank up on Mount Moriah. Then I listened to him pray over Yapper Jim, and then Grass Edwards. It's my turn. I've been countin' on that ol' man prayin' over me too. It ain't fair." Even in sorrow his voice had a lyric, musical quality.

13

TEXAS CAMP

Dacee June leaned back, her hands folded in her lap. "Daddy's always told us he wants you to sing 'Amazing Grace' at his graveside. You know that."

His voice became so soft she had to lean forward to hear. "I couldn't do it, darlin'. I'd choke up."

Dacee June peered at the soot-darkened ceiling. "Maybe you won't have to. I keep hoping one morning he'll wake up and say, 'Think I'll go huntin' in the Big Horns for a couple of weeks.'"

A soft smile broke across the old man's face. "He does love to hunt, don't he?"

"Hunt? My foot, we all know you old coots were always looking for another gold strike. Don't you talk to me about hunting and fishing. I was the only one who ever hunted or fished on those trips," she whooped. "That was a lame excuse for you to go running up and down frigid creeks trying to catch your death of ague." *Lord, it feels so good to smile and laugh and tease. I've been tense for so long. Too long.*

Quiet Jim took a sip of coffee, then wiped his narrow lips with the back of his hand. "It gets in your blood, darlin'. It's like a disease you cain't whip. It goes into remission for long periods, but then it breaks out at the most surprisin' times. Your daddy had it worse than me, but I was always willin' to follow along. Shoot, I reckon all of us would have ridden into Hades with that old man if he called it out."

"Now don't you get me all teared up," she insisted. "Would you like for me to get Little Frank and Quint to carry you up to see him?"

"Not yet. If he's sleepin', I might as well wait here. Besides, someone has to keep up the tradition. One of us has been here most every morning for twenty years. And now it could be I'm the last. It ain't fair. I've been in this blasted wheelchair for fifteen years. I don't know why I have to outlive them all." He rubbed his thighs and lifeless legs.

She stood up and kissed his forehead. "That's because you still have some songs to sing, Quiet Jim. I'll give you five other reasons why the Lord still has you around. Their names are Quint and Fern and Sarah and Jimmy and Brett. You've got a twenty-year-old and four teenagers, and Columbia has no intention of raising them alone."

"An old man like me has no business with a young wife. It ain't fair to her."

"Hush, you ol' Texan! That's nonsense. Columbia hasn't retreated a minute since you asked her to dance at Bobby and Jamie Sue's wedding reception."

"You remember that night?" he asked.

"I remember I had you dance the first dance with me."

"You made ever' one in the Texas Camp dance with you first."

"I was a rather determined young lady, wasn't I?"

"Was?" Quiet Jim spouted. "Never knew any woman who turned out the spittin' image of her mama more than you."

"Hah! Like my mother? Quiet Jim, you are always tellin' me I'm as stubborn as daddy!"

He stared back down into his coffee cup. "So was your mama."

"I better go rescue Todd and Rebekah's girls. I understand they are babysitting the Toluca trio. You tell Carty when you want to go upstairs, and he'll see you have a lift." She plucked his coffee cup from his hand, sashayed over to the stove, and refilled his cup. She stirred in two spoons of brown sugar, then opened a large octagon tin and pulled out two English tea biscuits.

"You spoil me, young lady," he said.

"Of course I do. And in case you forgot, Quiet Jim Trooper, I'm thirty-one years old now."

He shook his head and rubbed his freshly shaven chin. "You'll always be twelve to me. You know that."

"I feel like it sometimes when I'm so helpless to do anything for daddy. It's like the day Big River Frank got killed. All I did was sit

15

there and cry. Now enough of that. This is the day the Lord has made, and I'm not rejoicing and being very glad in it. I better hike up the hill."

"Kiss them babies for me," Quiet Jim called out.

Dacee June found Carty giving instructions to Little Frank and Quint. She studied her husband. *He works too hard, Lord. Look at his eyes. Dark, almost drooping. He needs a break. A vacation. Ever since Todd let him run the hardware store, he thinks he must do everything. We should take the train over to Yellowstone. The girls would love it. Maybe when Daddy gets better . . . or . . .*

"Mornin', Aunt Dacee June," Little Frank grinned.

"Good morning, Little Frank, Quint."

"How's grandpa?" Little Frank asked.

She gazed into her nephew's questioning blue eyes. "About the same, honey."

"Should I go up and see him?"

"He is sleeping now, and Uncle Sammy is with him. Maybe later."

Carty Toluca tapped his fingers against a clipboard. "I'm sending these two out to the Broken Boulder Mine. The Raxton sisters ordered these pumps three months ago, and they were just delivered yesterday. I'm not going to wait another day. Besides, these two want an early start so they can get back by dark."

"Miss Agnes is sponsorin' a dance at the arcade. We don't want to miss out," Quint explained.

"No, I imagine you don't." *He's got his mother's stunning looks and his father's gentle manner. If women ever get the vote, Quint Troop will be president!* "Who's the lucky girl tonight?"

"I'm not sure, Dacee June. I do know I promised the first dance to Veronica."

Little Frank put his arm around Quint's shoulder. "That was Patricia," he corrected.

Quint's brown eyes sparkled. "Was that Patricia we saw at Squibly's?"

"Yep."

Quint looped his thumbs in his suspenders. "You'd think after knowin' them most of my life I could tell them apart."

"You aren't the only one," Dacee June declared. "Usually I have to wait for Patricia to start chewing her lip."

"Or Veronica to tap her foot," Quint chimed in.

"You two take it easy driving out to the Broken Boulder. Those last six miles are rough. See if you can find out if the Raxtons are back in the Hills and coming to town for the Fourth of July activities. They've spent months in California. Quint, don't forget to check on your daddy. He might want you boys to carry him up to sit with Daddy Brazos."

"Yes, Mama." Quint winked at her.

Young man, that might be the most dangerous wink in Deadwood! Dacee June grabbed Carty's hand and tugged him toward the back room.

"Where are you taking me, Mrs. Toluca?" he quizzed as he stumbled after her.

"To the storeroom, Mr. Toluca," she lectured.

For the first time in days, there was a light, teasing expression in his voice. "For what purpose?"

"To give you your good morning kiss, unless you want me to embarrass these two young men," she announced in a loud voice.

"Good grief, Aunt Dacee June, we've seen people kiss before," Little Frank blurted out.

"Yes," she waved a long, thin finger at him, "but you have never seen *my* good morning kiss!"

Dacee June tugged her sheepish-looking husband down the bolt row, past a stack of sluice boxes, and in front of an unopened crate of Winchester '94 carbines. In the back room they wound their way through the narrow aisle of floor-to-ceiling crates, boxes, and cartons. Carty stopped near the glass-cutting table and tugged her to his chest.

He was only an inch or two taller, but with his straight-up posture and broad shoulders, Carty seemed to tower above her. "Now what's all this nonsense about a good morning kiss, Dacee June? You and I both know there's something else on your mind."

She caught a whiff of the spice-smelling tonic water on his clean-shaven face. She threw her arms around his neck and put her head on his shoulder and began to sob. Dacee June felt Carty's strong arms circled around her.

"Hold me," she whimpered.

"I'm holdin', darlin'."

"I mean, never let go."

"Never? Not even for dinner?"

"Never, ever. I don't want you to ever let go. Not for a minute. Not for a second. Not for a thousand years."

He rocked her back and forth. "It's Daddy Brazos, isn't it?"

She closed her eyes. Tears flooded his white shirt. "I want him to hug me just one more time, Carty. I'm dyin' inside. I hurt so bad. I've never ever felt anything like this."

"Worse than givin' birth to Ninete?"

"Oh yes, a thousand times worse than that. I feel so ashamed."

Carty rubbed her back as he hugged her. "Why, baby? It's OK to grieve."

"But we shouldn't grieve as those who have no hope. I've never known a man who trusted the Lord Jesus more than Daddy. I know he's going to heaven. I know he'll finally get to be with Mama. He'll see his own Patricia and Veronica again. It will be such a joy and delight for him. But I don't know, Carty." Her heart pounded against his chest.

He gently stroked her hair. "It's all right, darlin'. You cry all you want."

"I'm ashamed, Carty. Why aren't I trusting the Lord's timing? Why am I so scared? I thought my faith was stronger than this. But how can I survive without Daddy? He's always been there."

He put his calloused hand on her cheek. "I'll be here for you, darlin'."

"I know you will. See? That's why I'm ashamed. You're the most wonderful man, and I can't even relax in your arms. I'm worthless," she sobbed.

"Now darlin'," Carty corrected. "I've always been the second most wonderful man in your life. I've known since the first day I met you when you were twelve and spoiled rotten. But it's OK. I've never tried to compete with Daddy Brazos. I've never known a man like him in my life either. Coming in second to him is still ten steps ahead of every other man, except maybe your brothers. I know I'm not Daddy Brazos, but I'm all yours."

"Carty, I'm so selfish, I hate myself," she whimpered. "I think only of myself. I'm no good to you and the girls this way. And no good to Daddy. He needs to go on. This is no way to live. I hate feeling this way. Why can't I be strong like you and my brothers?"

He brushed away her tears with a thumb. "I reckon you have to be yourself. You're Dacee June Fortune Toluca. There is no one in the Black Hills like you, darlin'."

She laid her head back on his shoulder. "I've never been separated from Daddy my whole life. You remember how he took me everywhere?"

"How about the time when he first came up here to the Hills without you?"

"That was only a few months. He left me with Aunt Barbara and Uncle Milt. I cried myself to sleep every single night. Is that what it's going to be like now?"

He held her waist. "You won't have to go through it alone, darlin'. I'm here. The girls are here. Todd, Sammy, Bobby . . . their wives and kids . . . we're all together. You'll be OK."

"I know, I know. I'm so weak-willed, Carty."

"Darlin', no one in the entire states of South Dakota and Wyoming has ever called Dacee June 'weak-willed'."

"Then why can't I release him? Why can't I just say, 'Go on, Daddy. Go on and hug Mama for me.' I hate being this way, Carty." *Oh, Lord, I hope there is a big field of bluebonnets in heaven.*

"Darlin' go home. Wash up. Play with the girls. Hike up the hill where the air is fresh and you can breathe deep. The Lord will take care of us."

Dacee June finally released her husband's neck. "You're a good man, Carty Toluca. I've known that since the first day we met."

"You hated me when we met, remember?" he challenged.

"Oh, well, yes. But I was a silly, pudgy, ugly twelve-year-old."

"Darlin', you were never ever ugly. You've always been the cutest thing I've ever seen in my life."

"But I was silly, right?"

"Yep. And spoiled rotten."

She pulled back. "And pudgy. Mr. Toluca, you certainly know how to make a girl feel good."

"Thank you, ma'am."

She kissed his cheek.

"Is that all I get? I was promised a whole lot more than that!"

Dacee June brushed her hair back. "I hate to see a grown man beg." Her arms circled his neck, her lips pressed against his. She could feel his warmth, his chest pushed against hers, as he held her tight. For a moment, she forgot about Daddy . . . about the children . . . about Deadwood . . . about death and dying . . . and about the clerks in the next room. All she could think about was a strong desire that this kiss would last forever.

Then he pulled back.

And it was over.

"Darlin'," he winked. "You have never, ever been pudgy!"

BLY

▮▀ ▮▀ ▮▀

Dacee June was winded when she reached the top of the Williams Street stairs, seventy-two steps above Main Street. Glancing across the street, she saw two small eyes peering through the white gauze curtains. She blew a kiss and the eyes disappeared.

Before she could cross the street the front door flew open, and a young barefoot girl in a long beige dress ran out onto the porch. "Hi, Mama! I get to be the prairie sun!"

Dacee June was at the bottom of the steps leading up to the porch when six-year-old Ninete leaped into her arms. "Hi, punkin', what is this prairie sun?"

"In the play, I get to wear a yellow costume and be the sun coming up in the morning!"

Two other young barefoot girls, a little taller than Ninete, darted out on the porch.

"Isn't it wonderful, Mama? We are goin' to have a Fourth of July play after all!" seven-year-old Jehane squealed.

"You girls know, what with Grandpa Brazos sick, I haven't had time to write one this year," Dacee June said.

"But Amber wrote it, and she said she'd direct it!" Jehane insisted.

"Amber wrote a play?"

Eight-year-old Elita shuffled out on the porch, scooting her bare feet along the concrete. "Amber stayed up until three o'clock this morning writing it. I get to be the Elkhorn and Missouri Valley Railroad!"

Dacee June stared at the perfectly round, perfectly innocent brown eyes of her daughter. "My, that will be a challenging part."

"I'm the church!" Jehane announced.

"This is a fascinating play. Where are your shoes?"

"Camilla said we don't have to wear shoes today."

TEXAS CAMP

A thirteen-year-old with wavy, sandy, blonde hair down past her waist appeared in the doorway. "Hi, Aunt Dacee June. I meant they could go barefoot in the house, not outside."

With straight, black, bobbed hair barely down to her shoulders, twelve-year-old Nettie appeared next to her sister. "Aunt Dacee June, how's Grandpa Brazos?"

Dacee June surveyed the five girls who surrounded her. *Daddy Brazos, these are your treasures . . . your legacy. Your girls who will carry your memory in their hearts for the next seventy years! Oh, Lord, they are the most beautiful girls in the world.* "Nettie, Grandpa is about like yesterday. He's not doing too good."

"Daddy's really worried," Camilla added. "He always gets grouchy when he's worried."

"And he's been really grouchy lately," Nettie added.

Dacee June led her nieces and daughters back into the house. "I know exactly what you mean, girls. Your daddy's been that way his whole life! Now tell me about the Fourth of July play. I can't believe Amber wrote one overnight."

"She knows how to run a typing machine!" Elita announced.

"Yes, I know. I taught her," Dacee June said.

"Amber has the toughest part," Elita offered as they retreated into the living room.

"Who or what is Amber going to be?"

"She has to be you, Mama!" Jehane declared.

"What?"

Ninete squirmed out of her mother's arms and stood on the burgundy sofa cushion. "Amber is playing Dacee June Fortune Toluca!" she squealed.

"I'm in the play?"

"Yes," Elita instructed. "It's called Queen of the Black Hills!"

"Garret is going to be Quiet Jim because he never talks much in public anyway," Jehane said.

"Garret's just shy," Dacee June added. "Growing up in a house with Uncle Sammy, Aunt Abby, and Amber would make anyone a little shy. But just how are you going to have a play ready by to-morrow night? Girls, put on your shoes, and we'll go have some breakfast with Aunt Rebekah."

"We have to have three rehearsals today," Jehane announced.

"There's a part for all thirteen of us cousins," Elita said.

"That rehearsal schedule will be tough for Little Frank. He's working at the store and is headed out to the Broken Boulder Mine with Quint," Dacee June explained.

"Really? We'd better go tell Amber." Camilla tossed her long hair back over her shoulder.

"Where is she?"

"She's over at our house," Nettie declared.

"My, there is a houseful. I don't suppose the twins are there?"

Camilla stooped down to help Ninete tie her shoe. "No, Aunt Jamie Sue telephoned and said they were all going up to Mount Moriah and take flowers for the graves. Uncle Bobby is coming in on the morning train. Then we'll all be together."

☞ ☞ ☞

Rebekah and Dacee June sat on the covered porch and watched Amber lead nine neatly dressed, giggling children down the stairs toward Main Street. Abby Fortune, dressed in purple satin that whispered with every step, joined them with a cup of coffee in her hand. She stopped at the railing and eyed the rooftops of down-town Deadwood.

"Seems strange not to have you leading that," she teased.

"It's like I'm looking at a dream about myself. I can't believe how much Amber is like me in so many ways."

"That what Sammy says." Abby laughed and turned around.

"She is much more beautiful, like her mother," Dacee June added.

"Now don't you start on that again. She may not have Fortune blood, but she has a Fortune heart," Abby insisted.

"I don't think I ever commanded attention like she does. She's so dramatic . . ."

"What?" Rebekah and Abby began to laugh at the same time.

"Did I?" Dacee June demanded. "Oh, my, was I really that way?"

"Amber has patterned her entire life after you since she was six," Abby said. "Why do you think she wrote a play about the 'Queen of the Black Hills'? You are her ideal picture of feminine tenacity."

"You could have found her a better model."

"Honey, there has never been a Fortune who wasn't a good role model for others to follow," Abby insisted. "Even Sammy turned out all right."

"I don't feel much like a role model today. It is so difficult sitting by Daddy's bed. I sobbed all night long, then more on Carty's shoulder. I wish I could be strong."

"Poor Todd," Rebekah added. "He just can't take it. When he comes home, he goes up on the hill for hours at a time."

"To cry?"

"I'm sure he does. He just can't bear the thought," Rebekah explained.

"You notice how each of the brothers handle it different? Todd holds it inside, then has to be alone. Bobby tries working himself to death to avoid the pain, and Sammy . . . dear old soft-hearted Sammy won't hardly leave Daddy's side. He just sits there with tears rolling down his leather-tough cheeks."

"I've never met a more tender man than Sammy," Abby added. "Everyone treats him like he was still that notorious Oklahoma gunfighter, and yet he'll shed a tear when some alley cat gets run over by the milk wagon."

"I do have the greatest brothers in the world," Dacee June replied.

"You won't get any arguments from us," Rebekah added. The telephone rang, and she retreated into the house.

"Do you remember the first time I hiked up here to Forest Hill?" Abby asked Dacee June.

"Yes, I remember. You had on a beautiful green dress, and I was wearing that horrible buckskin outfit, thinking I looked quite nobby. Then I saw you and felt like I was a ten-year-old boy, in comparison."

"I can't believe how much my life has changed since then. The Lord has been very good to Abigail McNeill Fortune. I've received so much better than what I deserve. Sometimes it worries me."

"You mean, too much prosperity? Not enough testing and trials?" Dacee June said.

Abby sipped from a flowered china cup. "I suppose that thought has crossed my mind."

"Maybe that's why this struggle with Daddy is so painful to me," Dacee June murmured. "I'm not used to much adversity. Not since leaving Texas anyway."

"I, for one, figured I did my share years ago, but that's a selfish, narrow way of looking at things," Abigail added.

Rebekah strolled out on the porch. "The Fortunes are busy again. Looks like you need to get back to the hardware store," she told Dacee June.

"Is it Daddy?"

"No, it's some man named Wyman St. Luce. He wants to talk to the owner of the business, and the clerks don't know what do with him."

"Where's Carty?" Dacee June asked.

"It seems that Amber latched onto Little Frank for this play, and so Carty went out to the Broken Boulder with Quint Trooper," Rebekah reported.

TEXAS CAMP

Dacee June stared out over the top of Deadwood. "Oh, no. He's so tired and run-down anyway. I was hoping he'd have a peaceful day."

"Sometimes a ride can be peaceful," Rebekah offered.

"Can you imagine a visit with the Raxton sisters as peaceful?" Dacee June proposed.

"No," Rebekah added. "I suppose you're right. But with Todd being in Spearfish picking up the governor, and now Carty out on the road, that leaves Dacee June to negotiate."

"Negotiate what?" Abby pressed. "Who is this man, Wyman St. Luce?"

"I think he must have something to do with a circus," Rebekah said.

"A circus?" Abby echoed.

"Yes, Joey said this man wanted to know what you wanted him to do with the elephant."

CHAPTER
TWO

Just as Dacee June turned the corner toward the hardware store, their youngest clerk raced up the concrete sidewalk, shouting, "Mrs. Toluca, you ain't goin' to believe this!"

Joey claimed to be seventeen, but he gave the appearance of being about fourteen. He was also the hardest working, most dedicated clerk who wasn't related to the owners. At five feet, four inches and one hundred twenty-five pounds, Joey Plummer was mostly muscle and bone. He had to bounce on his toes in order to appear as tall as Dacee June. He refused to call anyone older than him by their first name.

"Mrs. Toluca, I ain't never seen a real elephant. Have you ever seen a real elephant?" Joey's dark hair was parted in the middle and slicked down to his ears. Everything below that was shaved off.

"Yes, I did, Joey. The last time I was in Chicago with Rebekah. Mr. Barnum's show was running, and he had several elephants."

She looked at the dead-axe paneled freight wagon parked in front of the hardware store. "Did they haul the elephant in that wagon?"

"Yes, ma'am. That's a big wagon, ain't it?" His dark tie hung loose and slung to the right as usual, but Dacee June had given up trying to straighten it months before.

"But that wagon is not as big as a mature elephant. I presume it's a small one." She paused and waited for a cloud of red dust from a speeding four-horse carriage to roll across the sidewalk in front of them.

"It's huge!" Joey turned around and walked backwards. "Ain't never been one that big in the entire Black Hills, so they say."

"Any size elephant would be an attraction around here. Why did they send it to the store?" She glanced down. A sprinkling of red dust peppered across her white lace cuffs.

Joey jammed his hands in his back pockets. "That's what it said on the bill of lading."

She stopped by the rear wheel of the unmarked wagon. "It must be something for tomorrow's parade. Perhaps Todd made some arrangement for the city to borrow an elephant and didn't tell anyone."

"It ain't borrowed. Nope, that's why you had to come down. To sign for it." Joey bounced on his toes. "It's a gift."

"A gift? Oh, my, Joey. What are earth are we supposed to do with it?"

"It's a fine-lookin' elephant, Mrs. Toluca."

She stepped to the back of the wagon, but the rear door was closed. There were no windows or iron bars. "How tall is this elephant?"

Joey raised his hand shoulder high. "About three or four feet, I reckon."

"Then it's just a baby." She surveyed the wood-paneled wagon. *It's a wonder it didn't suffocate!*

Joey rubbed his smooth, hairless chin. "I cain't imagine one any bigger."

Dacee June strolled to the front of the wagon. Two giant sorrel draft horses stood with heads down and blindered eyes closed. *Is this one of Sammy's jokes? Did he order an elephant just to fluster me? This could be a set-up. Maybe he'll be at the window . . . and Todd . . . and Bobby . . . and even Carty. . . . Maybe they are all here, and they just think they'll play a joke on me. It wouldn't be the first time they all ganged up on me!* She put her hand on the sleeve of Joey's gartered white shirt. "Go get the freighter and have him open it up so I can see what this little joke is all about."

He rolled his eyes as if searching for a response. "What?"

Dacee June glanced at her shadow on the sidewalk and immediately sucked in her stomach. "Have the teamster open the wagon so I can see this elephant of his . . . or ours."

"But it ain't in there." She noticed that even when Joey scratched his head, not a single hair was out of place.

"I thought you said they hauled it in this wagon."

"I did. But we done unloaded it."

Dacee June scanned the street filled with horses, carriages, and wagons. "What did they do with it?"

"I hepped 'em unload it in the back room."

"The elephant is in the back room of our hardware store?" *Why can't anything ever be simple? When all the men leave, there appears an elephant in the back room! 'Let's go get Dacee June, she'll know what to do. Dacee June knows everything.' Not hardly. Dacee June just pretends like she knows everything. And she's been pretending for so long she's really good at it.*

"Yep, I didn't think you wanted it out in the store with all the customers."

"Where is this freighter?"

"Mr. St. Luce said he'd watch the elephant until you got down here. You have to sign the invoice."

"We certainly aren't going to keep it in the storeroom," she fumed.

"That's what I tried to tell him. But I think he wanted to unload it and get on his way."

"Yes, I'm sure he did, but we've got to get it out of there right away."

"What are you goin' to do with it?" Joey asked.

"It's supposed to be in the parade, right?"

"I reckon you could if you wanted. I'm sure no one has seen anything like it."

"We'll just have to find a secure site for the night," she offered.

"Did you have any place in mind?" he probed.

She glanced north. "How about the Montana Livery?"

Joey burst out with a laugh. "Mrs. Toluca, you crack me up. You Fortunes is all that way. You string me along so serious and then slide in a jibe that catches me by surprise. You all got sneaky humor. I like it, but it always makes me think."

She let him into the hardware store and down a long aisle of steel pipe fixtures. "Joey Plummer, what on earth are you talking about?"

He trotted to keep up. "About keepin' that there elephant at the livery. That's the kind of thing Mr. Brazos Fortune would have said before he took sick."

She marched ahead of him toward the storeroom at the rear of the building. "You thought that was funny?"

"Yes, ma'am. Who but a Fortune would tease and say we ought to keep an elephant-shaped cake at a livery stable?"

She felt her neck, her mouth, her shoulders droop. "A cake?" It was more of a cough than a question.

"You surely didn't think someone brung us a real elephant, did you?" He cut in front of her and led the way into the storeroom that served as a warehouse and shop.

Perched on a wooden stretcher and sitting on top of the huge glass cutting table was a four-foot-tall, six-foot-long, gray-icied cake carved in the shape of a reclining elephant.

"My word," she gasped. "It's sort of . . . I didn't think that . . . it's . . . it's . . . why?"

A short man with a round bowler pulled down too low, like a man covering baldness, clutched a folded paper in his hand. "My name is St. Luce. Where's Mr. Fortune?"

"I'm Dacee June Toluca."

"I need a Fortune to sign for this," he mumbled.

"I can sign the invoice."

"Nope. Got to have a Fortune sign. It says so right here."

"Mr. St. Luce, I assure you I can . . ."

"Can't bend the rules. Where's a Fortune?"

"I am Dacee June Fortune Toluca, and I . . ."

"You been married twice?"

"No, I haven't. Fortune is my maiden name."

"Where's your husband? He can sign for it."

"My husband is Carty Toluca. He is Brazos Fortune's son-in-law and a co-owner of the store."

"He can sign for it then."

"I'm a Fortune by birth, but I can't sign for it? And yet my husband, who has never been a Fortune, can?"

"I'm sure you understand."

"I don't understand at all."

The man pulled off his hat and began to fan himself. "There ain't no reason to get your fur raised. Jist go get your husband and I'll be on my way."

"Mr. St. Luce, either I sign that invoice, or you can put that cake back in your wagon and haul it back to wherever you came from."

"Spearfish."

"You hauled that all the way from Spearfish?" she asked.

31

"Yep, I got damp sheets linin' my wagon. That keeps the dust off the cake, mostly," he bragged.

"Mr. St. Luce, please remove your cake from our storeroom."

"But it took four of us to unload it!"

"That really doesn't concern me. Remove that cake."

"But . . . but . . . but that's a hundred-dollar cake."

"A hundred-dollar cake?" Joey gasped. "I ain't never in my life heard of a hundred-dollar cake!"

"I am not paying a hundred dollars for it," Dacee June insisted.

"It's prepaid. It's a gift."

"A gift from whom?"

"Says right there on the invoice. Sandra and Augusta Raxton."

"The Raxton sisters sent us this?" Dacee June strolled entirely around the massive cake. "How in the world do you get it not to collapse?"

"It ain't all cake, of course. Just the top foot or so. Under that is a hollow screen-and-wire frame. You could hide a couple of hundred-pound sacks of potatoes under it."

"I'll keep that in mind."

St. Luce reached into his gray wool vest pocket and pulled out a long envelope. "There's a note with it."

Dacee June opened the stiff, rose print paper to see Augusta Raxton's perfect penmanship.

> For the Fortunes of the Black Hills:
> Dear Folks, we sold the Broken Boulder to Mr. Albert Sween & Company. You were right, we made it big. But, as you know, the mine's been on the decline for several years, and it seemed a good time to sell. We're finally moving to San Francisco. I hope they are ready for the likes of Sandra and me. Please cancel our hardware orders and forward the remaining balance on our bill. We know the big Fourth of July celebration is coming up, so we're sending this thank-you cake. We "went to see the elephant," and he was made out of gold. If you are ever in San Francisco, you know you are welcome at our

home. Oscar and Byron send their greetings. They went on ahead and purchased two homes on Nob Hill. Won't the boys in Miles City be surprised at what happened to the Raxton sisters? God bless you. We owe you more than a simple cake can ever express.

    Sincerely,

    Augusta Raxton Chambers & Sandra Raxton Puddin

☞ ☞ ☞

"A simple cake?" Dacee June mumbled.

"They canceled their hardware orders?" Joey echoed.

"Apparently."

"Then there ain't no reason for Mr. Toluca and Mr. Troop to take that load out there," Joey said.

Dacee June peered toward the main floor of the store as if hoping to see Carty standing there. "And that's such a hard trip," she murmured.

"What about this invoice?" St. Luce blustered.

"We're very busy, Mr. St. Luce." Dacee June plucked the invoice from his hand, snatched a lead pencil from Joey, and wrote her name on the bottom. "There, if that won't do, remove your cake from the storeroom." She swung around facing her young clerk. "Joey, how long have Carty and Quint been gone?"

"About an hour, I reckon."

"I'm going to check with Sammy. Is he still upstairs with Daddy?" she probed.

Joey's attempt to straighten his tie made it even worse. "I think so."

"My brother has some of the fastest horses in the state. I'm sure a rider could catch up with Carty and Quint and turn them around. It's too arduous a trip to be done for no reason."

"What do you want me to do with this here elephant?"

"We can't leave it there. We need to put it some place cool until we can figure out what to do with it. We need a basement." She

33

noticed the gray frosting on the cake had the same light red tint of dust as her sleeves did.

"We had better find one with big double doors."

"The church!" Dacee June led Joey out the store. "Take it to the church basement, and maybe we'll have it for dessert after the Fourth of July pageant." *I wonder if I need to hire a butcher to carve an elephant cake?*

"I thought you were too busy to have a pageant this year?"

"Amber wrote a play last night, so the pageant is back on."

"Is Miss Amber going to be in it?" Joey asked.

"Yes, indeed, she is."

"I'm goin'," he grinned. "She's probably the purdiest girl in all of the Black Hills, don't you reckon?"

At least we're keeping the title in the family. "Joey, I'll go upstairs and check with Sammy. You be in charge of moving the cake."

"You want me to just put it in the church basement?"

"Yes. Use the back doors and get at least three other men to help you. Have Amber show you some place to put it that's not in her way. Whatever she says will be fine."

"You said, 'Three other men.' I like that," he grinned.

"Joey, you've been doing a man's work for years."

"Thank ya, ma'am. Don't that look like the tastiest cake you ever did see?"

Dacee June peeked back through the storeroom door at the massive gray lump perched like a contoured manure pile on the stretcher. *Joey, there is absolutely nothing about that cake that looks tasty!*

☛ ☛ ☛

Sam was waiting for Dacee June when she reached the top of the stairs.

"How is he?" she asked.

The deep furrows at the corners of his eyes revealed no emotion. "The same." But the pupils of his eyes told a different story.

She took his arm. "How are you?"

He patted her hand. "The same."

"Sammy, have you got a fast horse I can borrow?"

"What's the problem, Sis?"

"I need to send a rider to catch up with Carty and Quint and turn them around. The Raxtons sent word that they sold the mine and don't need those pumps."

"Who would buy a played-out mine?"

"Sammy, we both know there are hundreds of men who will throw good money down a hole in the ground if they're convinced there is gold in it. Anyway, I want to try to catch up to Carty and turn them back."

"Why not just telephone them?" he suggested.

"At the Broken Boulder? How would that shorten their trip?"

"I meant call someone up on Dutchman's Flat and have them turn Carty back."

"Who on Dutchman's Flat has a telephone?"

"Spud Brewster."

"Last I heard he didn't have a roof on his cabin."

Sam Fortune brushed his drooping gray mustache with his fingertips. "He came to town and put down a year's deposit, so I sent Williamson out to patch him into the line going to the Broken Boulder."

"When was that?"

"A couple of weeks past."

"I'll try to telephone him. Carty's too tired and run down to make that trip for nothing."

"Speaking of telephone, if you have time to sit with Daddy, I need to go to the office and then to the dress shop and check on Abby. She's making costumes for the pageant Amber wrote. She's supposed to come up with decorations for the wagon the kids are riding on in the parade. Which reminds me, I need to find her some canvass grommets." He meandered to the back of the store.

Dacee June scurried down the wide stairs and through an aisle toward the counter in the back of the huge display room. She had just passed the bolt bins when someone called out behind her.

"Ma'am, do you work here?" He stood well over six feet tall, with a clean-shaven, dimpled chin. He chewed on a toothpick. His dark eyebrows were thick, his face chiseled.

"Eh, yes, but I need to run upstairs. Let me find you a clerk. On second thought, I don't know who's available. What can I do for you?"

"I want to buy a Winchester."

Dacee June tried not to stare at the broad-shouldered man's bright blue eyes or easy smile. "Did you see one you wanted in the case?"

"Eh, no ma'am, I jist rode into town."

He looks about my age . . . or younger. "The gun case is unlocked. Take a look and I'll make a quick telephone call."

He tipped his flat-crowned hat and ambled across the store.

☞ ☞ ☞

Dacee June held the black receiver to her ear. She waited for the operator, Anaconda Biggs, to hook her up as she stood on tiptoes to scan the stairs for a clerk.

In the middle of the second ring, a deep voice bellowed, "Yeah, what do you want?"

"Spud?" she questioned.

"Do I look like that mealy-mouthed, pint-sized, claim-stealin' Irishman?"

"Actually, I can't see you at all," she stammered. "Who is this?"

"Who are you?" the man demanded.

"I'm the one who's trying to call Spud Brewster," she snapped.

"He ain't here, and if he were, I'd shoot him."

"Why did you answer the telephone?"

"Cause it rang."

"Are you at Spud's house?" she quizzed.

"Nope. I wouldn't go over there if he was on his deathbed beggin' to see me."

"Isn't Mr. Spud Brewster two long rings?"

"That was a long and a short."

"That's because you picked it up too soon," she suggested. "If you had let it ring, it would have been two long rings."

"Are you tellin' me I don't know how to operate my own telephone?"

A second male voice boomed into her receiver. "You couldn't even operate an outhouse! That's my phone number and you know it!"

"Is that you, Spud?"

"Mordecai, you know it is. This is my line."

"The Broken Boulder's on this line too! You could have been from the Broken Boulder."

"I don't sound like one of them Raxton women, do I?"

"You sound like a claim jumper, that's what you sound like!"

"Spud?" Dacee June broke in.

"Who's that? You got a woman with you, Mordecai?"

"It ain't none of your business if I do."

"This is Dacee June Toluca, and I need . . ."

"There ain't no woman in Dakota who would be in your cabin."

She brushed her bangs out of her eyes and tapped the toe of her lace-up boot on the bare, painted floor of the hardware store. "Spud, this is important. I really need to talk to you."

"Then why are you over at Mordecai's?" Spud quizzed.

"I am here in Deadwood and I'm in a hurry to . . ."

"What's Mordecai doin' in town? It ain't Saturday," Spud interrupted.

"I kin go to town any day I please!" Mordecai shouted.

37

"Next time you leave that cabin, it might be burnt down before you get home!"

"You try it, Spud Brewster, and I'll put a bullet in your brain!"

"Please. This is important to me. I need to . . ."

"I ain't a bit worried," Mordecai boasted. "You couldn't hit a two-foot-thick ponderosa pine from three feet."

"Stick your fool head out the door!" Spud challenged.

"What?"

"Let's see how good a shot I am. Stick your head out the door."

"I will if you will!"

"Will you two shut up!" Dacee June yelled in the telephone.

"What?"

"I need to talk, so please be quiet."

"Lady, who do you think you are?"

"I'm Dacee June Fortune Toluca!" she found herself shouting as loud as she could at the two men.

"Dacee June Fortune is callin' me?" Spud gasped.

"How do we know she's Dacee June?" Mordecai cautioned. "Could be any old gal from the Green Door."

"If you two don't immediately be quiet, I'll send my brother Sammy out to collect your hardware bill," she blurted out. "And I'll see that your credit at the Merchant's Hotel is canceled, tell the girls at the Gem that you are two-bit, penniless prospectors, and inform the Homestake that you're squatting on their property!"

"It is Dacee June!" Mordecai acknowledged.

"Yes, and I need to talk to Spud. So, Mordecai, please hang up the telephone."

"You mean, I cain't listen?"

"No, you may not."

"OK, I'll hang up."

"He ain't goin' to do it, Dacee June," Spud Brewster insisted.

"Mordecai, are you still there?" she questioned.

She waited a moment, then shifted the earpiece to the other ear. "Mordecai, on the back wall of the Oyster Cafe there is a notice concerning you and a certain widow lady in Central City. I will personally see that she and the sheriff have a map to your cabin if you don't immediately . . ."

There was a definite click of a telephone disconnection.

"He hung up," Spud Brewster announced.

"Yes, Spud, I need to ask you a favor."

"What's on the notice at the back of Oyster Cafe?" he pressed.

"I have no idea," she admitted.

"You bluffed him?"

"Apparently. Most people have some secret they don't want revealed."

"Even you Fortunes?"

"Even the Fortunes. Spud, I have a favor to ask you."

"Yes, ma'am, I'm always available to hep Brazos Fortune's daughter. Him and that Texas Camp financed me more times than I can count. Why I was jist tellin' Mr. Carty Fortune . . ."

"Carty's name is Toluca," she corrected.

"You mean, he's not a Fortune?"

"He's married to me. I'm a Fortune. Dacee June Fortune Toluca."

"Brazos ain't his daddy?"

"Brazos is my daddy. He's Carty's father-in-law."

"I'll be swan. All this time I thought his name was Carty Fortune. I reckon he thought me the fool for saying that."

"When did you see him?" she asked.

"I was out there next to the road talkin' to him when this dad gum telephone rang. It don't ever ring when I'm close by. Shoot, it don't hardly ever ring at all."

"Carty is there now?"

"Nope. He and Quiet Jim's kid was headed for the Broken Boulder jist a few minutes ago."

"Spud, I need to get a message to Carty. Can you go flag them down?"

"Nope. They done passed me by."

"I know, but they can't be very far down the road. They have a heavy freight wagon. Perhaps you could ride down and catch up with them."

"My mule lamed up. I'm cabin bound."

"Don't you have any other animal?"

"There's Edison. She's my milk cow."

"Can you run out and holler at them and get their attention?"

"Nope, they crested the hill already. But I can catch them on the way back. They have to pass right here. What do you want me to tell them?"

"It will be too late then, Spud. I wanted to tell him to turn around and come back. The Raxtons have canceled their order."

"They run out of money?"

"No, just the opposite. They've sold the Broken Boulder," she explained.

"Who bought it? I heard there ain't much gold left in it."

"I believe it is Mr. Albert Sween and Company."

"From Virginia City, Nevada?"

"I suppose so. I don't know the man."

"He's a bigger crook than Mordecai!"

"Spud, I don't know anything about that, but if you think of any way to get Carty's attention, would you please do so, and tell him to come back to town?"

"Yep, I'll tell him to hurry home; it's an emergency."

"She didn't say it was an emergency, you dolt!" another voice boomed out.

"You're a dead man!" Spud hollered.

"You ain't never in your life got the upper hand on me!"

"You are a doleful, wretched, pitiful liar and cheat!" Spud screamed.

"Me? I didn't steal your claim. I didn't steal your gold. And I didn't steal your dad gum skinny-faced girlfriend."

"You told her lies!"

"Didn't need to. When it comes to you, the truth is scary enough!"

"Boys!" Dacee June hollered. "You are wearing me out. You live fifty yards from each other, and you're brothers! I can't for the life of me understand why you are so hateful to each other. I'm hanging up. If either of you can get Carty turned around before he goes all the way to the Broken Boulder, I would appreciate it."

"I ain't hanging up until he hangs up!" Spud snarled.

Dacee June dropped the black receiver in the cradle. *Lord, why is nothing ever simple? If Spud had answered the phone, he could have run back out and signaled Carty by now. Instead, I just wasted ten minutes of my life listening to two grown men rant and rave.*

"Did you get a hold of Carty?" Sam said from behind her.

She spun around. "No, he just passed by, but Spud won't go after him."

"Is he afraid Mordecai will burn his cabin down again?"

"I suppose. Did you know that Mordecai has a telephone?"

"No, only Spud has one."

"Mordecai has a phone," she insisted.

"He's not hooked up."

"Well, I just talked to him."

Sam Fortune pulled off his hat and ran his fingers through his short gray hair. "All right, one of these days I'll ride out and see if he's pirating a phone line." He jammed his hat back on. "You want to check on Daddy, Lil' Sis? I'll go see how my business and my family are doing. The doc came by this mornin' and said everything's the same. He figured most ever'thin' is shuttin' down but that big old heart of his."

"Did Quiet Jim go up?"

41

"No. He sat by the stove and sang hymns for an hour or so," Sam explained. "It really does seem like he is more peaceful with Quiet Jim singin' downstairs."

"The whole world is more peaceful when Quiet Jim sings."

"I reckon you're right."

"I'll go sit a spell. Rebekah will be here around noon for a couple hours."

Sam peered out the front window of the hardware. "What in the world are Joey and the boys loading into the back of Xang-Poo's yellow buckboard?"

"Does it look like a gray, three-hundred-pound elephant-shaped cake?"

"Not really," Sammy insisted. "What is it?"

☞ ☞ ☞

The square-shouldered man still hovered at the gun case. Dacee June strolled over behind the counter.

"Did you make a decision?"

"These are nice guns."

"I think they're going to be a very popular cartridge," she said.

"How much are they?"

"Twenty-four dollars."

She watched as he took a deep breath and let out a slow sigh. "And a box of cartridges?"

"The total would be $25.75. Would you like it?"

When Dacee June looked up he was staring into her eyes. She quickly looked down at the receipt book.

"Yes, ma'am. I need a good reliable gun. I don't have time to find out if a used one is any good." He counted out dollar bills and coins.

Dacee June dipped the pen in ink and wrote out a bill of sale. "I'll put your name on this receipt."

His voice was barely above a whisper. "Thanks, but it isn't necessary."

"Is there anything else?"

"I thought I might look at the pocket knives."

"Please help yourself." She took the money and put it in the cash box below the counter. "Joey is the young man in the blue shirt. When you are through looking at the knives, show him the receipt and he'll get your carbine and cartridges for you. Please excuse me. I need to go upstairs."

"Thank you, ma'am." He tipped his black felt, wide-brimmed hat and smiled in a way that made Dacee June want to peek in a mirror and make sure her hair was neatly stacked.

When she reached the bottom of the stairs, she glanced back and was surprised that he continued to watch her.

☛ ☛ ☛

The stairway was painted a light green. The mixing charts had called it sea-mist green. Dacee June had been the one who painted the stairs when she was fourteen. There were twenty-one steps to the landing at the top. When she was little, they seemed steep and fraught with daring deeds.

Back then she and her father lived above the store.

Robert served in the army.

Sammy lived on the run in the Indian Territory.

Todd built a house on Forest Hill and courted Rebekah, the banker's daughter.

And every day was full of wonderful adventure.

Everyone knew her name.

By the time she was sixteen, Dacee June was the Queen of the Black Hills. She took the stairs two at a time.

Now she pushed on her knees to reach the top, where the air was stale and starting to heat. She paused at the door, brushed her bangs to the side of her round face, and took a deep breath. She straightened the white lace collar on her dress, then fumbled to make sure the top button was fastened.

Without a sound, she swung the door open and strolled to the narrow bed along the north wall. "Good morning, Daddy!" she announced. She leaned into his bedside and plucked up a limp, seemingly lifeless hand, then stroked his still, calloused fingers.

"You need some light in here, Daddy. Sammy has everything so dark." She marched over to the Main Street window and swung open the shutters. "Daddy, there's a big old July Dakota sun out there this morning." She looked over the rooftops of other downtown buildings. "The white rocks on top of Mount Moriah are reflecting like a lighthouse. This is your kind of day, Daddy."

She dragged the oak rocking chair to the side of the bed. "I bet you'd like to be out in the hills with your gold pan and that Texas Camp of yours, searching for a little color. You need a little color yourself," she added.

She entwined her fingers in his. "Maybe when the boys get back I'll have them help me, and we'll scoot your bed over to the window. At least the morning sun could warm your bones. Did you hear Quiet Jim singing hymns this morning? He is such a dear friend. He misses having you downstairs at the stove."

She rubbed the corners of her eyes. "He said you had to pull through because you promised to read over him, and he had never known a time in your life when you didn't keep your word."

Dacee June lifted his rough fingers to her lips to kiss them, then began to weep. "Papá, jé suis ainsi effrayé," she sobbed. "I'm so scared of losing you." She dropped his hand to her knee and tilted her head back and tried to gasp herself silent. "Oh, Daddy, I hurt so bad. I don't want to be this way. I love you so. What's the matter with me?"

Lord, I don't know what to do. I seem to be losing control. I can't hold back my tears. I can't think straight. I get flustered with little things. I snap at the girls. I haven't been able to let Carty get close. I'm so tired, Lord. This isn't good. This isn't healthy. I need to go to bed and go to sleep and not wake up for two weeks, then have everything be perfect.

☞ ☞ ☞

Dacee June woke when a single drop of water splashed on her forehead. She reached up toward the top of the tent, then pulled her hand back. Daddy said don't touch the tent or more water will come through. She pushed back the heavy green wool blanket that smelled like campfire smoke, scooted toward the middle of the tent, and sat straight up. Her pigtails were trapped inside an old flannel shirt. She tugged them out to droop halfway down her back.

Sprawled on her bedroll, she pulled back the tattered gray blanket that divided the tent into two sections.

He's up, of course. I suppose he has a fire going even in the rain. Nothing stops him. She tried to stand in the middle of the five-foot tent but had to stoop to pull on her old brown ducking skirt. She tucked in the flannel shirt, then buttoned the sleeves. Her hands felt cold, rough, dirty. The wet rag almost iced up as she washed her face. Perched on an old dynamite box filled with her personal items, she stared down at her sock-covered feet.

I can't even remember how many days I've worn these stockings. They're so gritty. But at least they are warm now, and there is no reason to get another pair dirty, even if I had a clean pair.

She pulled on her mud-splattered, black lace-up boots. A sharp pain shot through her back as she leaned over to lace them up. *We've been sleeping on the ground for two weeks. My bed is going to feel really, really good when we get home.*

She jammed on the round-crowned, wide-brimmed floppy felt hat that smelled of wet beaver, sweat, and campfire smoke. It felt damp on her forehead. The braided horsehair stampede string rubbed rough against her cheeks and under her chin. Dacee June took one more look in the little mirror.

Miss Dacee June, you look like a fifteen-year-old orphan who's been lost in the woods. What a sight. Mama would be livid. "A lady always looks, speaks, and acts like a lady, Dacee June. No matter what her age." *Oh, Mama, your little daughter turned out to be a tomboy raised by men.*

A light sprinkle of raw rain hit her when she stuck her head outside the tent. She called it the cloudcamp, because this morning, like all the rest, the Wyoming storm clouds touched the ground like fog at the eight-thousand-foot elevation campsite in the Big Horn Mountains. Surrounding the clearing, dark-trunked pines stood as barriers to vision and made the whole world seem no more than fifty feet by fifty feet. She sucked in damp, cold, fresh-tasting air as she strolled toward a man in a yellow oilcloth slicker who hovered over a smokey, yet glowing fire.

"Good morning, Quiet Jim," she called out.

The short, thin man spun on his heels, a frying pan in his hand. "Good mornin', Dacee June, darlin'. How's the purdiest teenager in Dakota?"

She grinned. "We're in Wyoming, Quiet Jim."

"Yep, and you're the purdiest here too."

"Don't you go feeding me those lines," she grinned. "I'll start believing them one of these days."

Quiet Jim's mouth dropped open, and he stared at her.

She glanced away from his gaze. *Lord, he wasn't teasing. He means it.* "Where's Daddy?" she asked.

"It's a long story, darlin'," Quiet Jim began. "Grass went out for a . . . eh, stroll this mornin' and found some Liliaceae and . . ."

"Prairie onions this high up?"

"He moseyed back for a sack, and Yapper Jim went out with him. They couldn't find the onions, but they did discover . . ."

"Let me guess. They found color in a stream?"

Quiet Jim stood up from hovering over the big black skillet full of sizzling salt pork. "Yep. So your daddy grabbed his gold pan, and they all went out lookin' for a new claim."

She slowly turned around and surveyed the cloud-draped pine trees. "Which way did they go?"

He pointed toward the picketed horses. "West. At least, I think that's west. You aim to go after them?"

"No, I want to go the opposite direction. I think the ladies room is to the east this morning."

Quiet Jim stirred the fire. "I reckon you're right. Take a gun."

"I'm not goin' that far."

His voice was barely audible. "Please, take a gun. You may not need to, but it surely makes me feel better."

She strolled to the big canvas tarp-covered pannier and pulled out a carbine. "Daddy didn't take his Sharps?"

"I don't know if they have a gun among them. Talk of gold makes grown men act foolish."

"Then I'll take the Sharps." She dropped the lever and checked the chamber.

"You have a bullet?"

"Yes, and I'll have a bullet when I come back."

"Don't be gone too long. Stay where you can see the camp. If you get lost, give a holler or fire the gun, then stand still, I'll come find you."

"Yes, Daddy," she teased.

"Dadgum it, Dacee June. You know all of us in the Texas Camp think of you as our own daughter."

"I know, Quiet Jim, and that makes me the luckiest girl in the Black Hills, that's for sure."

The steady drip and drizzle tumbled off her hat and puddled on the back of her flannel shirt. She folded her arms across her chest and scooted out through the trees, careful not to graze against the water-laden needles or brush. Her target was a granite boulder about the size of a pony cart. When she got there, she drug the heel of her boot across the packed mud to form a line back to camp. Through the trees and foggy clouds she could still see the outline of one of the tents.

She had just stood and tucked her flannel shirt back into her skirt when she heard a muted sound strike granite somewhere down the mountain. She squatted back down and grabbed the wet, ice-cold Sharps converted carbine. She cracked the chamber, slipped out the fat, fifty-caliber cartridge, then slid it back in and slowly reset the lever.

Maybe it's an elk! Lord, that would be so great for me to be the one who put meat in camp. But if we had an elk, they'd want to stay another week. She found a dry spot on her shirt and wiped moisture off her fingers. *And I'm not sure I want another week of camping in the rain. However, if I shoot a big elk, they will brag about me for years. Of course, they brag about me now.*

She raised the carbine to her shoulder and gazed across metal sights at the thick clouds and pines. *He could be walking downhill. If so, then he'll get away. I'll just hike over to the trees and see if I can stop him.*

She knew that somewhere above the thick Wyoming storm clouds a bright yellow sun rose on the prairie to the east. But in the Big Horn Mountains, it was only light, and even the silent trees lacked definition in the mist. Seeing no movement, she waited behind a cluster of short pines and listened.

There it is! It's more than one elk! But I only have one bullet! I'll have to find the bull. I'll take the horns back for a souvenir and mount them at the store. Won't that Carty Toluca be jealous!

She slowly inched her way down the hill, then froze when she spotted a shadowy, misty movement. She pressed the carbine to her shoulder. *I won't shoot him until I see his rack. I won't have them making fun of my marksmanship.*

48

BLY

The big animal faded in and out of the cloudy haze. She tried to wipe the rain from her eyes.

I can't ever stay dry enough to get a shot off. I've got to get closer.

The drenched pine needles made no sound as she inched closer. The carbine still at her shoulder, the giant hammer cocked, her right index finger lapped around the cold trigger. She hunkered down at the edge of a clearing about the size of a lot up on Forest Hill.

Come on, boy . . . come on. Step out in the clearing! You've got one shot, Dacee June. Make it count, because four men will come running when you pull the trigger. Don't miss him.

The dark, shadowy long nose appeared across the tiny meadow. She began to squeeze. Then big eyes, pointed ears.

And in the dim distance, the silver buckles of a bridle.

A horse! I . . . I . . . I almost shot a horse!

With his hat down and shoulders slumped into the saddle, a misty rider trotted into view.

The carbine drooped to her side. I could have shot him! She pulled her finger off the trigger and slowly let the hammer down. Her hands began to shake. Cold sweat beaded her wet forehead. Beneath the flannel shirt she could hear her heart pound.

Lord, how easy it would have been to pull the trigger. I can't believe it. Within seconds I could have been a murderer! You're right, Lord. Sin is at the door. How close have I been to other such horrible mistakes and never known it?

She watched the rider lead a string of horses through the trees.

He's got saddled horses? They aren't pack horses. But why would you saddle four extra horses? In the rain? Unless there were four extra riders.

Where are the riders?

What are they up to?

Why would they be afoot?

Daddy!

Bushwhackers!

She crept forward, the carbine in her right hand, hung to her side. Every sixth step she dragged her boot in the mud and pine needle forest floor. The last horse in the string was a mahogany bay mare with wide rump. Dacee June kept the horse and trees between her and the rider as she circled what she thought was south, then turned west and dropped into a draw.

Lord, I'm getting further and further away from camp. If these trail marks I'm leaving wash away, I'm going to have a difficult time returning to camp. I hope I know what I'm doing.

The trail dropped lower and the trees thinned. Dacee June slowed her pursuit and kept out of sight. When the rider halted, she ducked behind a hedgerow of short whitewood trees and inched her way closer.

What's he looking at? It's just a little creek. Can't be more than three feet. The horses will . . .

As she inched closer, she squatted down and peered under the belly of the mahogany bay. Down the hill three men stood in the stream, hands raised up in the foggy, drizzling rain. Around them were four men, guns drawn. Dacee June could not see any of the faces clearly.

But she could hear.

"We want your gold, your grub, and your horses!" one man shouted.

"We don't have any gold," Grass Edwards protested.

"Like Hades, you don't. You're pannin' for gold, aren't you?"

"That doesn't mean we found any," Yapper Jim insisted.

She recognized her daddy's form as he stared up the hill toward the man on horseback with a string of saddled horses.

"Looks like you got plenty of horses, boys. So ride on out of here before you get into trouble," Brazos insisted.

"Mister, we've got the guns. You don't tell us what to do."

"Boys, you revealed yourself too soon. We know you got five, but you don't know how many we have," Brazos boasted.

"Don't try to bluff us."

"Did you count our horses? You haven't even found our camp. We could have thirty men just up this draw," Brazos said.

"There ain't thirty men in a hundred miles this time of year."

Dacee June cocked the huge hammer on the Sharps carbine. At the sound of the click, the man with the horse looked back over his shoulder, then returned his gaze to the scene in the creek below.

"Did you boys hear that hammer cock?" Brazos shouted.

"That was just a horseshoe on granite," the man with the horses called back down.

"Nope. That was the sound of a .50 Sharps. Have you ever seen what that can do to a man?" Brazos hollered.

On her hands and knees, Dacee June dragged herself through the mud. She crawled until she could stare under the belly of the tall bay mare. *Daddy, how could you hear that? You're losing your hearing. You are bluffing them, aren't you?*

The spokesman wore a flat-crowned gray felt hat. "We ain't fools!"

"That remains to be seen," Brazos replied.

She was only three feet behind the gun-toting horseman, partially shielded by a six-foot scraggly pine.

"You're goin' to lead us to your camp, and we're going to take what we want," the flat-crowned one declared.

"I don't think so." Brazos stared right up the side of the mountain where she crouched. "Go ahead, Lil' Sis, jam the Sharps in the back of that ol' boy up there!"

She leaped forward with such abandon the barrel of the carbine crashed into the man's backbone just above the belt. He yelped, staggered forward, and dropped his gun.

"What's goin' on up there, Brownie?" one man shouted.

Brownie still held the reins of the horses and raised his hands. "She got the drop on me!" he shouted.

"She?"

51

"Just some kid girl."

"I'm fifteen years old." Dacee June shoved the gun into the man's back.

"Take the gun away from her!" one of the men shouted. All four gunmen continued to point their weapons at the three men in the stream.

What am I supposed to do now? What if this man doesn't bluff? What would Daddy say if he were where I am? She glanced down at the men in the creek, then at the man's eyes that were looking over his shoulder at her. "Do you want me to kill this one now, Daddy?" she hollered.

The man in front of her slumped his shoulders and rolled wild eyes.

"You can kill him in just a minute, darlin'. But first, let's give them all a chance to ride away," Brazos insisted.

"She's crazy," Brownie hollered down to the others.

"She won't miss from that distance," Grass Edwards bellowed.

"She won't shoot you, Brownie. We've got her daddy and the others covered. She pulls that trigger, and they are all dead men."

"It ain't them that I'm concerned with." Brownie's voice cracked. "If she pulls that trigger, most my insides will be plastered on the big boulders on the other side of the crick."

"She's bluffin'," one of the men who had not spoken before insisted.

"Well, she don't have it pointed at you. I tell you she has a crazy look in her eyes. Look at her. She's covered with mud and looks like she's been living with the wolves!"

I'm just a little muddy and dirty and wet. "He insulted me, Daddy. Can I shoot him now? Please."

"I reckon that's fair."

"Wait a minute," Brownie screamed. "You ain't goin' to trade three lives for one, are ya?"

A man's voice blurted out like the lead singer in a Gilbert and Sullivan musical. "I figure it's three for three!"

It was the only time in her life she had ever heard Quiet Jim shout. It sounded like he was behind the boulders across the creek.

"What's goin' on?" one of the gunmen shouted.

"Now that's Quiet Jim Trooper," Grass Edwards explained, his hands still in the air. "He packs a Winchester '73 rifle. With good position he can take down two of you before you reach the trees. Say, you boys have heard of the Texas Camp, haven't you?"

"So," Yapper Jim blurted out, "that makes three out of five of you dead for sure."

"And with the other two separated from your horses," Brazos said, "the odds are gettin' slim."

"I ain't goin' to be shot by any little girl," Brownie grumbled. He reached back and shoved Dacee June's gun to the right.

She yanked it out of his hand. The barrel glanced off the man's shoulder and slammed into the side of his head, just above the ear. Even in the foggy rain, it sounded like a dry branch run over by a freight wagon.

Brownie crumpled to the mud, and Dacee June raised her gun at the men in the stream.

"Keep behind them trees, baby," Brazos called out.

"I reckon we've got four for your three," Grass informed the gunmen. "Dacee June will drop one of you with the first bullet and have plenty of time to shove in another cartridge for Brownie up there."

I only have one bullet, but they don't know that. Any girl "raised with the wolves" is bound to have plenty of bullets.

"Nice work, Lil' Sis," Brazos called out. "Your brothers will be proud of you."

"Say," Grass Edwards added, "you boys might know Brazos's sons. Perhaps you've heard of Sam Fortune?"

"Down in the territory?" the fattest man gulped.

"'Course, he won't stay down there if someone bushwhacks his daddy. Kind of touchy that way," Yapper Jim informed the men.

"You're Brazos Fortune?" another man asked.

"You boys thinkin' of ridin' off now?" Brazos challenged.

"Come on, let's go." One of the men holstered his gun.

"Keep that gun out!" the man with the flat-crowned hat hollered through the forest. The mountain-hanging rain clouds deadened all their sounds.

"He's the one that took down Doc Kabyo. I ain't goin' against him," another insisted.

"He doesn't even have a gun."

"It was Big River Frank, Dacee June, and me who took Kabyo," Brazos insisted.

"I think I can get three of 'em now," Quiet Jim said. "Now that the one holstered his revolver."

"Wait a minute. I'm ridin' out," the man insisted. "You can't shoot me. My gun's holstered."

"What's to keep you from yankin' that gun out the minute the shootin' starts?"

"We won't shoot an unarmed man," Brazos insisted.

The man unbuckled his revolver and let it drop to the mud.

"What do you think you're doin'?" flat-crowned screamed.

"I reckon I'm goin' to ride up to Bozeman and get really drunk, but I'll be alive come fall," the man reported.

The tall, thin man dropped his gun in the mud but left his holster on. "I'll ride with ya, Lanny. The stakes is too high in this game. A man has to know when to fold a hand."

"It don't look good," Brazos said. "You two take the old boy who Lil' Sis dispatched. No reason to waste a good bullet on him."

"I'll count to three. You shoot the skinny one, Quiet Jim. Lil' Sis can shoot the heavy one."

"Why can't I shoot the skinny one, Daddy?" she called out.

"Cause that big bullet of yours would divide him up like a fire-cracker in a tomato. There wouldn't be nothin' left to send home to Mama."

"I ain't playin' this game," the skinny one called out. He tossed his Henry rifle to the ground.

"Wait a minute," the last gunman growled. "I can't believe you let 'em bluff us."

The skinny man was halfway to the hill when he spun around. "And I can't believe you think any Fortune is bluffin'."

"This is rank. We get rused by four old men, three of whom are unarmed, and a little girl!" He shoved his gun in his holster and stormed up the hill after the others.

"Can I shoot him now, Daddy?" Dacee June called out. "He insulted me."

"I reckon it's justifiable," Brazos called out.

"What are you talkin' about?" the man screamed. "I put my gun in my holster."

"But you called her a little girl. That's a insult to my daughter."

"What in blazes am I supposed to call her?"

"A young lady," Yapper Jim insisted.

"A talented young lady," Grass added.

"A talented, beautiful young lady," Quiet Jim called out from behind the rocks.

"Call her a talented, intelligent, beautiful young lady," Brazos demanded.

"I cain't do that!" the man shouted.

"Go ahead and shoot him, baby," Brazos motioned.

She raised the carbine to her shoulder.

The man unbuckled his holster and dropped it to the mud. "I can't believe we let four old men and one talented, intelligent, young lady get the drop on us," he mumbled.

Quiet Jim strolled out from behind the boulders. "You forgot beautiful!"

"Absolutely stunning!" the man screamed.

Dacee June lowered her carbine. "Why, thank you!"

She met her daddy down the hill and tossed the carbine to him. "You look a little smudged, darlin'," he said. His voice sounded young.

"You look a little wet, Dacee June."

It was familiar, yet different, and she had to strain to see him, although he was only a few feet away. "Your face is sweatin' like a pig in a barrel."

She blinked her eyes open, and sat up. "What?" Her own voice sounded like a train whistle in a very long tunnel.

"It's hot in here and you're sweatin' something fierce." The voice was steady, deep, in control. A hand was on her shoulder. "Wake up, Lil' Sis."

Bright Dakota sunlight blasted through the glass of the Main Street windows. The room felt stifling. A tall, thin man with a graying goatee loomed at her side.

"Todd! You're back. Did you bring the governor?"

"The governor, Judge Young, and a passel of New York City businessmen. We had two carriages full. What did I miss around here, Lil' Sis?"

She gazed over at the shriveled old man in the bed. "Not too much. I just had a long dream about Daddy. Todd, I don't know why I do this. It just prolongs the pain. Does it happen to you?"

"Not yet. But I surely dream of Mama from time to time." Todd tugged open a window. A dusty blast of coolish air raced across her moist face. "Kind of hard to get excited about the holiday with Daddy on my mind. I suppose this one will be dull, what with no pageant or anything."

She took her brother's hand. "It won't be all that dull. Amber's written a play. And then there's the elephant."

"The what?" Todd gasped as his chin dropped.

"You see? You're getting excited about it already."

CHAPTER THREE

Joey met Dacee June at the bottom of the stairs. He rocked back on his scruffy heels and ran his tongue across his front teeth as his brown eyes danced.

Dacee June paused on the final steps. *Joey is so eager to please. Like a puppy, sometimes.*

"Mrs. Toluca, you look mighty fine today."

"Thank you, Joey."

"How's Daddy Brazos?"

"The same. Always the same, Joey."

"Whew-ee, you are the salesman, Mrs. Toluca. 'Course, ever'one always told me you could sell stereopticon slides to a blind man and make him the happiest guy in town. Do you think some day I'll be as good as you?"

She carried her straw hat in her hand and met him on the platform beneath the stairway. "What are you talking about, Joey?"

TEXAS CAMP

"Ma'am, we jist got that crate of 1894 smokeless powder Winchester 30 WCF in on Monday. I opened them up yesterday evenin' and put them in the case. Mr. Toluca and me was goin' to have a contest to see who could sell the most of them guns. If I beat him, he was goin' to buy me a beef-chop supper at the Merchant's Hotel."

She glanced back at the gun case. "How are you doing?"

"You got us beat already." The dark hair flopped down across his right eye, but she refrained from brushing it back. "You done sold six out of ten of them. We'll be needin' another case before August. You hardly left any for me and Mr. Toluca to sell."

Dacee June placed her hat on her head at a slight angle, then paused by a small mirror that hung from a twelve-by-twelve-inch post at the end of the bolt bin. "Not me, Joey. I sold one to that man, eh . . . that tall man with the broad shoulders. That's all. I've been too busy with Daddy to sell much of anything."

Joey jammed his hands behind the bib of the white ducking apron. "How about the man with the dark green shirt and brown leather vest? You sold to him, didn't ya?"

Dacee June studied her reflection in the little mirror. "That's the man I was talking about." *Sometimes I'm quite sure I look like my mother, but then her memory is so faded, so distant.*

"But you sold him six guns," Joey exclaimed.

"I sold him one Winchester for $24 and a box of shells. It came to $25.75. I stood there and watched his dimpled chagrin as he counted out the pennies."

"Pennies?"

"He had some dollar bills and the rest was in quarters, dimes, and pennies. I think it was most every cent the poor man had to his name. He said he wanted to look at knives, but he obviously couldn't afford one. I told him to show you the receipt and you'd get him his carbine and cartridges."

Joey's chin dropped. His eyes widened. "Are you joshin' me, Mrs. Toluca?"

She stepped over to the young man, their faces no more than a foot apart. "What are you talking about, Joey?"

His face turned red. "He gave me a bill of sale for six guns plus ten boxes of .30 caliber WCF smokeless bullets."

"He only bought one from me."

Joey spun a complete circle on his heels. "Oh, no . . ."

She grabbed his shoulders. "What's the matter?"

Joey pulled away and scurried to the counter at the back of the store, Dacee June right behind him.

Joey sorted through a dovetailed bullet box jammed with papers. "After you went upstairs he asked a dozen questions about that abalone-handled Barlow knife."

Dacee June folded her arms across her chest. "He didn't have enough money to buy anything."

"I didn't know nothin' about that. Finally, he looked around and asked where that good-lookin' woman clerk went to."

"He said that?"

"Yes, ma'am. I surmised he meant you. So I said you'd probably gone upstairs to see your sick daddy. Then he handed me a receipt for six guns."

Her hand flew to her mouth. "You gave him six guns?"

"He had your signature on his receipt, Mrs. Toluca. How was I to know?"

"Joey, are you telling me that man walked out of here with six rifles and only paid for one of them?"

"Six carbines and ten boxes of bullets."

"I can't believe this!" She stomped around to the front of the counter. "The man's a crook, and he looked so . . ."

"Broad shouldered?"

"No! He had beady blue eyes. At least, I think he did."

"I didn't look at his eyes. You want me to go upstairs and get Mr. Fortune to deal with this?" Joey asked.

"Yes . . . no, my brother needs to stay with Daddy. It's good for both of them." She pulled her straw hat back off her head and began to fan her face. "I'll take care of this myself. I just can't believe it!"

"Here's the receipt!" Joey handed her the slip of paper. "Ain't that your signin'?"

"Yes, it's my receipt. But the one's been changed to a six, and the one box of shells turned to ten! He got ten boxes of .30 caliber Winchester center-fire cartridges?"

"Yes, ma'am. That's what's on the receipt."

"When did he have time to forge it?"

"When I was in the storeroom!" Joey blurted out. "He asked if we had any more knives in the storeroom, and I went back to check. That surely does look like a six and a ten, don't it?"

"He is a very good forger."

"What else could I do? I know I should've checked with you, but you went up to see Daddy Brazos, and I seen the hurtin' in your eyes and jist didn't want to bother you none. I'll make it up. I'll save up and pay you back, honest. Just don't fire me 'cause this is the best job I ever had in my life."

She stared at the teenage boy. *Honey, just how many jobs have you had to work in your life? Way too many, that's for sure.* "Joey, the man's a crook. You didn't do anything wrong. You're like family to us. You aren't ever going to get fired."

"I didn't think he was suspicious lookin'. Was he suspicious lookin' to you?"

Why is it, Lord, that handsome men are never suspicious looking to me, but ugly ones always are? What a foolish woman I can be. "The fact is, he stole those guns. He will face Deadwood justice. I'll go talk to the sheriff."

She kept the receipt in her hand, and he piled the others back into the wooden box.

"Yes, ma'am," Joey replied. "The sheriff will take care of it as soon as he comes back."

"Where is he?"

"I seen him at the Silver Dollar Cafe when I was at lunch. I heard him tell Jewel Spinner that he had to deliver a warrant on some old boy named Primkiss in Crook City. Ain't that a funny name? The man, I mean, not the town."

"When will he be back?"

"Cain't take very long to ride to Crook City and back. He'll want to be back by dark. Some of them ol' boys down across the Dead Line will be actin' up tonight with firecrackers and dynamite, even if it is only July 3rd. And there's a dance. Are you goin' to the dance?"

"I thought it was for young people."

"You ain't exactly old, Mrs. Toluca."

"Thank you, Joey, but your compliment doesn't overshadow the fact there is a crook to catch."

"The broad-shouldered man?"

"The one who needed a hair cut and had beady eyes," she fumed. "When did he leave the store?"

"About an hour ago, I reckon. Maybe a little less. We could telegraph down to Rapid City for them to be on the lookout. Your brother, Robert, could check the trains."

She tapped the toe of her black lace-up boot on the wooden floor. "I don't need my brothers to help. I'll take care of it."

His eyes widened. "All by yourself? How about Sam? I bet that broad-shouldered man would back down if he faced Mr. Sam Fortune."

"I said I'll take care of it, Joey!" she snapped.

"Yes, ma'am."

"Do we know the serial numbers on the stolen guns?"

"I wrote 'em down on the ledger."

Dacee June once again jammed her straw hat on her head and pinned it to her dark hair.

"Where are you goin' to look for him?" Joey asked.

She stared out the front window and spotted a black leather hack trotting north toward the depot. "If the man's still in town, where do you think he'd be?"

"He won't be up at this end of town, that's for sure, Mrs. Toluca. I reckon he'd be down at the Piedmont or at the Green Door. You ain't goin' into them by yourself, are you?"

"Joey, I will go into any building in this town to find the man with the . . . ."

A slight grin broke across his narrow lips. "Broad shoulders?"

"Green shirt and brown vest," she glared.

"If Mr. Todd Fortune comes down, you want me to tell him where you went?"

"No, don't tell him, Joey. He has enough to worry about besides a man who just stole five rifles."

"Carbines."

"A man who just stole five carbines isn't likely to hang around town very long, is he?"

"So you don't think he's in town?"

"Maybe not, but I believe there's someone who saw which way he left. Perhaps I can at least find a name or a route to have for the sheriff when he returns. I just can't stand by and do nothing."

"You make it sound personal."

"It is personal."

Dacee June stormed out into the bright afternoon sun. A dull thundering roar flooded down the gulch from the Homestake Mine's gigantic stamp mill up at Lead. Dust fogged up from the wagons and coaches and hung suspended in the air. Every breath was seasoned with red dirt.

BLY

She adjusted her straw hat and stopped at the boardwalk toward Deadwood's Badlands. *I simply will not allow a man to take advantage of me like that. If he thought he could get away with stealing from Dacee June Fortune, he has another thing . . . I mean, Dacee June Fortune Toluca. There is such a thing as Deadwood justice. Mister, you will regret this day for the rest of your natural life, no matter how short it might be.*

Skeeter McAllister lounged against the redbrick wall of Barry's Smokes and Pawn, chewing on an unlit cigar. He stood at least a foot taller that her. He tipped his hat. "Afternoon, Dacee June."

"Skeeter, maybe you can help me. I'm looking for a man."

"What's wrong with Carty?" he drawled.

A stern furrow of her eyebrows brought Skeeter's round-brimmed hat off his head. "Sorry, ma'am, I was funnin' ya. Who are you lookin' for?"

She glanced up and down the wooden sidewalk. "A thief."

"What did he steal?"

"Some goods from the hardware."

"What kind of goods?"

Another glare from Dacee June silenced his narrow, unshaven face. "Eh, what did he look like? Can you give me some description?"

"He was about six foot one, approximately 175 pounds. His dark brown hair was shaggy and curled out under his dirty gray felt hat. He needed a haircut. He had blue eyes, with sort of a dark blue ring around the pupils. His face and chin were strong and chiseled. He looked about my age, and he had a small scar about one inch long on his neck under his right ear. And he sort of had . . . broad shoulders."

Skeeter stared at her with an open mouth.

"Well, have you seen him?" she questioned.

"I couldn't even describe myself with such detail."

TEXAS CAMP

She clamped her arms across her chest and was surprised to feel the receipt still tucked in her fingers. "Have you seen such a man or not?"

"What was he wearing?"

"A green shirt and tan buckskin vest that looked almost new. The brass buttons had buffalos on them, and the second button needed to be resown. His jeans were so faded they were sky blue and he wore a woven leather belt, you know the kind they make in prison. His scruffy brown boots had one heel tacked with a horse-shoe nail."

"Was he packin' a pistol?" Skeeter asked.

"Not that I could see. He wasn't wearing a holster, and he didn't have a gun stuck in his belt."

"Was he carryin' a rifle?"

"Maybe a carbine or two." *How does a man carry six carbines out of a store in broad daylight without being suspicious?*

"What did you say?"

Dacee June leaned close enough to smell the smoke on the tall man's vest. "Skeeter, have you seen a man that matches that description or not?"

"Yes, ma'am. I seen a man with a green shirt and brown leather vest."

"Where was he?"

"He was headin' into your hardware store about an hour and a half ago."

"No, I mean after that. Where did he go when he came out?"

Skeeter leaned back against the brick wall. "He didn't come out."

"What?"

"I mean, I never did see him come out. So I don't know where he went."

"Have you been here all day?" she asked.

"Right here. You know how I am, Dacee June. I like stayin' put and lettin' the excitement come to me."

She studied the lanky, sandy-haired man with tattered duck-ings and faded flannel shirt. "Are you sure you've been here all day?"

"Yep. Except for a lunch break. A man's got to eat, you know. I jist got back when you hiked up here."

She bushed her dark bangs out of her eyes. "Thanks anyway, Skeeter."

"You're welcome. If I spot him, you want me to tell him you're lookin' for him?"

"Absolutely not! I want to find him, not him find me. Do you understand the difference?"

"Yes, ma'am. It reminds me of my second wife. It was always best that I find her, not that she find me." Skeeter's grin revealed a wide gap in his lower teeth.

"Have you seen Jenng Wing? He knows everything that goes on in China Town."

Skeeter rubbed his eyebrows with his fingertips. "Not since I helped him at the depot early this mornin'."

"At the depot?"

"Fresh fish came in iced down all the way from San Francisco. Ain't that something? I hepped him unload over five hundred pounds. I heard that they got a machine in San Francisco that makes ice. What will they invent next?"

"Perhaps I'll stop by and see Mr. Wing."

"Are you goin' clean down to China Town?"

"If I need to. I really want to find that man."

"You want me to walk with you?" Skeeter offered.

She looked at the puffy red circles around the tall man's eyes.

"Thank you, Skeeter, but this is my town. I can go anywhere I want."

He tipped his hat. "Yes, ma'am. I reckon you can. Sorry I was such lame help to ya today. We's still pals, ain't we?"

"Skeeter, you've been my friend since the first day you came to Deadwood and wanted some work and Daddy put you to chopping wood while I stacked it. Do you remember that day?"

"Like it was yesterday, Dacee June."

She reached over and patted his shirtsleeve. "That was fifteen years ago."

He stood straight and threw his chest back. "It was fourteen years and two months, but who's countin'?"

☞ ☞ ☞

The high, stiff collar buttoned under her neck felt confining as she hiked on the boardwalk, but Dacee June resisted the urge to unfasten it. She marched through the ten-foot-tall open doors of Beano Billy's and into a fog of cigar smoke and coarse laughter.

The long, narrow saloon grew silent. Even in the shadows, she knew she was the only woman in the building, the object of every blurry-eyed stare.

Dacee June paused in the middle of the room. A young man about twenty years old, and at least three inches shorter, staggered up to her.

"You're lookin' mighty fine tonight, darlin'," he drawled.

A bartender with a white shirt and black tie and carrying an axe handle marched up to the man. "Son, this is Miss Dacee June, you don't talk to her that way."

The young man jerked his revolver from his holster and waved it at the man. "I seen her first. You'll just have to wait your turn," he slurred.

The first blow from the axe handle caught the man on the wrist. The scream drowned the sound of the gun crashing to the floor.

BLY

The second blow creased the man's hat above his right ear. The now silent young man dropped to the gray-painted wood floor of the saloon.

He didn't move.

Nor did Dacee June.

The crowd broke out in applause.

"Sorry, Dacee June," the bartender hollered above the roar. "He's sort of new in town. He don't know better."

She stared down at the young man. "I certainly hope you didn't do any permanent damage."

"Don't worry about him. I'll give him free drinks when he wakes up. Now what can I do to help you?"

"Beano, I'm looking for a man who stole something from the hardware."

"What did he look like?"

"He was . . . *broad shouldered and* . . . six foot one, about my age, wore a dirty gray hat, and a green shirt with brown leather vest."

Beano glanced around at the waiting patrons. "Did you hear that, boys? Dacee June is lookin' for some old boy with a green shirt and leather vest. He took somethin' that belonged to her, and that jist ain't tolerated in Deadwood. Any of you sober enough to have seen him?"

"I seen him!" a short man with a long scraggly gray beard offered.

"Cabbage Charley, where did you see him?" she asked.

"He was headed into your brother's hardware," the old man announced, as if he had won a hand of poker.

"Did you see him come out?" she pressed.

When the man shook his head, the beard waved like a flag. "Nope."

"I think I seen a man like that," another offered.

She spun around to see a heavyset man in a tight wool suit at the big mahogany bar. "Tiny, where did you see him?"

"I'd rather not say, Miss Dacee June."

Hoots and hollers exploded in the room.

"Tiny, I won't say anything to your mother."

He tugged on his tight collar. "You promise?"

"Not a word."

"There was a man of that description over at Lizzie's Club."

"When were you there?" she asked.

The big man paused. "I wasn't ever there, remember?"

Again the room broke out in a roar.

"When was the man with the green shirt and leather vest at Lizzie's?"

"I reckon he got there a little over a half-hour ago."

She strolled closer to the big man. "You think he's still there, Tiny?"

"If he's got enough money, I reckon so." He pulled off his hat.

"I think he's broke, unless he sold the goods already."

"What goods?"

"My goods."

"If he's broke, he won't be at Lizzie's very long. She don't give credit to no man."

"Thank you, Tiny. I think I'll go check it out," Dacee June said.

"You're welcome, ma'am. You need me to go over there and check if he's still there?"

She laughed and noticed that everyone in the saloon was still focused on her. "No, I think you've spent enough time at Lizzie's today."

"I reckon so. You sure you ain't goin' to tell my mama?"

Beano stuck the axe handle below the bar and began wiping glasses with a white tea towel. "Dacee June is Brazos Fortune's daughter. That means she don't lie, ever," he huffed. "Now a couple of you drag that old boy back into the corner, so we don't trip over him and hurt ourselves."

Even the dust-laden air that hovered above Main Street tasted sweet compared to the smoke in Beano Billy's.

Lizzie's Wayfarer's Club is not the only two-story building along the Badlands section of lower Main Street that has no windows, but it is the only one painted autumn plum. I should know. I mixed and sold her the paint. She came in and said, "I want a color so memorable even a drunk in a blizzard can spot it." Lizzie, you certainly achieved that. Some say that if it weren't for the mountains, Lizzie's could be seen from Chicago.

The man who stood at the door of Lizzie's Wayfarer's Club rocked back on his heels and grinned as he saw Dacee June approach. His new black beaver felt hat was cocked to the side. He had no neck.

"Howdy, Dacee June, you out collectin' for the library?"

Lord, everyone in this town sees Rutt as a dangerous hulk of a man. But I know he's a soft-hearted man who would give a needy dove his last dime. "Hello, Rutt. No, it's not collection time. Is Lizzie in?" *I can never understand how he pulls those shirts on over the immense muscles on his arms.*

"Yep. Should be in her office. You want me to check?" He reached over and took her hand.

It is as if my hands were those of a child. So tiny, so lost in his. "I'll go see her. Thanks anyway, Rutt."

He didn't let go of her hand. "What's the trouble, Dacee June, darlin'?"

She glanced away. "Trouble?"

His voice was low, like a submerged boulder rolling down the creek during snow melt. "I can see it in your eyes."

She stared up at the massive three-hundred-pound man with a scarred face and wide brown eyes. "I can't slip past you, can I, Rutt?"

"No, darlin'." He released her hand. "I spend my life studying people."

"And singing Gilbert and Sullivan."

Among the pockmarks a wide smile broke across his face. "Yes, ma'am. Did you catch the show?"

"Of course I did, Rutt. My daughters think you are the greatest tenor ever to sing in Deadwood."

"How about their mama? What did she think?"

"I agree with them completely."

He rubbed the corners of his leather-tough, creased eyes. "Dacee June, you don't know how good that sounds. There ain't no one in the Black Hills whose opinion I value more than yours."

"That's a very nice compliment, Rutt."

"I meant it."

She stared into his deep brown eyes. "I know you did. You are a good friend."

"And you are a troubled friend. Eyes don't ever lie."

"Just a little trouble at the store. Sammy always says I worry too much about the business."

"I ain't seen your brother much lately. He used to stop by and we'd visit about life down in the Indian Nation."

"He's been stayin' close to Daddy."

"How is Mr. Fortune?" Rutt asked.

"Not gettin' any better."

"You reckon he has any idea how important he is to some of us down in the Badlands?"

"What do you mean?"

"He always took a man for face value. Didn't care where a man hung his hat, just as long as he was honest. A lot of us feel mighty proud to have Brazos Fortune for a friend."

Dacee June wiped her eyes. "Thank you, Rutt. Perhaps you can help me. A man stole some things from the hardware this afternoon, and I'm tryin' to track him down. Tiny said he might have seen such a man come in here. He had a . . ."

He held up his hand. "Don't ask, Dacee June. You know I cain't tell. I swore to Lizzie I would never ever tell anyone who comes to her place. I just cain't, really. It's a pledge I made, and I want to keep all my pledges."

"I understand, Rutt. I'll go see Lizzie."

"Thank you, Dacee June. And thanks for always talkin' to me. Most folks rush right by and never say a word."

"You and me are pals, Rutt. I always talk to my pals."

"I ain't never known a nice lady who had so many pals in the bad part of town."

Dacee June pushed through to the large entry room lit by a crystal electric chandelier. Oak wainscoting lapped up the wall to the yellow floral wallpaper. A lady with long red hair peeked her head around the corner.

"Dacee June!" the woman shouted out.

"Hi, Rosie." Dacee June pulled off her straw hat.

The short woman bustled out in the middle of the room, her black silk skirt swishing as she strutted. Dacee June gave her a brief hug.

"It ain't time for the doctor's checkup, is it?" Rosie asked.

Dacee June took the woman's pale, thin hand. "No, I just came by to see Lizzie."

Rosie clutched Dacee June's arm. "We still ain't had that cup of tea you promised."

"When are you coming up to see me? I still have that assortment of French teas."

Rosie glanced down at her bare toes that stuck out from under the satin dress. "I don't reckon many would be happy to see me up on Williams Street."

"I would be," Dacee June replied.

"Yeah, all you Fortunes is different."

"I'm a Toluca."

"You is a Fortune, through and through, Dacee June. You know what I mean."

"I need to see Lizzie."

"And I need to steam my face," Rosie added.

Dacee June stared at the weak brown eyes of the shorter woman.

"Ain't you going to say it?" Rosie asked.

"What?"

"You know, what you always tell me."

"About quittin' this line of work?"

"Yeah, that part. Ain't you goin' to say it?" Rosie insisted.

"No."

The red-headed woman looked hurt. "Why?"

"Rosie, I've told you that for almost five years, and here you are. It's your choice. I can only wish something better for you, but I can't do anything about it."

"Say it, please," the woman insisted.

Dacee June folded her arms across her chest. "Rosie Benoit, you have to take better care of yourself. This is no place for a beautiful girl like you to work." She watched Rosie's eyes soften. Tears formed in the corners.

Then the woman dropped her chin to her chest. "I been thinkin' about it. Thinkin' about it real hard, Dacee June."

"You have?"

"I couldn't do it without help."

"You know that the Lord would help you . . . and so will I."

"I know. Sometimes that's the only good news I have. Dacee June and the Lord haven't given up on me yet." Rosie scooted across the room. "You need to see Lizzie?"

"Is she in her office?"

Rosie glanced up at a brass clock on the wall above the plum velvet settee. "It's 2:21. She will be sittin' in her chair, a New York newspaper spread across her desk, and sound asleep."

72

"Nap time?"

"Yes," Rosie said.

"Perhaps I shouldn't disturb her."

"No, you go right in. She always claims she isn't sleepin'. If we leave her be, she gets upset."

"Are you sure?"

"You can trust me, Dacee June."

She's right, Lord. I do trust her.

Dacee June lightly rapped her knuckles and pushed open the door a few inches. "Lizzie?"

The heavy woman slumped over the English walnut rolltop desk sat straight up. Her words were flung out like darts. "Dacee June? Darlin', what are you doin' here today?"

"May I come in?"

"Of course you can. I was just readin' the newspaper. Did you know that demi-saison gowns from Paris are quite the rage in New York City this summer? Look at this one in *Harper's*. It's wood-colored with a small check in the front and in the back, trimmed with gold embroidery and a yoke of fancy silk. That's velvet embroidery on the cuffs. And the hat . . . look at that hat, girl . . . that's a rosette of yellow mousseline de soie. What do you think?"

Dacee June stood behind the large woman and stared down at the illustration in the magazine. She put her hand on the woman's shoulder. "It's absolutely beautiful! But if you wore a hat with that many plumes in the Black Hills, some old boy would mistake you for a wild turkey and shoot you for sure."

Lizzie let out a deep belly laugh. "You're right about that girl. How about the dress?"

"Now, Lizzie DeShey, you and I have discussed bustles many times, and you know I think they are absolutely horrid. I have no idea in the world why they are making a comeback."

The woman with rings on every finger reached up and patted Dacee June's hand. "You're right, darlin'." The fifty-year-old woman stood and took Dacee June's arm. "You know, I used to be as skinny as the woman in that picture."

"I know. You've shown me the photographs."

"I was a looker, wasn't I?"

"Lizzie, you had the looks every woman in the world envies. I never in my life looked that good. You remember how I looked? A pudgy little tomboy."

"Darlin', you were always the Queen of the Black Hills. And you never looked like a tomboy, except maybe in that buckskin outfit. Now, what are you raisin' money for? You know you can count on me for a contribution."

The two women strolled arm in arm to the middle of the large, over-furnitured room.

"No charity work this time, Lizzie. I've got a problem."

Lizzie stopped and faced her. "You came to the right place. That Carty Toluca is treatin' you good, isn't he?"

Dacee June's shoulders and neck relaxed. "He's an absolute jewel. You know that."

"Brazos is your daddy. Todd, Sam, and Robert are your brothers. And then you married Carty Toluca. You just might be the luckiest woman on the face of the earth, girl," Lizzie giggled.

"I know. I know. I never have a problem with them. The truth is, Lizzie, I had a man steal some items from the hardware store, right under my nose and I'm . . ."

"You are really steamed about it? You take it very personal and plan on catchin' the culprit by yourself."

"How did you know all that?"

"You're easy to read, darlin'."

"That's exactly what Rutt told me."

"So what can I do about this stealin' scalawag?"

Dacee June strolled around the office and studied the French Impressionist painting of two girls at a piano. *Lizzie's office always smells like lilacs, whiskey, and chocolate.* "Tiny said he might have seen the man over here." She turned toward Lizzie. "I'm tryin' to track him down or find out what direction he went."

Lizzie laced her fingers in front of her ample waist. "You think he might be at my place now?"

"Maybe." Dacee June took a deep breath. "Or at least within the last hour." Using her hands to express herself, she described the man.

Lizzie shook her head. Dangling earrings slapped against her rouge-painted face. "I don't know his name. But I could tell he was a thief when he walked in the door. That's why I asked for his money before I let him in."

"His eyes are rather beady, aren't they?" Dacee June said.

"Yep, that's him. I think he's visitin' with Trudella."

"Now? He's here now?"

"Yep." Lizzie fingered her pearl necklace. "But I can't tell you that. In this business ever'thin' has to be private. So I can't fetch him, or even let you confront him. But I can shoo him out into the street, and you can coldcock him there."

The air was stuffy, and Dacee June could taste the perfume in the air. "I'm not going to coldcock him. I just want my guns back."

"Guns? He stole guns?"

"Oh, Lizzie, I wasn't going to say what he stole. Don't tell anyone. Did he have them with him when he came in?"

"No guns, or they have to face the wrath of Mr. Mangin. If he stole guns, you should get the sheriff, darlin'."

"The sheriff's at Crook City." Dacee June surveyed a three-foot-tall, porcelain Japanese woman that sat on a teakwood pedestal.

"Don't you go gettin' into trouble. But to tell you the truth, he looked more like a footpad than a gun thief. I didn't think he had it in him."

"He changed the bill of lading and walked out the front door when I wasn't looking. I seldom work at the store any more, but I don't want anyone to think they can get away with anything while I'm there."

Lizzie rubbed the bridge of her wide nose. "You want him at the front door or the back?"

"The front. I suppose it would be safer to have Rutt standing nearby."

"You carrying your pistol?" Lizzie asked.

"Not since the girls were born."

Lizzie pulled open the top drawer of the rolltop desk. "You want one of mine?"

"No, I don't want to shoot him, Lizzie. I just want our guns and bullets back."

Lizzie waltzed over to her. "Sometimes it takes a gun to get a man to take you serious. You can trust me on that one, darlin'."

"I'll have to chance it."

"Confront him with Rutt lookin' on. Maybe that will calm him down a little."

"Thanks, Lizzie. I'll wait outside."

"You can wait in here, darlin', you know that."

"I'd rather be outside, that way it won't come back on you."

Lizzie sauntered with her arm in arm to the front door where Rutt loomed like a massive iron statue. "Did you buy them hymn-books like I asked you to?" Lizzie asked.

"I ordered them from Chicago," Dacee June explained.

"The girls will be surprised." Lizzie paused in front of a big oval swivel mirror.

"I imagine they will."

"They need to know those good old hymns." The big woman let out a deep sigh. "I used to be skinny."

Dacee June kissed the woman's sagging, rouge-covered cheek. "I know, honey. I know."

☞ ☞ ☞

Dacee June paced the sidewalk in front of Lizzie's Wayfarer's Club. Every time a wagon or carriage rumbled down the dirt road she turned aside, her back toward the travelers.

Carty is out of town. The girls are at church with Amber. Todd is upstairs at the hardware. Robert is coming in on the Rapid City train. Sammy is . . . where is he? Lord, I just don't want to have to explain to my family why I'm down here. If you could, let me confront this crook, get my guns back, and go home in private. The children will be done with play practice and be starved. Unless they ate some of that cake. That horrid elephant cake!

Dexter Norris drove his hack up the middle of the street, and Dacee June darted into the alley.

This is crazy. You are a mature woman. What are you doing down here, Dacee June Toluca?

OK, perhaps not mature. But at least old enough to stay away from the "suspicion" of evil. At least the alley is empty, which certainly won't be true after dark. Lord, I want to get this over. I'll just walk up to that broad-shouldered man and say . . .

What am I goin' to say?

"Mister, you owe me $129.50. I want the money or the guns immediately, or else . . . or else . . . I'll tell my brothers, I mean, my husband . . . or the sheriff . . . or . . ."

Lord, why do we women always have to have the authority of a man behind us before anyone listens? Even Mama, bless her soul, out on that hill country prairie threatened those by appealing to her men. What does a widow with no sons do?

What on earth am I doing here? A man who steals guns will certainly use one. This is crazy.

Maybe I should just say . . .

"What in the world are you doing here, dear?"

Dacee June spun around to see Dexter Norris's hack with a white-haired lady seated in the back drive into the alley between Lizzie's and the Iron Bucket Saloon.

"Mrs. Speaker?" Dacee June choked.

"Dexter is driving me home from Mrs. Treadway's. Her gout is better today, but she still sits in that rocker and won't even cook. Now, is that any way to live? I made her a big pot of potato and onion soup with ham hock, but she'll probably let it grow cold. Anyway, we were driving down the road and I saw someone step into the alley, and I said, 'That looks like Dacee June Fortune,' and Dexter said, 'You mean, Dacee June Toluca,' and I said, 'Yes, of course that is what I mean, but what is that girl doing down in the Badlands,' and Dexter said maybe you were doing some social work, but there was no one around, and I thought perhaps you lost something and we could help you find it, but Dexter said you weren't looking down but seemed to be examining the paint on the wall."

Even though she wore a flat-brimmed straw hat, Dacee June shaded her eyes with her hand. "It's autumn plum."

"What is, dear?"

"That's the color of paint on the wall. I mixed it myself. I was curious as to whether it faded more on the east side of the building than here on the west."

Mrs. Speaker leaned back on the leather bench. "I should have known our girl was working. Dexter, did you know that she helps with the store and at the phone company, and teaches her darling girls French? She is quite an amazing young lady, isn't she?"

The chiseled-faced driver nodded his head.

"Can we give you a lift, or do you have your own rig?" Mrs. Speaker asked.

"I walked down. I needed to stretch my legs."

"We can certainly give you a lift back uptown. No one needs that much exercise."

"That's not necessary."

"Nonsense, I won't go off and leave you down here. How would I explain that to your Carty and your brothers?"

"Really, Mrs. Speaker, I'll be a few minutes. I don't want to keep you."

"I'm in no hurry."

Dacee June searched the silent driver's unemotional eyes. "Dexter might need to . . ."

"You aren't in a hurry, are you, Dexter?" Mrs. Speaker questioned.

The driver shook his head.

"You see, it's settled. Go ahead with your work."

"Dacee June?" The voice sounded like an alarm. A deep, rumbling alarm.

She looked up to see Rutt Mangin standing at the corner of the building. "Hate to interrupt, but he's about ready to leave," he reported.

"Who dear?" Mrs. Speaker asked.

"Mrs. Speaker, wait right here in the alley. I have to go talk to a man about some, eh, hardware."

"What did I tell you, Dexter? She is a hardworking girl, just like her mama. Did I tell you that Sarah Ruth, that's Dacee June's mother, and I were very good friends? Why one time . . ."

Thelma Speaker's voice faded as Dacee June looped back out on the Main Street sidewalk. Rutt chatted with the man in a green shirt and leather vest.

Dacee June shuffled along by the front wall of the building, keeping Rutt between her and the man.

If I can sneak up on him, he won't bolt and run. Maybe.

She caught a glimpse of the shirtsleeve.

The shirt has more blue in it out in the sunlight.

Then the unfastened vest drifted into view.

And that vest is more stained than I remember. Everything looks a little different in the sunlight.

She darted around Rutt. "Mister, I want to talk to you."

Dacee June found herself staring at an overweight, bald man, with a button missing on his shirt. A watch chain without a watch hung loose from his vest.

He had round shoulders.

"Who are you?" she demanded.

"I reckon I'm the man you wanted to talk to."

"I don't want to talk to you!" she snapped.

"Ain't this the man, Dacee June?" Rutt asked.

The man surveyed Dacee June from boot to hat. "The man for what?"

"Of course he's not the man!" she fumed.

"But you said he wore a green shirt and a leather vest."

She could feel the back of her neck grow warm. "That shirt is blue."

"It most certainly isn't," the man huffed. "It's paradise green. I should know. I work for the mill that made the cloth."

"You aren't the one I want," she insisted.

He attempted to button his vest. "And you aren't the one I want."

Rutt Mangin stepped up to the man. "Don't talk to Dacee June like that," he growled.

"This is extremely strange," the man said. "Melvin Philips warned me that Deadwood was different, but I just wasn't prepared to be castigated by bouncers and . . ."

"Careful with your choice of words," Rutt pressed.

"And, eh, society ladies."

"You don't want to talk to him?" Rutt asked Dacee June.

"No."

Rutt clamped his hand down on the salesman's shoulder. "Then get out of here, mister."

"I . . I . . I certainly intend to," he stammered.

The bald man scurried up the wooden sidewalk toward the El Dorado Club, and when he reached the open front door, he darted inside.

"Don't you know something about him besides his shirt and vest?"

Dacee June let out a deep sigh. "He has blue eyes, with sort of a deep blue circle about them, looks about thirty or so. He has broad shoulders, and his hair is thick as it curls out under his hat, and he has a slight scar . . ."

"On his neck under his right ear?"

"Yes, that's him!"

Rutt wiped his hand across his lips. "Why didn't you say so in the first place?"

"I, eh, I just wasn't thinking clearly, I suppose."

"You're lookin' for Wade Justice."

"Wade Justice? Where have I heard that name?" Dacee June watched the street as a small Mexican boy led a milk cow by the ear.

"In Pierre." Rutt studied three well-mounted cowboys as if looking for an assassin. "I heard yesterday that Justice was the one that was on trial for stealing the steamboat loaded with contract beef."

"But he wasn't convicted?"

"Nope. One of the jurors disappeared during the trial, and some of the other jurors got scared and went home. The judge threw the case out, then left town too."

"Oh! Oh, my. What's a man like that doing stealing six guns?"

Mangrin chewed on his tongue. "Guns? I reckon he needed them. Glad to know Justice is in town. I'll warn Lizzie."

"But why steal six guns? That seems strange."

"Not if you have five friends."

"A gang?"

"Justice had five men with him when he hijacked that steamboat. And it would be a desperate gang if they now have no guns.

I hear Justice is mean, Dacee June. Don't you go confrontin' him without me or one of them brothers of yours around."

"Or Carty."

"Who?"

"My husband."

"Yeah, don't go tacklin' the likes of Wade Justice without good help and a gun. You still carry that .38?"

"No, not for many years."

"You ought to," Mangrin insisted.

"Are you saying that Justice is the type to shoot an unarmed woman?"

"If you was tryin' to take away his guns, he might."

"I can see I've acted rather hasty. I will proceed with more caution. Frankly, he didn't look that mean."

"Them are the most dangerous kind, Dacee June."

"Thank you for the assistance, Rutt. At least I will have a name to give the sheriff."

He tipped his hat. "You're welcome, Dacee June. Say, I'm goin' to sing some patriotic numbers on the Fourth. You're invited to come listen."

"Where at?"

"Right here at Lizzie's Wayfarer's Club. You're always invited to come listen."

"Thank you, Rutt. You know I'd like to hear you sing, but there's a pageant at the church and my girls are in it."

"What time is the pageant?" he asked.

"I think it's at 7:00 P.M."

"I ain't singing until after 9:00. Bring along them girls with you and we could . . ." Suddenly, Rutt backed away. "I'm sorry, Dacee June, I wasn't thinkin'. That ain't right. Them girls should never come down here. I meant no harm by it."

"Will you be singing the 'Battle Hymn of the Republic'?" she asked.

"Yep, that's one of them."

"How would you like to sing that at the patriotic pageant at the church?" she probed.

His stare burned into hers. "You joshin' me?"

She took his muscled arm. "You know me better than that."

"They ain't goin' to let me sing up there. What would the deacons say?"

"Now, Rutt Mangin, do you think there's a man in Deadwood that can tell me no?"

He began to laugh a deep, guttural laugh that was so infectious Dacee June giggled. "No, ma'am, I don't reckon there's a man in Dakota or Wyomin' who would say no to you."

"Then, will you come sing for us?"

"Yes ma'am, I believe I will."

"I'll let you know what time for sure."

"I won't embarrass you, Dacee June."

"You never embarrass me, Rutt Mangin."

When she twirled around the corner she spied Thelma Speaker leaning back on the carriage seat as if trying to hear the conversation on the street. She sat up as Dacee June approached. "Did you speak to the salesman?"

"The wh . . . what?" Dacee June stammered.

"I believe you said it was hardware you needed to discuss?"

"Oh, yes, I spoke to him. But it was the wrong man."

She climbed up in the carriage next to Thelma Speaker, who leaned over and whispered, "You really don't expect me to believe the story about examining the paint, do you?"

Dacee June patted Mrs. Speaker's dress-draped knee. She could smell the older lady's familiar Morning Poppy perfume. "OK, I was down here to talk to Mr. Mangin too."

"My, he does have a lovely tenor voice, doesn't he?"

"Yes and I asked him to sing at the church Fourth of July pageant."

"How delightful. But what will Mrs. Majors say?"

"I imagine she'll pitch a fit. But it won't be the first time. I want Mr. Mangin to sing. I've been tryin' to coax him to church for years."

"He was always Louise's favorite in the operettas, rest her soul." Thelma Speaker dropped her head and brushed her cheeks.

Dacee June slipped her arm around Mrs. Speaker's shoulder. "You miss your sister, don't you?"

"I miss Louise, and the professor, and Sarah Ruth and am startin' to miss your daddy, Henry, as well. I'm goin' to be the last one, Dacee June."

"Now you sound like Quiet Jim."

"Quiet Jim Trooper is several years younger than me."

"And I predict both of you will be around for many years."

"It's a lonely thing, Dacee June . . . being the last leaf on the tree is very, very lonely."

"Enough of that. We all need you very much. You are the only grandma my children have known, and they dearly love you."

Thelma sat up and took a deep breath. "Yes, you are right. I was just overcome by a maudlin moment. I need to think of other things."

"Precisely," Dacee June encouraged. "Why not look forward to the pageant? Did you hear Amber stayed up all night writing it?"

"Oh yes, and I heard it was a story about Dacee June Fortune Toluca, the Queen of the Black Hills."

"Silly, isn't it?"

"She does remind me of someone," Thelma mused.

"Now don't you start in on me. Abby is constantly blaming me for everything Amber does."

"She is rather ambitious," Thelma Speaker said. "She has her mother's stunning good looks, and I'm surprised she reached twenty without any marriage offers."

"Mrs. Speaker, that girl has had marriage offers since she was fifteen. But she wants to wait until after she's twenty-one. She's supposed to be in line for some inheritance from her father's estate. She didn't want anything to cloud that matter, as if it weren't clouded already."

Mrs. Speaker patted Dacee June's knee. "Was it really fifteen years ago when Abby and Amber came to town?"

"Yes, but don't you start in on that 'we're all getting old' routine again."

"All right, dear, why don't I change the subject?"

"Good idea."

Thelma Speaker sat back and folded her hands in her lap as the carriage rumbled up the street. "Tell me this: who was the man with the green shirt and leather vest, and why wasn't he the one you were looking for?"

CHAPTER FOUR

Dacee June insisted on getting out of Mrs. Speaker's carriage at the corner by the BuzzNut Cafe. When she marched up Main Street, two dogs stopped barking and scurried behind a pile of bricks in front of W. Keller's Fine Men's Clothing Store. A thick dark cloud sailed in front of the bright Dakota sun, causing an avalanche of shade to race right past her. For a moment even the easterly wind stopped blowing.

Joey Plummer stood at the door of the hardware as she approached. His white canvas apron hung to one side, matching his long bangs. His hands were shoved into the back pockets of his denim jeans. "I was beginnin' to worry about you, Mrs. Toluca. I was feared you found that ol' boy down in the Badlands and he was givin' you a hassle."

She held her thin hands out in front of her and spun her wedding ring around on her finger. "The one you really ought to be worried about is Mr. Wade Justice."

"Justice?" Joey's hands shot out of his pockets as his brown eyes surveyed Main Street. "I heard he's the one that shot them four cowboys dead up on the Yellowstone River last December?"

Dacee June tramped into the store. "I know nothing of that. All I know is that he was the one who cheated Fortune & Son Hardware out of five Winchester rifles and . . ."

"Carbines," Joey attempted to correct.

She pranced over to the gun case and stared at the remaining carbines. "He will account to me because of them."

"That was Wade Justice?" Joey bounced from one foot to another.

"Yes, so I'm told."

"I thought Justice was older than that." Sweat popped out on Joey's smooth, tanned forehead. "Imagine that . . . I sold guns to Wade Justice and lived to talk about it!"

Dacee June tried to rub the tension out of the corners of her eyes. "We sold him one gun. He stole the others."

"Oh, brother, am I ever glad I didn't rile him." Joey was almost dancing around the aisle. "I can't believe it . . . *the* Wade Justice? Right here in our very store. I mean, your store. He's the most famous person I ever met in my life. Did you ever meet Wild Bill Hickok?"

"Yes, I did. He was a very dashing man."

"Ol' Jack McCall did him in before I ever moved to town. But Wade Justice? I've got to mail my mama. She's always askin' if I've met anyone famous. This will impress her. Did you hear about the time Wade Justice and two others robbed four banks in one day? That must have been a sight to see. I surely wish I could have been there."

Dacee June untied her hat and tried to brush her hair back over her ears. "If Mr. Justice is such a fearsome man, why did he resort to deceit to get our guns?"

Joey's eyes grew big. "Yeah, you would have thought he would've just walked in here, examined a gun as if to purchase it, shot us all dead, and stole ever'thing in sight."

She yanked a Winchester 94 out of the glass case and ran her hand along the smooth wood of the buttstock. "Now there's a happy thought."

Joey strutted back and forth with a scowl. "You better not tangle with him, Mrs. Toluca. That's a job for someone like your brother Sam. Yes, ma'am. You don't want to mix it up with the likes of a gunfighter like Wade Justice."

Dacee June threw the carbine to her shoulder and traced an imaginary target across the high ceiling of the hardware store. "Mr. Wade Justice, I will not allow you to get away with this. Vous n'avez aucune idee la colere que vous avez juste encourue."

Joey stepped back as she shoved the carbine into his hands. "What does that mean?"

She spun around at the sound of boot heels. "It means he has no idea the wrath he has just incurred."

Todd Fortune descended the stairs with the precision of a Prussian officer, his short, graying hair neatly combed, his tailored suit crisp and precise, his black tie perfectly tucked into his gray vest, mustache and goatee groomed.

Dacee June scooted over to him. "How's Daddy doing?"

Todd tapped on the worn oak stair railing. "He's sleeping. Jamie Sue came over to sit a spell. She said she could be with him until the play practice started over at the church. I need to stretch my legs and check on some things at the bank. Did I tell you I've decided to sell the iron frame building next to Abby's?"

"Did you find a buyer?"

"Some outfit that wants to manufacture a self-propelled carriage using a steam-driven engine."

"Like a train without tracks?"

"I suppose. But they are willing to pay cash."

"Just don't take any payment in stock," she encouraged.

"Now you are beginning to sound like Rebekah."

Dacee June took her oldest brother's arm as they strolled toward the front of the store. "Did Daddy wake up at all?"

Todd laced his strong fingers into his sister's. "Long enough to drink some water and let me feed him some of your soup."

Lord, I have always known I have the best brothers on the face of the earth. Patricia and Veronica missed out on knowing that. "The soup must have been snow cold."

"He didn't seem to mind. I don't think he can tell hot from cold anymore. Anyway, I told him his Dacee June made the soup for him, and he slurped it right down."

She leaned her head on Todd's shoulder. "Did he say anything?"

"No, but he knew what I was sayin'. There was that little sly smile of his and the tears rolled down his cheeks."

"Tears?"

"When I mentioned your name, darlin'."

She hugged her brother's arm. "Why doesn't he just let go, Todd? He was the most independent . . . most . . ."

"Stubborn?"

"Yes, the most stubbornly righteous man on earth. He would not let anyone do anything for him. And now, we have to feed him and wipe his chin and change his soiled sheets. That's not the way Daddy Brazos should have to live. And he misses Mama so. Why doesn't he let go? Why doesn't he just let Jesus take him home?"

Todd stroked her long brown hair. "Sis, darlin', Daddy can let go of life. He knows that he's lived a good and faithful one. He can let go of the store and the other businesses. He put all those in my hands years ago. He can let go of his friends. Just Quiet Jim left. I believe he can let go of the grandkids, though he loves them dearly. And you know what, Lil' Sis, I reckon he's ready to let go of me, Sam, and Bobby. He's done all he can. He's ready to release us into the Lord's hand. But, Dacee June, I don't think he knows how to let go of you."

She pulled away from Todd and dropped her chin to her chest. She struggled not to sob. "Are you saying it's my fault?"

"No, Lil' Sis." He put his left hand on her shoulder and lifted her chin. "I'm sayin' that when Mama died, us boys went every direction. You were all he had, and he pledged himself to look after you. You've been his life, his crutch, his purpose, his delight. I just don't think he knows how to let go of his Dacee June. Your love gave him thirty more years of life, and Bobby, Sam, and I are grateful."

"But now I have Carty and you boys are around. There is no woman in South Dakota surrounded by finer men. I think he can let go now."

"None of us can be Daddy, of course. The Lord only made one Brazos Fortune. But I don't reckon he wants you to not need him anymore. Can you remember when Mama died?"

"He sat on the bed for twenty straight hours holdin' her dead body until Rev. Tasker and Dr. Shaney came and pulled him away."

"He doesn't turn loose easy. It's not in him. He just doesn't know how, darlin'." He let his arms drop to his sides. "Now, Sis, don't pay me too much mind. I just don't know how to handle this either. I'm not ready to be the oldest Fortune. I feel helpless. Helpless for Daddy, helpless for you, helpless for Rebekah and the kids. When he's gone, I'm not sure what I'll do."

She brushed down his coat sleeve and picked off a piece of lint. "You'll do fine, big brother. Daddy knew what he was doing when he put you in charge of everything." She looked him straight in the eye. "Do you know what he told me last month about you?"

"You been holdin' back something?"

"I thought I would be so smart and wait for the eulogy. But the words have been clawing at my heart from the inside trying to escape. One night about a month ago when he was hurting and couldn't breathe very good and kept coughing up blood, I sat at the head of the bed and held him up so he could catch his breath. He had one of those clear-thinking moments, so I started talking about Mama and how nice it would be to see her again. He perked up. His tired eyes cleared. He started talking about us kids one at a time."

"And you never told us? What did he say?"

"I was going to wait until I could get through it all without crying," she offered. "Daddy said Robert was just identical to Mama . . . smart, faithful, sensitive, and a bulldog if you ever crossed him."

"He gets more like Mama every year, it seems to me."

"And he said Sammy was just like him. Strong-willed, reckless for whatever he believes in, not willing to back down from any man, any time, and has a hard time ever admitting a mistake."

"Which is why the two of them went toe to toe for years. Now they understand each other with just a nod or a glance."

"Daddy said he figured Patricia and Veronica were just like Grandma, but they didn't live long enough to prove it. And me, well he said I was a pure cross between him and Mama. He said I had every one of their strengths. He didn't mention that I have every one of their weaknesses too. But we all know that."

"And how about me?" Todd asked. "What was his verdict on his oldest son?"

"He said, 'There's never been a finer man in the Black Hills than my boy Todd. He's smart, courageous, wise, self-controlled—things I could only wish for. Todd turned out to be the man I always wanted to be but never could.'"

She heard him gasp as she watched him march out the front door of the hardware store, not looking to the left or right.

Joey finished helping another clerk with a barrel of nails, then scurried up to her side. "Is Daddy Brazos all right? I thought I seen Todd cryin'."

"No, he's not very emotional. He hides his feelings."

"I'd have sworn it was tears."

"It was probably just the dust in the air," she said.

"Did you tell him about them missin' guns?" Joey quizzed.

"No, did you?"

Joey's brown eyes blinked hard. "No, ma'am, I was hopin' you'd tell him."

"I'll take care of it, Joey. It's my sale, and I'm responsible. If anyone asks about the carbines, just refer them to me. Now, do you and the other clerks think you can take care of things for a while? I'll go check on the gang of little hooligans with Amber at the church."

"Yes, ma'am, we'll take care of the store. Tomorrow bein' a holiday and all, I don't reckon there will be too much business."

"Jamie Sue is upstairs with Daddy. If you need someone to make a decision, just ask Jamie Sue. She'll tell you what to do."

"Yes ma'am," Joey gulped. "I'm sure she will."

Dacee June grinned. "Joey, there is no one in the Black Hills more opinionated than men with the last name of Fortune, unless it is the women with the last name of Fortune."

☛ ☛ ☛

The white double doors on the church stood wide open. Dacee June heard giggles and shouts as she approached.

Elita ran to greet her. "Mama, this is the most fun Fourth of July play ever!"

Lord, I will not be jealous. I have begged you to find someone to work with the children and now that you have, I refuse to mope. Dacee June hugged her oldest daughter and could feel the thin, bony shoulders through the light cotton dress. "That's very nice, darling. Elle est tout a fait une jeune dame etonnante."

Elita nodded. "Yes, Amber is a very amazing girl!"

Dacee June stopped in the entryway and picked a white sock off the small book table. "I trust you are all minding her."

"All except Garrett and Casey," Elita said.

"They are the youngest boys. That's to be expected, I suppose."

Ninete bounced up. "Hi, Mama, guess what I've been doing?"

"By the looks of the gray icing on your chin, young lady, I'd say you've been examining the elephant cake a little too closely."

Ninete wiped her mouth on her burgundy dress sleeve.

Amber Fortune led a swirl of cousins halfway down the aisle. "Aunt Dacee June! Something horrible happened."

Who got sick? Hurt? Where's Jehane? "What is it?"

"Mother has that cough in her throat that she seems to get every summer. I don't know why the doctors don't do something with it. Anyway, she has a sore throat and said she doesn't think she'll be able to sing the closing song tomorrow night at the pageant! What am I going to do?"

Dacee June took her hand, and the two women strolled to the platform at the front of the sanctuary. "Amber, you are twenty-one years old. You have a lovely voice. You can sing the finale."

"I'm not twenty-one for a few more weeks," Amber said.

"That's not my point."

Amber clutched Dacee June's arm. "I can't sing. I give a dramatic interpretation of the song that I'm performing. It is essential that someone else sing. You'll have to sing for me . . . please." Amber's face reflected rehearsed anxiety.

Dacee June hugged her niece, Nettie, who leaned at her right side. "The last time I sang at a pageant was right before my wedding, and I was absolutely horrible. I believe that's the first time I ever saw my father grimace when I was on stage. That was my last song."

"What am I goin' to do?" Amber wailed.

Dacee June peered under the front pew and retrieved another white sock. "What song is it?"

"The Battle Hymn of the Republic," Amber announced.

Dacee June rubbed her chin. "How would you like the best tenor between San Francisco and Chicago to sing for you tomorrow night?"

"You mean," Amber gasped, "David Myer O'Campo?"

Dacee June shook her head. "I have a friend who makes Mr. O'Campo sound like a twelve-year-old with his voice changing."

"He's here in Deadwood?"

"Just happens to be."

"What's his name?" Amber pressed.

Dacee June leaned close but still had to speak up to be heard above the chatter of the children. "I think it would be better not to reveal that yet, if you understand what I'm saying."

Amber clapped her hands. "Oh, yes! Mother told me that when she was in the theater famous actors would sometimes stop by to visit and would be talked into minor parts for fun, as long as they didn't advertise their names and try to make money off it. Is it that sort of thing?"

"You'll understand when you hear him sing," Dacee June said.

Amber laced her hands straight on top her head. "Oh, dear, maybe I should rewrite the script."

"Why?"

"Because I have the soloist standing off stage! I don't want to insult him."

"Off stage will be fine, honey. He's a very gracious man."

Amber rocked up on her toes. "Is he someone you met from college back in Chicago? Was he in the opera? Has he ever sung in Europe? Is he handsome? Is he tall? Does he have a wonderful smile? Is he single?" Amber let herself slowly down. "Aunt Dacee June, what are you staring at?"

"Amber Gordon Fortune, sometimes when I look at you, it's like looking back in time at myself. I can't believe you and I are so much alike."

Amber grinned. "And we're not even related. I mean, by blood."

"Young lady, you and I are related by marriage, by the blood of Jesus, and by a kindred spirit so similar it's uncanny. I don't think you can get closer than that."

Amber threw her arms around Dacee June. Both women were the same height, size, and hair color. "I wish you were going with me to Kentucky to settle my father's estate."

Dacee June stepped back to glance at the red, white, and blue display at the front of the church. "Your mama will be with you. That's a beautiful banner."

"I know, but Mama has so many hurts back there. She'll be too melancholy to give much advice. Thank you, I sewed the banner last night."

"I heard you were up until three writing the script."

"And then from three until eight this morning I made the banner."

"You do plan on sleeping, I presume."

"Aunt Dacee June, sometimes life is just too exciting to sleep. Do you know what I mean?"

"Yes, I think I can still remember those days."

"Won't you come with me to Kentucky? Bring the girls with you. We can practice French all the way back on the train."

"Amber, you are a bright, intelligent woman. You know how to make good decisions. Just do what's right. Do what you won't have regrets about later. The Lord will be with you."

"I know," Amber said. "But I'm much wiser after I talk things out with you. I feel panicked when you aren't around. Do you know what I mean?"

"Yes, I do." *And that is precisely one of the reasons I just can't turn loose of Daddy.* "When are you going to be done here?"

"In about an hour. Little Frank went home to get Grandpa's Sharps carbine for a prop. Then we'll go through it one more time. We couldn't have a story about the Black Hills and not have Grandpa Brazos's Sharps."

"Would you like for me to stick around and help see everyone gets home?"

"The twins will help me."

Dacee June glanced around the room. "Where are Patricia and Veronica?"

"They went downstairs to try to fix up the elephant cake."

"What happened to it?"

"It sort of got bumped," Amber said. "Little Frank and Quint carried it downstairs by themselves."

"Bumped it against what?" Dacee June asked.

"The communion table."

"The communion table has gray icing all over it?"

"Oh, no, we cleaned that up. But it made a large dent in the elephant. But don't worry, the twins got a round loaf of sourdough bread, and it filled in rather nicely. Now they are smoothing the icing over the loaf of bread. No one will be able to tell."

Dacee June strolled to the back of the sanctuary and down the stairs to the basement. *The person expecting a piece of cake and getting sourdough bread will be able to tell! Lord, I can't believe anyone would give such a cake to their friends. This is the kind of thing you send to an enemy. Hmmm, I wonder if I can send it to Mr. Wade Justice?*

The twins were busy with spatulas trying to skim off enough red-dirt-dusted gray frosting to paint the loaf of bread. Both wore long green calico dresses with short puffy sleeves hemmed in white lace, their long brown hair down, and matching calico ribbons in their hair. And both had a trace of frosting on the left side of their up-turned noses.

"Hi, Aunt Dacee June. I think it's atrocious looking," Veronica declared, rocking from one foot to the other. "Cakes weren't meant to be this size. They can't hold up."

"I don't think it's cake all the way down. There is some sort of wire frame under it, isn't there?" Dacee June said.

"That's why Little Frank couldn't run Daddy's sword clear into the middle!" Patricia declared. "We thought it was just a tough cake."

"Now that is something I wish I had a photograph of . . . Little Frank Fortune slaying the cake elephant!"

"Little Frank said it looks more like the manure pile out behind the Montana Livery," Patricia giggled. "If you close your eyes, the frosting is rather tasty, in a gritty sort of way."

Dacee June circled the cake. "Even if it does stay edible, we will never eat such a monstrous cake. We'll have to throw most of it away."

Veronica smeared gray frosting on the bread crust. "Aunt Dacee June, where do you throw away a cake the size of a small elephant?"

"Now that, girls, is a very good question. We could dump it outside town and attract every varmint for a hundred miles. Or perhaps we could haul it to the border and abandon it in Wyoming. But that might start a war."

Seventeen-year-old Patricia brushed her straight brown bangs back out of her eyes, leaving another trail of gray frosting. "Little Frank suggested we toss the cake down an empty mine shaft."

"Your brother is very bright." Dacee June leaned over and surveyed the cake. "Is that a stick in there?"

"It holds the loaf of bread in place," Veronica announced.

"It looks like a twig off a tree."

"Yes, it was out in the alley," Patricia said.

Dacee June tried to brush the wrinkles out of her forehead. *Lord, this might be the most awful cake ever made on the face of the earth. Another Deadwood first!*

TEXAS CAMP

Patricia sidled up to Dacee June. "Did you know that Little Frank is sweet on Quint's sister?"

"Yes, I did hear about that." *That young man could melt a glacier with those dancing eyes.* "How are your brother and Fern Trooper getting along?" Dacee June asked.

"Oh, not Fern, Aunt Dacee June," Veronica gasped. "Little Frank likes Sarah."

Dacee June's hand flew to her chest. "Sarah? Oh, my word. When did this happen?"

"Sunday, after church," Veronica said.

"And you didn't tell me?" *Little Frank is nineteen. That makes Fern eighteen and Sarah seventeen. This sounds like trouble, young Mr. Fortune.*

Patricia licked gray icing off the spatula. "We thought you saw them slip off on that ride."

"Ride? Where?" *How could I miss so many important things at church?*

Veronica tilted her head, folded her hands on her cheek, and batted her thin eyelashes. "We don't know, but he sure came back home smiling big."

"Just how big was he smiling?" Dacee June asked.

"Real, real big!" Patricia raised her eyebrows as she talked.

"And what does Fern Trooper say about all that?"

Veronica wiped the frosting off Patricia's nose. "Quint said Fern and Sarah aren't speaking to each other."

"Which is hard, since they share the same room," Dacee June added.

"One time Veronica and I got mad and didn't talk to each other." Patricia grabbed a tea towel and wiped the frosting off her sister's face.

"How long did that last?" Dacee June asked.

"Not talking or getting mad at each other?" Veronica quizzed.

"Not talking to each other," Dacee June replied.

"About an hour," Veronica said.

"It was seventy-six minutes," Patricia added.

"That's about an hour," Veronica shot back.

Patricia folded her arms across her chest. "It is not."

"Why do you always have to correct me?" Veronica's arms were folded identically to Patricia's.

"I only correct you when you are wrong," Patricia chided.

Dacee June shook her head. "Girls, when you are through with the cake, Amber needs you upstairs." *Some things never change. They panic if they have to go a day without each other yet spend half their time getting on each other's nerves. Like a marriage, I suppose.*

"Are you goin' to sing the finale, Aunt Dacee June?" Patricia asked.

"No, but I understand a quite well-known tenor has been secured."

"Wow, just like that." The faint freckles on Veronica's nose seemed to jump up and down when she smiled and talked. "Amber has a lot of contacts among actors and singers."

Patricia's expression mirrored her sister's. "She should. Aunt Abby was the best actress to ever play the Black Hills. All the Fortunes say so."

☞ ☞ ☞

Dacee June hiked up the church stairs while the twins giggled in the background. The air was hot, dusty, heavy. She tromped past the hardware store without going in. She was just about to turn toward the Williams Street stairs when a familiar figure rode a buckskin gelding up the middle of Main Street.

One wave from Dacee June and the gray-haired man with the long drooping mustache rode over and tipped his hat. "Afternoon, Dacee June. It's July hot, ain't it?"

She tugged on the sweat-drenched collar of her dress. "Yes, it is." Dacee June pulled off her straw hat and began to fan herself with it. "Sheriff, did you know that Wade Justice was in Deadwood today?"

He sat straight up in the saddle. His right hand went for his gun. "Justice is in Deadwood?"

"Yes, he came into the hardware, but I must confess I didn't recognize him."

The sheriff surveyed the second-story windows of the hotel across the street as they talked. "What did he want?"

Dacee June glanced down at the toes of her black lace-up boots. "He, eh, purchased a gun, a new Winchester '94 smokeless carbine."

The sheriff spat a wad of tobacco out into the street, then took his hand off the grip of his revolver. "You sold Wade Justice a gun?"

She squinted up at the older man on horseback. "I didn't know who it was. We can't really ask for identification when we sell a firearm."

The sheriff's eyes narrowed. "How many bullets did he buy?"

Dacee June felt about twelve years old. "He purchased one box of .30 caliber Winchester center-fire, smokeless bullets."

The sheriff pulled off his hat and ran his fingers through his graying hair. He glanced up at the cemetery on Mount Moriah. "So this is the day?"

"What day is that, Sheriff?"

"Dacee June, when I took this job, Seth Bullock told me the day would come when some scoundrel, some gunslinger, some crazy violent drunk would show up and I'd either have to kill him or he'd kill me. I've been gettin' up ever mornin' for six years wonderin' 'Is it today?' If Wade Justice is plannin' something in this town, then I reckon this is the day."

She felt a heaviness on her chest. Each word came out forced. "He was in town, but I'm not sure he still is. I asked around, and no one has seen him since. I believe he rode on off."

"Justice ain't goin' to stay in plain sight. You got to know who to ask in this town."

She tied her hat back on. "I asked Skeeter, Beano, Rutt, and Lizzie," she replied. "Not a one of them had seen him in town."

He studied her eyes. "You asked the right ones, Dacee June. Sometimes I forget all the folks you know. If the likes of them ain't seen him, he's gone . . . for a while anyway. But tell me, just why were you lookin' for him?"

"After he left the store, I, eh, I got suspicious and tried to find out who he was."

The sheriff glanced up the street toward a big brick building. "Is Sammy around?"

"I suppose he's over at the phone company. You goin' to depu- tize him?"

"Dacee June, to tell you the truth, if I couldn't count on Sam Fortune backin' me up, I'd lay down this badge and ride off to Cheyenne in a minute."

"You know he'll be there. Bobby's due in on the train, and Todd . . . he's probably up on Forest Hill, but I'll find him if you need him."

"I might need them all. First, I'll check around. Your brothers are Deadwood's insurance policy." The sheriff pulled his Winchester '73 carbine from the scabbard and laid it across his lap. "Before anyone cuts too big a swath in this town, they know they have to deal with the law and with the Fortunes. That's enough to force many a would-be outlaw to seek easier pickin's. But Justice, he's a different type. He's the only man I know wild enough to take on ol' Stuart Brannon head-to-head down in Globe City, Arizona."

"And he lived through it?"

"Oh, you know Pop Brannon. I heard he marched straight up to Justice and coldcocked him before he ever knew what was happenin'. According to the rumors at the depot, that was a couple years ago. But from the sounds of things, Justice has only got meaner."

"Perhaps he was just passin' through Deadwood. He could be halfway to Spearfish by now."

"Maybe so. But he bought that carbine of yours for a reason. I'd like to figure out the reason before I get it pointed at me. If you see any of your brothers before I do, fill them in for me. Afternoon, Mrs. Toluca. I reckon I knew this day was comin'." He tipped his hat and rode his buckskin toward the Montana Livery.

Lord, forgive me for not telling the sheriff about the guns Justice stole. I wanted to. I planned on it. But I just couldn't. I can't tell him I'm so pigeon-headed that I let a desperate man steal five more guns from our store. Lord, this is frightening. The sheriff is right. This might be a deciding day. I'll tell Carty when he gets home. He can tell the others.

☞ ☞ ☞

Dacee June paused at the small wood platform halfway up the seventy-two stairs leading to Williams Street. She glanced back over the top of Main Street to the Mount Moriah Cemetery on the far side of the gulch.

Lord, I was in this town the first time they buried a man on that mountain. It was Big River Frank, after he took a bullet that was meant for me. There have been lots of folks buried up there in the past twenty years: Preacher Smith, J. B. Hickok, and the babies that took sick one winter. I knew that someday I would wear black and follow that empty saddled pony of Daddy's up there. One more season, Lord. Give me one more season with him. Please.

The telephone was ringing when she shoved open the unlocked front door to her mansard-roofed house. Her boot heels tapped the hardwood floor over to the wall-mounted telephone.

"Yes, this the Toluca residence." She untied her straw hat.

"I know that."

Dacee June jammed the hat on a wooden peg near the telephone. "Joey?"

"Hi, Mrs. Toluca."

"Is it Daddy?"

"No, ma'am. You got a telephone call here, and I surmised you wanted to know about it."

She unfastened the three tiny simulated pearl buttons on her high collar. "Who called?"

"Mr. Brewster."

"Which one?" She ran her fingers over the top of the cherry-wood hall table and stared at the dust tracks they left.

"I don't know. Does it matter?"

"No, I suppose not. What did he want?"

"He wanted to talk to you."

"What about?"

"He didn't say."

"I'll ring him back," she declared.

"Your brother's here and wants to talk to you."

"Which one?"

"Does it matter?"

Dacee June sighed and rolled her eyes. "No, put him on."

"What?"

"Let him have the telephone."

"Shoot, he owns the whole company."

The voice was so deep it always tickled her toes. "Hi, Lil' Sis."

"Hi, Sammy."

"The sheriff said Wade Justice was in the store."

"Yes, and I didn't even know it was him. Are you deputized?"

"Yep, I'm wearin' a badge under my vest. Sis, don't tell Abby. She always worries when I help out."

"Please be careful. I hear Justice is a very violent man."

"If the rumors are true, he's a violent man without reason or accountability, Dacee June. Those are the worst kind. I heard someone say just the other day that Wade Justice and five half-breeds stole a thousand head of cattle. He sold the cows and shot the half-breeds."

"He didn't look that despicable."

"Does despicable always show?" he asked.

"Apparently not. How about Robert? Is he deputized?"

"Bobby just came in on the train. The sheriff was at the depot to meet him. Bein' a railroad detective means he's already deputized. Have you seen Todd?"

"Not for a while. He might be behind the houses on the hillside. I can go check."

"Don't bother him, but when you see him, tell him to get deputized. We might need his 'Flying Fist of Death.'"

A brief, tight smile flashed across her face. "I won't mention that. Has anyone spotted Justice still in town?"

"Nope. But that's a tad frightenin' in itself."

"Be careful, Sammy."

"Don't worry, Sis. I know types like Justice."

"I will worry, because I know types like Sam Fortune."

After her brother hung up, Dacee June sat down on the deacon's bench in the hallway and unlaced her boots. She could feel the heat of the sweat-drenched cotton stockings. There were hot spots on her feet where the leather had rubbed as she hiked up the stairs. She tugged off her shoes and socks, then wiggled her pink toes.

Spud Brewster probably wants to tell me that Carty just passed by heading back to Deadwood, which, of course, doesn't get him home one bit faster.

She stood in front of the mirror next to the umbrella stand. "Lord," she mumbled, "I know that a lady should not expose her bare toes in public, but if I was really poor and owned no shoes, it would be acceptable. So what I want to know is, Why do poor women get all the fun?"

I'd call Spud Brewster, but Mordecai would answer too, and they would bicker and fight. I'm not in the mood for any more of that.

Dacee June padded across the living room carpet toward the kitchen, then straightened the leather pillows on the sofa. She felt something hard poke her bare foot.

"A grapefruit seed? On my carpet?" *But we haven't had a grapefruit since Christmas! Why, I've run a carpet sweeper over that place a hundred times since then.*

The linoleum floor felt cool to her warm feet. She slowed her pace as she entered the pantry. *I really must get a new carpet sweeper. We'll hang the carpets next week and make sure they're well beaten. It's been a year or more.* She took a deep breath and sighed. "Now, what will I fix for supper?" *It was much simpler when we had a big dinner and a small supper. But the children never want to eat much at noon, and Carty . . . my wonderful Carty. He loves everything I do for him. Lord, I can't believe all the torment I caused him when we were young. I guess I knew it was him even back then. I was only twelve, but I could tell.*

And now, Elita is eight. When will she know the right one? Will she be twelve? Oh dear, I hope it's not the Poulson boy . . . he's so aggressive. On the other hand, Thomas Smylie is a dud. I know he's only eight, but the future seems cast.

The ringing of the telephone caused her to jerk her head back.

I trust it isn't Joey asking if I called Spud Brewster. She scurried back through the living room to the entryway.

"Yes? Toluca residence."

"I thought this was Dacee June's house."

"I'm Dacee June Toluca."

"Oh, yep. You told me that."

"Is this Spud?"

"It sure as Hades ain't Mordecai."

Suddenly another voice boomed into the telephone. "Don't you start ridin' me, Spud Brewster!"

"Get off the line or you'll get the business end of a double-barreled shotgun."

"Boys!" Dacee June hollered. "I've got to fix supper, so tell me the message and then let me go. You can argue all day long, but I don't have time."

"We've been arguin' all day long."

"No we ain't. We just started when Dacee June Fortune called the first time."

"If we have, it's all your fault."

"Boys, I'm hangin' up now!" she announced.

"Ain't you going to listen to what I have to say?"

"Go ahead then. Has Carty passed by on his way back to Deadwood?"

"Nope. There's some kind of gunfight goin' on up at the Broken Boulder Mine."

Dacee June rubbed the back of her neck. "What?"

"We hear gunshots, but we can't figure out what's goin' on."

"When we tried to call the mine, no one answered."

"We thought you might want to know."

"Did either of you ride up to check it out?" she asked.

"Ain't got no horse. Besides, if I pulled out, that thievin' Mordecai will steel ever' thing I own."

"You ain't got one thing in there worth stealin'!"

"I surely ain't goin' to let you steal it anyway."

"Are you telling me that Carty hasn't come back by your place and there is gunfire at the mine and you won't go check it out?"

"Yep. That's why I'm callin' you."

"I'll tell the sheriff immediately."

106

"About what? About me and Spud?"

"No, about the shootin' at the Broken Boulder," she murmured as she hung up.

☛ ☛ ☛

By the time Dacee phoned Sammy and Robert, then grabbed her .32 caliber Whitneyville revolver and scurried down the steps, Rebekah had signaled Todd. He was ten steps behind her.

"Do you know if Carty is in that gunfight? Or is it just a guess?" he called out.

"I know nothing more than what the Brewster brothers told me. I know Carty is still out there some place."

He caught up with her at the bottom of the stairs, and they scurried arm in arm to the store. The sheriff stood beside Sam and Robert Fortune as they entered the two-story brick building.

"I tried to call out to the mine, or to the Brewsters, but the line must be dead," the sheriff replied.

"I've got to go check on Carty," Dacee June insisted.

"We'll go with you, Lil' Sis," Robert said.

"I got a question," the sheriff pondered. "Now, I came over here the minute Sam called. I figured on ridin' out with you. But on the way I got to thinkin' about Wade Justice. What if he was going to do something in Deadwood? Wouldn't it be good to send me and all three Fortune boys on a wild-goose chase?"

"That would purtneer leave the town wide open," Sam agreed.

"What do you think we ought to do?" Dacee June asked.

"How about Bobby and me goin' with Lil' Sis, and Sammy and the sheriff stayin' in town?" Todd suggested.

"I was hopin' you'd say that," the sheriff said. "But I didn't want to be selfish."

"One of us needs to be around Daddy anyway," Robert added. "I'll go upstairs and tell Jamie Sue."

"And I'll phone Rebekah," Todd said.

"Ask her to watch my girls," Dacee June said.

"I'll get three horses from the livery," Samuel announced. "Lil' Sis, do you want a sidesaddle?"

Dacee June scowled.

"Eh no, I reckon you don't."

☞ ☞ ☞

Robert led the way out of town on a sorrel gelding.

Dacee June followed on a bay.

Todd rode a long-legged black horse named Martinez.

All three carried brand new Winchester '94 carbines across their laps. When they reached the Butler Creek Road, Robert waited for the others and they rode up the hill, three abreast, with Dacee June in the middle.

"You armed us with pretty good weapons, Lil' Sis." Todd fingered the receiver of the carbine. "I haven't had time to check these out yet."

"Sammy says he likes these new '94s," Robert added. "I looked for Daddy's Sharps, but Little Frank must have it."

"It's at the church for a prop," Dacee June explained. "The .30 caliber cartridge should be enough. I wanted us to match the opposition."

"Who is the opposition?" Todd pressed.

"I have no idea," she said. "I don't even know if Carty is in trouble, or if he and Quint stopped to shoot coyotes. I think I may have overreacted."

"Are you sayin' we should go back?" Bobby asked.

"I'm saying that I've had a lousy feeling about Carty going out to the Broken Boulder all day, and it's still nagging at me. He's been so run down and tired lately."

"Daddy hanging on has taken a toll on all of us," Robert admitted.

The black horse whinnied and pulled left. One kick from Todd's spur corrected him. "I haven't had a good night's sleep in months. It's wearin' Rebekah out, I'm sure, but she's not one to complain."

"Kind of interesting how it works. How many hours of sleep do you reckon Daddy has lost over the years worrying about us?" Robert murmured.

Dacee June tried brushing down her long, full skirt across the horse's shoulders. "And now everything is turned around."

Robert chuckled. "I would guess he didn't lose as much sleep over the three of us combined as he did for Sammy by himself."

"We all had our moments to cause him grief," Todd replied.

"Even little Bobby?" Dacee June challenged.

Forty-one-year-old ex-army captain Robert Fortune gritted his teeth. "Don't you two start in on the Bobby stories. It's bad enough when Sammy is here."

"Just one," Todd said. "I don't think I've smiled in six months, so humor me. It was the last Fourth of July parade before the war."

Bobby groaned. "Not this one."

"Be quiet, little brother."

"Go on, Todd. It's nice to think of those days," Dacee June insisted.

"We were down in Austin and Daddy had been talkin' to Sam Houston about what Texas would do in case of war. So we all went to the parade. Mr. Houston wanted to have the flags flying to invoke patriotism. It was the most marvelous parade I ever attended in my life."

"I was only five," Robert murmured.

"We were all lined up," Todd continued. "Mama had one twin on each side. They were about three years old or so. Sammy went off to stand with Aunt Barbara and Uncle Milt."

"If I remember right, he went to stand with some little blonde-headed girl," Robert said.

"How old was he?" Dacee June asked.

Robert pulled off his black felt hat and wiped the sweat off his forehead. "Eight. But Sis, he charmed the little girls just liked he does the ladies still."

"Anyway," Todd continued, "I'm standin' next to Daddy, and Mama has the twins, and then all of a sudden, we look around and can't find little Bobby."

"Was he chasing girls too?" Dacee June chided.

"Bobby? He never looked a girl in the eye until he was seventeen."

"Eighteen," Robert said.

"Anyway, Bobby was gone and Mama was beside herself. He was never just Bobby to her. She always called him *my* Bobby . . . *my* darling . . . *my* sweet boy . . . but she had to care for the twins. So Daddy and I started searchin' up and down the crowd."

Todd sat straight backed in the saddle as he rode. "Daddy was in near panic. You know how he always was with us kids. He made it clear every day of his life that we were his most precious possessions."

Dacee June surveyed both of her square-shouldered, square-jawed brothers. "Where did you find him?"

"The parade started. The drum and bugle corps marched. The soldiers came riding prancin' horses. Daddy and I looked up, and here came Mr. Houston riding that big white horse of his, all decked out in a Texas general's uniform. The crowd was hollerin' and wavin' and there, sittin' in the saddle just ahead of Mr. Houston, was you-know-who."

Dacee June clapped her hands and giggled. "Bobby?"

"Yep." Todd put his right hand on the rump of the horse, leaned back, then faced the other two. "So Daddy was hoppin' mad and dashed out in the street to grab him and tan his hide for runnin' off."

"What happened?" she asked.

"Mr. Houston said, 'Let him ride, Brazos. He'll remember this day the rest of his life.'"

"It's the only memory I have before I was ten," Robert admitted. "I have never forgotten that day. That's when I knew I would be a soldier."

"Later that evenin', back at the hotel, Daddy quizzed him about why he ran off like that," Todd said.

"What did he say?" Dacee June asked.

Todd sat back up with his reins hand resting on the saddle horn. "He said that he just wanted to do something to make Daddy proud of him."

"What did Daddy say?" Dacee June asked.

"Do you remember, Bobby?" Todd challenged.

Robert Fortune stared straight out over his horse's ears. "Oh, yeah. I can hear that crusty low voice. 'Son, there has never been one second of any day that I haven't been extremely proud of ever' one of my children.'"

Dacee June glanced back at her oldest brother. "And then did he paddle Bobby's tail?"

"No. Mama wouldn't let him. He was her Bobby. I'm afraid me and Sammy were the only two who felt Daddy's paddle. Sammy mostly," Todd admitted.

"I don't remember Daddy ever paddling any of us," Dacee June said.

"I don't think he ever did after the twins died," Bobby said. "He said he just didn't have the heart for it any more. 'Course all of us but you, girl, were pretty big by then."

"Is every story going to lead us back to Daddy?" she asked.

Todd loosened his tie. "I suppose it's that time of our lives."

Dacee June stopped at the top of the hill and gawked down at the row of ponderosa pines that served as telephone cable poles. "Really, boys, this trip is seeming more irrational all the time. I have to go just for my peace of mind. But you two can go back," she offered.

"That's the silliest thing I ever heard of," Robert said.

"Besides," Todd added. "I was getting tired of hiding up on Forest Hill. I needed a ride."

"What do you know about the new owners of the Broken Boulder?" Robert asked.

Dacee June kicked the bay's flanks and started down the hill, her brothers still by her side. "A Mr. Albert Sween and Company bought the mine from the Raxton sisters."

"Sween of Virginia City?" Robert asked.

"That's what I hear. The Brewster brothers said the Sween company was crooks, but they say that about everyone."

"Including each other," Todd said. "Have you heard of Albert Sween, Bobby?"

"Yeah. We have orders to forbid Mr. Albert Sween, his family, or anyone known to be employed by him to set foot on the Elkhorn Railroad."

"Why?" Dacee June asked.

Robert stood in the stirrups and rubbed the top of his calves. "There was some kind of dispute over a rail line up in Idaho. Folks claim Sween bribed the judge to award the line to him."

"I thought that was the way all railroads operated," Todd said.

"This time, they found that the judge's daughters had been kidnapped and held until the verdict came down. Then the judge left town soon afterward. Created quite a stir. Two months later Sween sold the short line to the Northern Pacific."

"For a handsome profit, no doubt," Dacee June added.

"The Raxton sisters told me the Broken Boulder played out last fall. Wonder why Sween would want it?" Todd said.

"Whatever the reason, I'm glad we're out of the mining business," Bobby said.

"It's like roulette," Todd added. "The odds are you are goin' to lose, but the few that win, win big."

Bobby eased back in the saddle, his carbine rested on the saddle horn. "And the stakes are higher."

Todd nodded to the south. "Are those the Brewster cabins up there on the side of that mountain?"

"Yep. But I haven't been back here two times in the past five years," Robert admitted.

They rode single file as the road began its zigzag ascent up the tree-scattered mountain. Two identical one-room, unpainted clapboard cabins stood in mirror reflection on each side of the dirt road facing each other. The one on the right had a yard of neatly swept dirt. Daisies grew in an old mine cart.

The one on the left had a rusted iron bathtub, two skunk hides tacked to a tree, and a wheelless buckboard perched up on stumps. Coffee grounds and globs of a green moldy substance littered the yard like calf droppings.

"Spud is the neat one," Dacee June explained.

Robert leaned over and stared into a steel drum. "Doesn't look like anyone is at home. Are those peach pits in there?"

"I can't imagine them both bein' gone," Todd said.

Dacee June took a deep breath, and the air tasted somewhere between skunk and pine. "It's the only way they would go. They don't trust each other enough to go off on their own."

"I'll double-check the cabins," Robert offered.

Dacee June and Todd remained in the saddle as Robert scouted inside one cabin, then the other.

"You reckon they went on up to the Broken Boulder?" Todd asked.

Robert mounted his horse.

"They hiked if they did," Dacee June offered. "They didn't have a horse between them, and didn't want to go to the mine while the shooting was going on. That's why they called me. If they went on up, the shooting must have stopped."

They rode fifty more yards and heard a distant gunshot.

Then another.

And another.

CHAPTER FIVE

Robert reined up next to Dacee June, his back military straight. She fought the urge to salute.

"Just because there's gunfire doesn't mean Carty's in trouble, Lil' Sis."

She hiked up her straw hat and tried to tuck a strand of hair underneath. She fought to keep her voice from shaking. "He hasn't returned down this road. It's the only passable trail by wagon to the Broken Boulder Mine. So he has to be up there."

Todd brushed down his light brown chin whiskers, then cocked the lever on his carbine. Immediately Robert and Dacee June did the same.

"I suppose it would be better to ride up there expectin' trouble than to get caught unprepared," Todd said.

"Let me ride up ahead," Robert offered. "I've been down this telephone pole line a time or two with Sammy. You two go slow along the right side of the road. If you hear two quick shots, get Sis out of here."

She studied her brother's eyes. "Bobby, there is no way I'm turning around."

"This is no time to argue, Dacee June. If it's a gunfight, you belong some place safe. Todd will take care of you, and I'll go see what I can do."

Her right hand held the carbine. The left was clenched knuckle-white. "If it's a gunfight, Captain Robert Fortune, I belong at Carty's side. I'm a daughter of Brazos Fortune. It's the way I was raised. You know I couldn't do anything else."

Robert's eyes darted to his brother's.

Todd loosened his tie and unfastened the top button on his white shirt. "I reckon she's right, Bobby."

"I reckon she is." Robert turned the head of his sorrel horse to the left, then spurred the horse's flanks. "Lord, help us, again," he mumbled.

Robert trotted his wide-rumped horse off the trail into the trees and followed the telephone line that paralleled the road most of the way.

There were two more distant shots.

Dacee June studied the horizon. A rolling mountain. Scattered Ponderosa pines. Boulders and abandoned tailing piles. Other than Robert tracing a telephone wire, she could see no activity whatever. "We need to hurry," she called out.

Todd continued to lead the way. He never took his eyes off the dirt road ahead of them. "Daddy taught you better than to go gallopin' into a gunfight you can neither see nor know anything about."

She thought of her father's narrow scowl and big drooping gray mustache. "Yes, but he never told me what to do when my husband's life is at risk," she called out. When her horse broke into a trot, she felt the hard saddle leather slap against her backside.

Todd reined up when they reached to top of the next mountain. The road dropped down for a mile across a treeless mesa scattered with rocks, boulders, and abandoned, rusted mining equipment. Robert wound through the boulders.

Across the mesa, Dacee June spied the twelve-by-twelve-inch beams of the headworks of the Broken Boulder and a few unpainted buildings. There was a puff of gray smoke and a split second later, a report from a rifle filtered across the mesa.

She stood in the stirrups to brush down her full skirt and relieve the aches. "Todd, it is a gunfight and not all of them have smoke-less cartridges."

He pulled a handful of bullets from his pocket and slid them through the loading gate of the carbine. "You're right about that, Lil' Sis. But I still don't have a bearing on position or intent."

When she put her hand to her temples, they were taut, throbbing. She threw the steel buttplate of the carbine against her shoulder and watched the mine building through the gun sights. "Who would want to shoot at Carty and Quint? They don't have anything but a wagon of mining supplies. Water pumps mainly. I don't understand. This is 1895, not '75."

"I expect we'll find out. Are you ready?" Todd asked.

She lowered the carbine as another rifle report sounded. This time there was no gunsmoke. *I would guess that six of them are shooting smokeless powder.* "What will we do?"

"One bunch is behind those boulders to the east. The others are in the buildings near the main mine shaft near the edge of the cliff. We'll race straight up to the gate."

She scrunched around trying to find a comfortable position in the saddle. "How will we know which side is which?"

Todd pulled his dark gray hat down tight above his ears. "The ones shooting at us are the other side."

She squinted her eyes but couldn't see her other brother. "What about Robert?"

116

"He'll be there for us. Bobby is money in the bank. Like all Fortunes, he won't back down. And unlike some of us, he has never been late for anything in his life."

The stillness of the air harbored a faint scent of pine and a taste of clay. She leaned across the saddle horn and rubbed the horse's neck. "Todd, let's gallop."

His narrow lips peeked out from the beard and goatee. "Why?"

Dacee June shoved the sleeves of her dress halfway up to her elbows. "It will stir up dust and divert their attention. Maybe they'll stop shooting at each other for a minute and give Carty better position."

A tight smile broke across his lips. "You are your daddy's daughter. 'Course, they'll be shootin' at us."

"We'll be too far away to make a good target, won't we? And none of them will know which side we are on. So they won't shoot."

"Or they'll both shoot."

"We can pull up over to those boulders at the edge of the cliff." She pointed her carbine at barn-size rocks just to the right of the mine gate.

"Are you serious?"

"We have to do something."

"Then take off your hat and unpin your hair, Sis."

"Why?" she demanded.

Todd shook his head. "Do you see how much all of us are getting to be like the old man? I was thinkin', if you are determined to ride into a gunfight straddlin' a horse with a carbine across your lap, then use all your weapons. Let 'em know a pretty lady with beautiful long brown hair is in the saddle."

A wide, easy smile broke across her face. "I like that! A woman straddling a horse. That should give them pause." Dacee June pulled off her straw hat and tied it to the saddle horn. She unpinned her hair, and it tumbled halfway down her back. "And thanks for the 'pretty lady with beautiful hair' compliment."

"You know I meant it."

"And I know I have the best brothers on the face of the earth. Rebekah, Jamie Sue, and Abby tell me that almost every day."

"Any accolades go to Mama and Daddy. You know that."

"It's like he's here riding with us, isn't it?"

Todd looked away. "Now, are you ready, Sis?"

She took a deep breath and held it, then let it out slow. "Todd, I've been cooped up with Daddy for so many months I almost forgot what it was to breathe and live. This is exactly what Daddy would do, isn't it?"

"He never did know how to sneak up on a fight."

"I'll race you to those boulders. The loser has to milk the cows in the morning!" she shouted, then kicked her heels into the bay horse. *It's been twenty years since we owned a milk cow. But we still argue over who has to milk the cow.*

Her right hand clutched the cold steel receiver of the Winchester '94. Her left hand grabbed the reins as Dacee June thundered down the mountain road half a length ahead of her brother.

The warm Dakota wind blasted her face and flagged her hair.

She clenched her knees to the horse's flanks and caught the rhythm of the gallop.

He's letting me win.

They always let me win.

I was twelve years old when Daddy and I galloped across the Dakota plains after a gang led by a man I can only remember as Stump. When we caught up with them, Daddy set me on a busted wagon, propped a shotgun in my hand, and told me to shoot anyone who came within fifty feet. I cried all that night because I never got a chance to use the gun.

I was there in Deadwood Gulch when Daddy and Big River Frank confronted Doc Kabyo.

I was in the telephone office when those two from the Indian Nation tried to gun down Sammy.

118

Lord, I know that isn't very ladylike, and I don't know how to explain it, but this is me. This is when I really feel alive.

I guess it's what happens when Mama and sisters die early and you're raised by Daddy and the boys.

Two shots were fired as they galloped up to the boulders, but she had no idea who fired them and at whom. She was out of the saddle and running before the horse ever stopped his stride. Dacee June darted behind a boulder and was startled to find two men hunched down among the rocks. One held a shotgun and clutched a piece of twisted tobacco. The other was unarmed, and he had field glasses around his neck. "Mordecai? Spud?"

Mordecai Brewster spat a wad of tobacco in the dirt at his feet. "Miss Dacee June? Did you come to watch the show too?"

She studied the small man's unshaven face. "Show?"

"He means gunfight." Spud Brewster kicked dirt over the tobacco spit. "I had no intention of coming down here myself. But he forced me at gunpoint."

Mordecai wiped his mouth on his sleeve. "I wasn't goin' to go off and let you plunder my valuables!"

"He has never in his life owned one thing that I wanted."

Todd scooted in behind her. "What's goin' on here, Spud? Who's shooting who?"

"Don't reckon we know yet," Spud said.

"They both stopped when you two rode up. I figured you might be the sheriff, until I see a lady on one of the horses. Sheriffs don't ride with no lady. 'Course, if he did, I reckon he'd have an easier time findin' a posse," Mordecai declared.

"There is some of 'em behind them boulders. And they are shootin' at those in the engine room at the mine. And there's a wagon parked in between," Spud explained.

"And a man's down by the wagon," Mordecai announced.

"A man down?" Dacee June said.

"I reckon he's shot dead," Mordecai declared.

"We don't know that for sure," Spud insisted.

"He ain't moved since we got here." Mordecai spat in the dirt again.

Once again, Spud kicked dirt over the spittle. "He might merely be judicious."

"I ain't never called bein' dead, bein' judicious."

"Have you seen Carty?" she asked.

"Carty Fortune?" Mordecai asked.

"My husband, Carty Toluca. That's his wagon."

"Ain't seen him. But no one has been out in the open since we snuck up here."

Dacee June's heart raced as she peered over the boulder. Todd held her shoulders. Her chest heaved. She could barely breathe.

"I can't see clearly, Todd. In the shadows, next to the wagon . . . I can't tell. Who is it? Oh, Lord, not Carty." *Father, that was so selfish. I don't want it to be Quint or any woman's husband or mother's son.* "We have to do something, Todd!"

"Let me get my bearings, Sis. I've got to figure out the line of fire."

"I've got to figure out if I'm a widow!" She shoved her carbine in his hands.

He grabbed her arm. "What are you doing?"

"I'm going to find my Carty."

"Sis, you can't."

She jerked away. "Je dois etre la femme que Dieu m'a cree pour etre."

"Which means?"

"I must be the woman God has created me to be."

She took a step out into the clearing. A bullet blasted the dirt twenty feet in front of her.

Todd shot back at the boulders.

Dacee June stood up straight, her fingers laced at her waist. *Lord, I have no idea what I'm doing. I just know that I can't do anything else. I am going to keep walking. "Show no fear, darlin'." Alright, Daddy, I'm not afraid.*

Two more shots blasted, each one coming a little closer. The second kicked dirt up on her green skirt. This time Todd did not respond.

I am not afraid.

She marched straight for the man lying in the dark shadows beside the hardware wagon. This time there was a blast and a buzz over her head.

I am not afraid.

"Lady, what are you doin'?" someone shouted from the boulders.

"I came to get my husband!" she hollered back, her voice much shakier than she wanted.

"I didn't know ol' Oakes was married," a different man screamed from the building.

As she reached the back of the wagon, her eyes adjusted to the shade. She gaped at the bearded, grubby man lying on his back in the dirt beside the wagon.

"That's not my husband!" she hollered. *I don't see any blood. Where did he get shot?*

"Get out of there, lady!" a man from the boulders shouted.

She put her hands to her cheeks. "Who is this dead man?"

"That's Oakes," a voice from the unpainted buildings screamed. "He's the cook, but he ain't dead. He passed out with cheap whiskey, and we ain't had time to revive him."

"Get out of there," a deep voice from the boulders bellowed.

She brushed her long hair back over her shoulders. "Where's my husband?"

"Who is your husband?"

"Carty Toluca," she shouted. "Have any of you seen Carty Toluca?"

"We ain't never heard of him. Now move it, lady, or you'll catch a stray bullet."

Dacee June jammed her arms across her chest. "I am not leaving without my husband. This is his wagon. He and Quint Trooper came up here with these pumps. Where is he?"

"The hardware clerks?"

"He is not a clerk; he is the general manager of the store." Her voice began to crack. "Where are Quint and my husband!"

Someone in the mining buildings cracked open the door. The barrel of his rifle poked out. "They went down in the bucket."

She turned her back to the boulders and faced the buildings. "They went down in the mine shaft?"

"Shoot no, they took a ride in the cable bucket that hauls ore from the floor of Spearfish Canyon. They wanted a ride, so we let them ride it down."

"Where are they now?" she demanded.

"In Spearfish Canyon, I reckon," he shouted. "These bushwhackers came along and we haven't had a chance to bring them up. Besides, Oakes is the only one who can operate that sucker."

"Move it, lady! This is your last warnin'," someone from the boulders demanded.

When she glanced down she could see both of her hands start to tremble. "He's not here?"

"He's in Spearfish Canyon!"

"But . . . but . . . what am I doing out here?" she stammered.

"About to get yourself killed! Get out of there."

Carty Toluca, I risked my life for you and you're playing in an ore cart?

Now I am afraid.

"I don't suppose you can stop long enough to raise him up and let us leave?" she demanded.

"Nope."

"Get out of there!" a man from the boulders roared.

A gunshot blasted from behind the boulders, followed by a stream of cursing. Dacee was still staring in that direction when someone shot back at the mining buildings. She spun around as the door was flung open.

"I got these. You got those, Bobby?" Todd shouted.

"Got 'em, big brother." Robert Fortune shouted back.

"Then march them out to the wagon," Todd demanded.

From the east, five gunmen raising new carbines above their heads stalked out from behind the boulders.

Then eight men trekked out from the headworks building, hands high, followed by Todd Fortune.

Spud and Mordecai Brewster scampered out into the clearing.

"I ain't never seen nothin' like this in all my born days. Them Fortunes are fearless, they are," Mordecai chattered.

"Did you see that? Dacee June diverts ever' one of 'em, and the brothers sneak in behind," Spud boasted. "It was just like one of them Hawthorne Miller novels! You boys ought to be smart enough not to buck the Fortunes of the Black Hills."

"Ain't it somethin'?" Mordecai crowed.

"What's your stake in this?" one of the men with Todd complained.

"We have no stake except to get Carty and Quint and go home," Robert replied. He stared at one of the men huddled in front of Todd with the bottom part of his left ear missing. "Don't I know you?"

"I ain't never seen ya." He held a Winchester '73 rifle with half the barrel hacked off above his head as he spat in the dirt. "Are you teamed up with Wade Justice?"

Robert studied the man. "I don't know Wade Justice. But I know who you are. I was in a cafe in Chipaso when the Mexican lady in the blue dress cut your ear with a twelve-inch knife."

"I don't know what you're talkin' about."

"You grabbed her goods, and she grabbed a butcher knife."

"What of it?" the man sneered.

"That makes you Prairie Bill Turner," Robert said.

123

"Ever'one knows that. Who are you?"

"Captain Robert Fortune, retired."

"You the railroad marshal?"

"That's me." He shoved his carbine barrel into one of the men standing next to him. "Put the carbines on the ground."

"I ain't puttin' mine down until they put theirs down too," the man snarled.

"Sounds fair. Put them all down!" Todd ordered.

"And who do you think you are?" one of the men gruffed.

"That there's Todd Fortune," Mordecai Brewster announced.

"The one with the Flying Fist of Death?" one of the mine shack men questioned.

Mordecai spat on the ground. "He's the one."

Among curses and mumbles, the gunmen laid down their weapons.

"I don't suppose any of you know how to run that donkey engine bucket?" Todd asked.

"We don't know nothin' about minin'. We're jist mine guards."

"My brother can run it," Mordecai announced. "Ain't never been a machine he couldn't operate."

"Mordecai, you and Spud go with Dacee June and get Carty and Quint back up here," Todd ordered.

"What do you aim to do?" the red-bearded man asked.

Dacee June marched over to him. "We are going to get my husband and Quint and take our wagon and ride out of here." In the background she heard the giant steam-driven engine begin to chug like a train engine.

"You ain't arrestin' us?"

"Nope," Todd replied.

"Are you arrestin' them?" the man pointed across the clearing.

"Nope. We're not arresting anyone."

"But they attacked us!" one of the men grumbled.

"What are gunmen like you doin' out at the mine?" Todd asked.

"The boss bought the mine."

"Who's your boss?" Todd asked.

"Albert Sween. We were just watching the place for him. Just doin' an honest day's work."

"They're lyin'!" someone across the yard shouted. "They are a bunch of hired guns and murderin' cutthroats!"

Dacee June stomped over to the men Robert held at bay.

She bent down and gathered up the carbines.

"What are you doin'?" one of them growled.

"Retrieving our guns."

"Those belong to us!"

"They were stolen from Fortune & Son Hardware," she insisted. Dacee June stood up with all five carbines cradled in her arms.

"They were?" Robert asked.

Dacee June blew her bangs back out of her eyes. "Wade Justice paid for one and stole five others. These are the guns."

Robert looked over at Todd. "Did you know that?"

"Not until just now."

She shoved the guns into the back of the hardware wagon next to the unloaded crates.

"You ain't goin' to leave us here without weapons!" one of the men by Robert groused.

"You do have horses, don't you?" Robert barked. "You can turn and ride off right now."

The chug of the steam-driven donkey engine was now joined with the squeal of a cable drawn tight around the five-foot drum.

"Are you takin' their side?" a white-faced, clean-shaven man with short hair snarled. "Wade Justice ain't goin' to like that."

"We have no part in all of this," Dacee June explained.

"You ain't seen the last of us," the white-faced man snarled.

Dacee June stalked over to the man and leaned close. "What did you say?"

He tried to step back, but the barrel of Robert's gun prevented his retreat. "What are you talkin' about?" he muttered.

"When you said, 'You ain't seen the last of us'? Do they teach you that in bushwhacking school, or what? Do you practice it down at the Piedmont in front of a mirror? That's the stupidest thing I ever heard. I 'ain't seen the last of you'? I didn't want to see you this time. I don't want to see you next time. I don't ever want to see you again. Bobby, just shoot them all."

Robert raised the barrel to the back of the man's head. "OK, Lil' Sis."

"What? Wait!" the man screamed. "You can't do that! We're unarmed. You can't kill us."

Dacee June studied the man from head to toe. "If that's the only way I can make sure I never have to see you again, then so be it."

A tall, heavy man with tattered flannel shirt tucked into ripped duckings glanced back over his shoulder. "She ain't serious."

"She looks serious enough to me. I'm leaving," the man at the end of the carbine barrel declared. "We ain't got no guns, so only a fool would stay."

"You riding out?" Robert challenged.

"I sure as Hades ain't going to stay and get shot up."

Five men sulked back behind the boulders. A few minutes later, they rode straight up the hill to the east.

She and Robert walked over to where Todd held the others.

"OK, Lil' Sis, you bluffed them back," Todd grinned.

"Who was bluffing? Were you bluffing, Bobby?"

"Nope."

"You're both getting as crazy as Sammy," Todd chided.

"It's in our blood."

"Do we get our guns back now?" one of Sween's men whined.

"No!" Dacee June blurted out. "Bobby, toss them in one of those ore buckets."

"The gunmen or the guns?" he asked.

"Now there's an idea," she smiled. "No, I meant the guns. Run them down to Spearfish Canyon. It will take them a while to re-trieve them."

"What if that bunch with Wade Justice comes back before we get our guns?" one of the men demanded.

"You'll have to duke it out with two-by-fours and rocks, because they don't have any guns either."

"They all just got out of prison," Robert reported.

"How did you know that?"

"The haircuts, worn but clean clothes, trimmed fingernails. Trust me, darlin'. Maybe they escaped. Whichever, they are ridin' light. Not a one was totin' a pistol."

"The buckets are coming up!" Spud Brewster hollered.

Dacee June and Robert packed the guns to the platform while Todd kept his carbine on the men. The guns rattled as they tossed them in the huge bucket.

"Oh, my!" Dacee June caught her breath as she stared at the floor of Spearfish Canyon, eighteen hundred feet below. "I forgot how steep that is!"

"Looks like them a wavin' down there," Mordecai Brewster called out.

Dacee June spied two men standing on top of an ore-filled four-by-seven-foot steel bucket as it climbed the cable along the side of the rocky cliff.

"Why didn't they ride an empty bucket? That looks dangerous!" Her temples relaxed as she watched the taller of the two men. *There he is, Lord. My own heart's delight. Oh, I miss that man. It's been a long day.*

A grinning Quint Trooper waved at them.

Her eyes caught sight of Carty's. His smile dropped off his face. He cupped his hands and shouted. But the roar of the steam engine behind her drowned him out.

When Carty leaped off the ore-filled bucket, he sprinted over to her.

"It's Daddy Brazos, isn't it?"

She threw her arms around him and hugged. "No, baby, no . . . he's the same."

Carty pulled back a few inches. "What is it, then? What are you three doin' out here?"

"Whew-eee, Dacee June, that was quite a ride," Quint blurted out as he scooted beside Carty. "Boy, Little Frank is goin' to die when he hears I got to ride the bucket. We've been dreamin' of doin' that for two years." He looked at Robert and over to where Todd held a gun on the men.

"Is ever'thin' OK?" Quint asked.

"It is now," Robert replied.

"We got stuck down there. I mean, we must have been down there for over an hour. Was afraid they wouldn't get it goin' again. We figured they wouldn't crank it up until they stopped blasting," Quint mumbled. "Is Todd holdin' a gun on those men?"

"You didn't tell me why you came out here." Carty pressed. "Did you know the Raxton sisters sold out? We came out here for nothin'. The new owner has different plans and doesn't want these pumps. So Quint talked them into lettin' us ride." Carty stared out at Todd. "Bobby, what's this all about?"

"Lil' Sis came out here to get her man," Robert announced.

Carty brushed her bangs back off her eyes with his fingertips. "Help? I didn't need any help. Did I?"

"Yes, you did," Robert insisted. "And your wife put her life on the line for you."

Carty's eyes surveyed the yard. "What are you talkin' about?"

"I'll tell you on the way home." Dacee June grabbed Carty's hand and led him toward the loaded hardware wagon. "Quint, you take my horse. Spud and Mordecai can ride in the back of the wagon with the pumps until we get to their cabins."

Todd, Robert, and Quint rode the horses behind the wagon as they headed back up the dirt road to the crest of the hill.

Carty pulled off his black tie and shoved it in his pocket. He unfastened his top button and rubbed his sweaty neck. "Now what's this about you putting your life on the line for me?"

"The Brewsters told us there was a gunfight at the mine. I thought your life was in danger, so I came out to help you. I stepped out in the middle of a gunfight looking for you."

"I can't believe you'd do something that dangerous."

"And I can't believe you went on a joyride down the cliff."

"You told me to relax, that I was workin' too hard."

She leaned her head on his shoulder. "Mr. Toluca, can you relax and drive this rig with just your left hand?"

"I reckon so."

"Then do it. I expect that right hand to be around me all the way back to Deadwood."

☛ ☛ ☛

The only thing that remained on the white china plate with blue flowers were two stalks of asparagus and a small partially chewed piece of gristle.

Dacee June scraped the scraps into the garbage pail and slipped the plate into the basin of hot soapy water. She stared out the window at the blackness that covered Forest Hill. She could see her reflection in the glass.

My eyes look tired.

My lips drawn.

My hair.

Oh, my hair looks horrid.

It has been a very long day.

It has been a long year, Lord.

And it will be another long night.

In the glass reflection she noticed a man in the doorway behind her. He looked forty, but she knew he was younger. His white shirt was unfastened at the collar, sleeves rolled up to his elbows. His coat and vest had long since disappeared.

There was a sly smile on his face.

That smile! Oh, Carty, your smile makes my heart sing. We need some time together.

"Are you staring at me, Mr. Toluca?"

"Yes, I am, Mrs. Toluca. This is a very good view."

"You can't see anything but the back of my dress and apron."

"This is a very good view."

Her face flushed. "Are the girls asleep?"

"Yes, they are. Hmmm."

"I heard that," she challenged.

"Just a sigh," he laughed. "I still can't believe you got your brothers and drove all the way out to the Broken Boulder to find me."

"You know I'm a very possessive woman. I was worried when the Brewsters said there was a gunfight and the phone lines went dead."

"I have no idea what's going on out there." Carty strolled over to her. "None of them are mining men except maybe the cook."

Dacee June continued to wash the dishes. "He slept through the whole gunfight," she said. "Where was the great Wade Justice through all that?"

"That's a good question. Sam said things were quiet in town." Carty's arms slipped around her waist and gently held her.

She pulled her hands out of the hot, soapy water and patted them dry on her apron. "It's not been too quiet since we got home."

"The Badlands bunch on lower Main Street are shootin' off Chinese fireworks a day early." He nuzzled through her hair and brushed a kiss on her neck.

Her slightly damp hands on his, she laid her head back and closed her eyes.

"What are you sighin' about, baby?" Carty whispered.

"How absolutely wonderful it feels to be in your arms."

"Even after all these years?"

"Yes."

"Even after three children?"

"Yes."

"Even standin' here at the kitchen sink?"

"Carty Toluca, my heart jumped the very first day you ever hugged me. And it's still jumping."

He kissed her neck again, then stood up straight. "Do you remember that first hug?"

"I certainly do. We were both sixteen."

"We were fourteen."

"We were not, Carty Toluca! That must have been some other girl." She pulled her long hair back and pointed to a spot on her neck.

"Dacee June Fortune, you know for a fact I've never hugged any girl on earth but you." He gently kissed the exact spot she indicated.

She immediately found another place and pointed. "What about Martha McCray?" she challenged.

Carty kissed her several times, then burst out laughing.

"What's so funny?" she challenged.

"One time in my entire life I went some place with another girl, and you never forget it."

Her forehead tensed. "You know I never did like Martha."

Carty kissed her earlobe next to the dangling gold earring. "Why do you think I asked her to the play?"

She turned her other ear toward his lips. "Just to spite me?"

He kissed that ear. "I remember, you had told me to get lost and that you never wanted to see me again."

"You didn't have to believe me." She pulled her hair completely on top of her head, exposing all her neck.

TEXAS CAMP

"I didn't believe you." Carty kissed his way across the back of her neck. "That's why I took Martha to a play that you were in. So I could see you."

Dacee June reached behind her head and ran her fingers through Carty's dark brown hair. "If you were trying to make me jealous, it worked."

"I noticed. That's why I never bring up her name even though that was fifteen years ago."

"You just brought up her name."

"No, that was you."

She twirled around in his arms and looked straight up at the ceiling so he could kiss her neck.. "Why did I do that?"

He repeatedly kissed her neck. "Because I laughed when you accused me of hugging Martha."

"Why did you laugh?"

He stood up straight. "Because the only touch I had from Martha McCray was when she slugged me."

"Why did she hit you?"

"Because during intermission, I snuck back stage to see you."

She pulled his face to her neck. "I don't remember that."

His arms slipped around her waist and held her tight against his chest. "That's because you were talkin' to Tommy Norton, and I slunk back out to the audience."

She raised his chin up with her fingers and looked straight into his eyes. "You never told me that before."

His wink coincided with the dimpled smile. "It was not my finest hour."

Dacee June leaned forward and pressed her lips on his. "I love you, Carty Toluca."

"Baby, I've loved you since I first saw you."

She laid her head on his chest. "You threw rocks at me the first time we met."

"See? How else does a twelve-year-old boy show love? Doesn't that prove it?"

"And you didn't hug me until we were sixteen and we went horseback riding out toward Cheyenne Crossing, and we stopped by the mouth of Cougar Creek."

Carty rocked her back and forth. "That was not the first time I hugged you."

Dacee June closed her eyes. *When it's my turn to go, Lord, I want to be right here in my Carty's arms.* "Oh? Just when do you think it was?"

He continued to rock her and rub her back. "We were fourteen. It was your birthday party, and we were playing musical chairs. There was only one chair left when Mrs. Speaker stopped playing the piano."

"I grabbed the chair," she said.

"And I grabbed you from behind."

"That wasn't a hug."

"It was a hug to me, Dacee June."

"We were playing a game!"

"I wasn't. I dreamt about that hug for two years."

"You did? You never told me that before either."

"There's a lot of dreams about you I've never mentioned."

She slipped her arms around his neck. "Oh?"

Dimples bracketed his wide grin. "You don't want to know what goes through the mind of a teenage boy."

She kissed his suntanned cheek. "Maybe I should know. One of these days they will be showing up on our front porch."

"And I'll be standin' there with my shotgun."

Dacee June pulled her head back. "Carty Toluca, now you are sounding like Daddy."

He raised his thick, dark eyebrows. "That's OK, isn't it?"

She laid her head on his chest. "Yes, it is."

He stroked her hair. "Do you have to go down there tonight?"

She pulled away and wiped her hands on a limp white cotton tea towel. "Yes, I do. Carty, I made myself and the Lord a promise that one of us would be with him until he died. Daddy is not goin' to die alone."

"I know, baby. I'll take your shift tonight. You stay home."

"Absolutely not. Carty Toluca, you are running yourself into the ground, you are working so hard."

"Darlin', you know I don't know any other way to work."

"I know . . . I know . . . sometimes I wish . . ." Dacee June pulled off her apron.

He turned his back and leaned against the wooden counter. "For that ranch?"

"Oh, Carty. Wouldn't it be wonderful? Just wide-open prairie acres with a barn and corrals and a big old Texas ranch house. No customers. No town. No Badlands. No footpads and sneak thieves. No shadows of the gulch. Just you and me and the girls and my brothers livin' down the road a spell. And Sundays at a country church. Everything so peaceful."

He rubbed the back of his neck and stared across the room. "Is that what you want?"

She stepped over and held his strong arm. "Carty Toluca, what I want more than anything in the world is you!"

"You know, darlin'," he patted her hand. "I always figured I'm the luckiest person in Deadwood. Except tonight."

"Poor baby . . ." she brushed his thick brown hair off his forehead. "It's a crazy season we're goin' through."

"You want me to walk you down to the hardware?"

She stared at him, then a slight smile broke across her face. "You say that every day and night. You know I've hiked every square foot of this town all my life. I'll be fine. But I like it when you ask. It feels good to know how much you care."

He gave her one more hug and kissed her cheek, then sighed out loud.

She raised her eyebrows. "Are you lusting after your wife, Mr. Toluca?"

"I most certainly am."

"Good. Then I know you'll miss me."

☞ ☞ ☞

The Williams Street stairs were shadowy even on a full-moon night. It was not a full moon, and Dacee June took the steps slowly. The iron rail was cold, though it was July 3. The crocheted dark green shawl felt good on her shoulders. A China rocket exploded somewhere above the buildings of lower Main Street and cast a brief light. In those wild, multicolored streaks, she continued the descent.

At the next red-and-white flash she spotted a man's form at the bottom of the stairs. His hat was pulled down. He leaned against the brick wall at the Dakota Brewery.

Her hand slipped inside the deep pocket of her ducking skirt. She fingered the rosewood grip of the .32 caliber pocket pistol. *Lord, I tell everyone I can go anywhere in Deadwood. I ask you to go with me, then I secretly carry my pistol. I am a woman of weak faith . . . but a deep desire to grow. Sometimes, it seems we're too busy, too hectic to contemplate spiritual matters.*

I wonder who that man is? I do wish he would move.

Mama always had time to meditate. She would hike out to the garden and hoe weeds that weren't there. When I asked, "What are you doin'?" she would say, "Baby, Mama's meditatin' and ponderin' . . . you go back in the house."

Lord, why did I remember that? It's been almost twenty years since she died. And I have not thought of that scene once in these twenty years.

135

He's smoking a quirley. Please, Lord, make him move.

Leaving her pistol and hand buried in her pocket, she slowly cocked the hammer one click, then the second.

That's right, Dacee June. Trust the Lord and cock the pistol.

She pulled the hammer back further with her thumb, then squeezed the trigger and let the hammer down slowly.

I will trust you, Lord.

Dacee June pulled her shawl up over her long brown hair and scooted to the landing at the bottom of the steep stairs.

A gravelly, whiskied voice rambled out of the darkness. "I've been waitin' for you."

She held her breath.

The tall man moved away from the wall just as another China rocket burst above the gulch. The wide grin of the thin man towered over her.

"Skeeter?"

He tipped his hat. "Evenin', Dacee June."

"You were waiting for me?" She sauntered toward the lights of Main Street.

He strolled alongside her. "Yep."

"How did you know I'd be here?"

"'Cause it's Wednesday night. Ever' Wednesday night for six months you've hiked down them stairs between 10:00 and 10:15 to go to the hardware store and relieve your brother Samuel to sit by your daddy's side," Skeeter explained.

A chorus of barking dogs greeted each new blast of fireworks.

She stopped to watch a green-and-yellow Roman candle streak across the night. *Am I that predictable that everyone knows where I am at any given moment?* "What did you need to talk to me about, Skeeter?"

"You was lookin' for a man with a green shirt and brown vest right after lunch?"

"Yes."

"There's a man at the back table at Beano Billy's wearing a green shirt and brown leather vest and totin' a new Winchester carbine. But I need to warn you that it's . . ."

"Wade Justice?"

Skeeter pulled off his flop hat as they continued to stroll. "You knowed it was him all along?"

"I found out this afternoon." A strand of brown hair flopped against her eye. She blew it back.

"Shoot, I wish I would have knowed that. I wouldn't have been pokin' around."

"I'm sorry, Skeeter. I didn't know it at the time we talked. Did you get in trouble?"

"He marched right up to me with that new carbine in his hand and growled, 'You lookin' for me?'"

"What did you say?"

He jammed his hat back on his head. "I, eh, I said a purdy lady was lookin' for him and I promised to be on the lookout, that's all. Sorry, Dacee June, I figured he was goin' to shoot me."

"Just because you were askin' about a man in a green shirt and brown vest?"

"Justice is mean. Did you hear what happened up at Ft. Benton, Montana?"

"No."

"You know that big new hotel they have?"

"I've heard about it." Dacee June tucked the wild strand of hair behind her ear.

"I heard tell this afternoon that Justice was in a poker game there last January. He was losin' and called the gambler out. But when the man didn't show, Justice broke into the man's room in the middle of the night and threw the gambler right out the third-story window. That old boy hit on the brick and broke his neck. He was dead as a lead weight in a fishin' contest. I talked to a man whose brother saw him lyin' there dead."

"I'll make sure not to play poker with Justice."

"At least, don't ever win," Skeeter added. "He is mean, Miss Dacee June. Don't rile him."

She paused at the corner of Shine and Main Streets. Competing piano tunes rolled up the street like a cat fight. "I have no intention to."

Skeeter stayed back in the shadows, against the building. "Do you still want to see him?"

"No, I've settled that business."

"That's good, 'cause Wino Jack said he heard Beano say he heard Justice was mumblin' about gettin' even."

Dacee June ignored the hair that flopped down. "Who was he talking about?"

"I don't know, but I hope it ain't you Fortunes."

"Skeeter, did Mr. Justice have any money?"

"Yep, he bought himself some supper. He didn't buy me none though. I reckon he didn't completely believe the purdy woman story."

"Did you tell the sheriff that Justice was at Beano Billy's?"

"Shoot no. That's all I need is to have him find out I was gabbin' with the sheriff. I'd be a dead man for sure."

"Thank you for the information, Skeeter."

"You're welcome, Dacee June. I think I'm goin' to call it a night. With fireworks startin' already, and Wade Justice in town, somethin' bad could happen. I have no intention of it happenin' to me."

"Do you have a place to stay tonight, Skeeter?"

"Yes, ma'am, I surely do. Long LeRoy done set up a tent along the crick, and we have fine quarters at least until winter."

"Good. I'll see you tomorrow."

"Night, Miss Dacee June." He tipped his hat and then ducked across the street.

Dacee June lingered at the corner and stared to the left, across the Dead Line. All the stores and saloons were wide open and sounding wild. To the right all the stores were closed. Not a soul stirred on the street.

But there was a carriage parked in front of the hardware.

Why would Sammy have a carriage? Is he going somewhere? Has he gone somewhere?

As she got closer, she recognized the driver.

Dacee June hiked straight up to the carriage. "Dexter, what are you doing up at this end of town tonight?"

He nodded and smiled, revealing straight white teeth.

A woman's voice broke in from the back seat. "Evenin', Dacee June."

Dacee June stepped closer. "Rosie? I didn't see you back there."

"I know I'm not supposed to be above the Dead Line this late, but Rutt sent me. He said if I keep the shawl over my head and didn't get out no one would know it was me."

"I'm sure it's fine for you to be here. What are you doing?"

"Waitin' for you, of course."

"How did you know I'd be down here?"

"It's Wednesday, Dacee June. You always go to sit with your daddy between 10 and 10:15. You're a little late tonight."

"Eh, I was detained." *This is embarrassing. I'm living in an aquarium and I didn't even know it.* "What can I do for you, Rosie Benoit? Do you need a place to stay for the night?"

"Oh, no, I got me the best room in the house and . . . oh, now I ain't quittin' yet," she announced. "It's comin' up on the Fourth of July. I wouldn't want to put Lizzie in a bind."

Lord, I don't understand job loyalty in a brothel. It's not exactly like packing peaches during harvest.

"Why did Rutt send you?"

"He wanted to tell you to be careful because Wade Justice is in town."

"Over at Beano Billy's?"

"How did you know that?"

"This is my town, remember?"

"I should have known," Rosie said. The woman leaned out of the carriage far enough that Dacee June could smell her pungent lilac perfume. "Dacee June, did you hear what Justice did over in Pierre?"

"I don't think so. What did he do?"

"He sliced up one of the girls at Kleptie's."

I have no idea what Kleptie's is, nor do I want to know. "Did they arrest him?"

"He took off before they caught him. Nevada Nellie said she met a girl in Rapid City whose sister was there and seen it with her own eyes. Rutt said he won't even let Justice into Lilly's. He's even carryin' a shotgun tonight. He wanted you to watch out."

"Thank you, Rosie, for the message."

"You're welcome." The dark-haired girl sat back up in the carriage. "It's nice and quiet up here, ain't it?"

"Yes, I suppose it is."

"I really liked sitting up here in this carriage. Made me feel sort of important. If someone would have told me to move on, I would have said, 'I'm waitin' for my good friend, Dacee June.' We are good friends, aren't we?"

"Yes we are, Rosie Benoit."

"See there. I knew it."

"And you know what else?"

"What?"

"I believe you and I could be really good friends if . . ."

"If I'd give up workin' the houses?"

"Yes."

"What would you be willin' to give up, Dacee June?" the woman challenged.

Dacee June stepped back from the carriage. "What do you mean?"

"You're asking me to give up the only occupation I've known since I was fifteen in order to be your friend. What would you have to give up to be a good friend to me?"

Lord, you set me up for that, didn't you? "You are right. I've made demands. So I guess I'll have to think on it a bit."

"You ain't mad at me, are you?"

"Of course not."

"I've got work waiting. I hope Daddy Brazos has a good night."

"Thank you, Rosie."

Dacee June pulled a brass key out of her pocket and opened the front door of the hardware. One bare electric bulb illuminated the top of the stairway. When she entered the upstairs apartment, a candle burned near the bed. Tucked under a plain white sheet was a wrinkled old man with white hair and white drooping mustache. His eyes were closed. His hands folded on his chest moved up and down as he breathed.

A tattered, dark brown stuffed leather chair crowded next to the bed. She could see Sammy's gray hair and narrow head.

He didn't turn around. "Evenin', Sis."

"Hi, Sammy. Sorry I'm late."

"That's all right, darlin', nothin's happenin' much. Me and Daddy were discussin' the war."

She scurried to Samuel's side. "He woke up?"

"No. I was doin' all the talkin'." Sam pulled himself out of the chair and faced her.

Sam Fortune, you are forty-three years old and you look fifty-five. "Go on home and get some sleep," Dacee June insisted. "Tomorrow's a big day."

"Garrett's lookin' forward to the play. Abby taught him all his lines tonight."

Dacee June held her father's limp hand. "What part does he have?"

141

"For the first half of the play, he's Preacher Smith."

"And the rest?"

"He's a stamp mill up at Lead," Sam laughed.

"Oh, my, it sounds like an interesting script."

"It sounds like a Dacee June script. Listen, Lil' Sis, I heard that . . ."

"That Wade Justice is in town and is at Beano Billy's. Yes, I know."

"He is?" Sam scratched his head and stared out the second-story window toward Main Street. "I didn't know that."

"What were you going to say?"

"I heard that Chop Lin's store was broken into tonight by a man with a new carbine."

Dacee June stroked her father's hand and didn't look at Sam. "Did the sheriff check it out?"

"Not yet. He was waitin' for me to go with him, I reckon."

"Are you goin' down there now?"

"Yep." Sam Fortune pulled on his hat. "Now don't you go tellin' Abby."

"Sammy, be careful." She held his arm as they walked over to the apartment door. "You don't have to do that, you know."

"Of course I do, Lil' Sis. Who else in this town would go with the sheriff into the Badlands district to face Wade Justice?"

She laced her fingers in front of her waist. "I would."

Sam Fortune laughed, then looked back at the man in the bed. "She's right, Daddy," he called out. "You raised yourself a firecracker who is as headstrong as you and Mama combined."

"Are you braggin' or complainin,' Sam Fortune?"

"Braggin' darlin'. Me and Todd and Bobby have been braggin' on you since the day you were born." He hugged her, then ambled out the doorway. "But not nearly as much as the old man in the bed."

CHAPTER SIX

Dacee June paused before she cracked open the upstairs window and listened to the quiet. No carriages or wagons rolled up the street. No one scurried in the shadows. No shouts. No curses. No pianos playing. No drunken laughter. No gunshots.

Her fingers traced patterns in the cool dust on the wooden window sill.

It's like two different towns, Lord. It's as if there's a line drawn in the dirt. Everything and everyone respectable stationed above the line. The others below. The strange thing is, everyone respects the invisible line.

Most of the time.

Two separate towns coexist beside each other. Only a few are comfortable in both places.

Like Brazos Fortune. And his daughter, Dacee June.

I was here before the Dead Line. Not more than a hundred men in the whole northern Black Hills. At twelve I ran from tent to tent, camp to camp, diggings to diggings, peeking in their pans and listening to their stories. I was the only kid in camp when the streams thawed in the spring of '76. They showed me their gold. They wouldn't show one another their pokes, but they showed me. They patted me on the head and shared their peppermints and sometimes their last biscuit when I was too dumb to realize how poor they were.

They begged me to climb up on a boulder and sing them a song. It didn't matter if it was off key or if I forgot the words. Oh, dear Lord, wasn't that horrible?

But they loved it.

Somehow I reminded them of a girl somewhere. A daughter. A niece. A granddaughter. A neighbor girl. They were old men. Some only in their twenties, but they looked old. Tired. Worn out. Some would not make it until summer.

But when I took sick and couldn't make the rounds, they came up here and lined up in the snow and freezing rain just to stick their heads into the old hardware and wish me well.

They were the boys of '76.

There will never be anything like that again.

Not in these hills.

Not for me.

She swung the window wider and felt a rush of fresh air flood into the room bringing the aromas of pine, tobacco, and fried meat. Up the gulch the stamp mills in Lead kept waves of dull thunder rolling like an ocean on a still Pacific evening. She tugged on the gold chain around the sweat-drenched collar of her dress. She brushed her slightly chapped lips with her finger-tips. They tasted salty. A lone China rocket exploded somewhere on lower Main, and she thought she heard a baby cry. Or an alley cat.

When they started building saloons and gambling joints, they were still open to Dacee June Fortune. Day after day I'd run giggling up the alley and slip in the back door. The bartender or owner or one of the girls *saved me a piece of candy or a bright ribbon. They'd let me sit on a stool and tell about when they were my age. Stories about fast horses, handsome ladies, and men who were dangerous with a gun. They would introduce me as "MY Dacee June."*

It was as if I owned the entire Black Hills. They would have shot on sight anyone who treated me rough.

Deadwood was brand new then.

It was still Sioux land. We barricaded Main Street when we heard about Custer and prayed Bobby had been spared.

In those days, Lord, Dacee June Fortune was everyone's Lil' Sis.

Lord, I'm not twelve anymore.

And the town has changed.

We're like anywhere else. Miles City. Cheyenne. Bozeman. Deadwood. Just a town. Crammed with people trying to find their place.

It was a game back then.

Oh, such a great and glorious game.

The next generation will never know that game. They will read about it in books and think it is all make-believe.

A game, a race, a battle.

To see who would strike it rich.

To see who would build a big house on Forest Hill.

To see who would live through the winter.

And who would catch ague, dysentery, cholera, and lie buried on Mount Moriah.

To see who would turn tail and sneak back to the states.

It was rough. Primitive. Dangerous. And the most exciting time in my life.

There were no lawmen.

No judges.

No laws.

But there was the Texas Camp! Grass Edwards. Yapper Jim. Quiet Jim. Big River Frank. And Brazos Fortune.

She turned back to the white-haired old man in the bed.

His glance was law. They knew that. He didn't bluff. He didn't back away. And he would never admit to being wrong.

Even when he was.

I think, inside, he didn't care if he died. It meant he would be by Mama's side, and that's all that old man ever wanted. She stared back out into the darkened street.

Some said he would remarry.

I knew better.

I think Thelma Speaker knew it too.

Dacee June managed a tight-lipped smile.

But she tried. Oh, my, how she tried.

The boys are probably right. For better or worse, I kept him alive. If he hadn't had me to worry and fuss over, he would have gone off and wrestled a grizzly bear or taken on Crazy Horse's legions single-handed.

She leaned her backside to the windowsill and stared at the bed.

Now everything's different.

There are two Dakotas, Daddy. Both of them are states now.

A train runs into Deadwood. I can ride it clear to Chicago.

Big companies own all the mines, run by men who live in some fancy house in San Francisco or New York. Men who never stood in a freezing stream for eight hours with a gold pan in their hand.

No one is finding gold nuggets in the streams any more.

No one is afraid of a Sioux attack. And if anyone doesn't like the cold weather, they take a train to Santa Barbara and spend the winter.

There are only a few left who've seen the steely glance of Brazos Fortune and felt their hearts stop and their throats go dry.

She studied the irregular breathing of the narrow-faced man in the bed.

Daddy, you were something back then.

Oh, Daddy, you are still everything to me even now.

"Mr. Henry Fortune, your baby girl is melancholy tonight. Enough of that! The water's warm and it's Wednesday night and time for your bath. Now, I don't want any argument from you."

The shriveled-up, gray-haired man didn't open his eyes as she pulled the cotton sheet back and tugged off the nightshirt. She moved the steaming porcelain bowl of water to the nightstand and retrieved a white rag and beige towel.

She started with his face, neck, ears.

His cheeks are so sunken. His mustache covers almost everything. Eyes that could melt a steel rail seldom open. He never really sees anything any more. And look at those skinny shoulders and arms. Arms that carried me so many times I could never count. They can't lift a pillow now. That's OK, Daddy. I'll lift everything for you.

She rubbed his chest and arms with a slow circular motion. "Daddy, I'm going to roll you on your side so I can wash your back. You need to roll over so you don't get those sores on your backside again. Come on, Daddy, that's the way."

After she washed his back she rubbed his shoulders and neck with her bare hand.

My little Daddy. You were always so big in my eyes. You towered above all men, if not in stature, certainly in character. And now, you're my little Daddy.

Lord, it is the end of his life. He has no complaints. He didn't blame you for Mama's death. Nor the twins. He wasn't bitter at you about losing the place in Texas. It was his lot. I believe he accepted that. He made the most of what you gave him. He raised three splendid boys, although one broke his heart for a few years. And he raised one very spoiled daughter.

He made his world better and never lost faith in you.

So his reward awaits him.

But what about me? This is the end of an era for me too. And I don't know what's up ahead. Carty's right. Sometimes I want to live out on the prairie in the wide-open spaces away from everyone.

147

She tucked the sheet up around his waist and continued to rub his back.

"Oh, Daddy, how I wish I could visit with you and tell you what's on my heart. And ask for your advice like I have for over thirty years."

She quit rubbing but left her hand on his shoulder.

"Come on, Dacee June, that's enough being maudlin. I'll get a clean nightshirt and let you get back to sleep."

As she started to pull her hand away, she was startled by his right hand as it lifted off the covers, reached up to his bony shoulders, and patted her hand.

"Oh Daddy . . . je suis ainsi effraye . . . I am so scared . . . et je suis trop vieux sois effraye . . . and I am too old to be scared."

Tears streamed down both cheeks as she rubbed his shoulders once again.

☛ ☛ ☛

At midnight a sudden burst of China rockets and Roman candles set off by the residents and patrons of the lower end of town welcomed the Fourth of July. Brazos slept soundly on his side.

Dacee June stuck a pale yellow ribbon on page 24 of *Le Crime de Sylvestre Bonnard*, then laid the leather-bound volume on the side table and strolled to the window.

Mr. Jacques-Anatole-Francois Thibault, I don't believe I share your fanaticism with books. However, some days I too am bewildered with everyday life.

She put her hand on the window to swing it closed but hesitated. The night air felt pleasant as she gazed at the street lamps and shadows.

This is such a strange place to build a town, Lord. Just a steep, narrow gulch where Whitewood and Deadwood Creeks converge in the northern Black Hills. Now, Rapid City is a good place for a town. Or

Spearfish, or even Custer. But Deadwood? I can't imagine anything left standing one hundred years from now. Maybe a rundown cemetery and busted markers overgrown with weeds and brambles.

She felt chilled and hugged her arms across her chest.

What's happening to me, Lord? It's as if my love of this place is dying with Daddy. I think it's because I'm just so very, very tired. No more reading. Perhaps I'll sit in the rocker and sleep a little. I will hold Daddy's hand and sleep. I will be able to tell if he needs me . . .

"Mrs. Fortune!" The man's voice was deep, powerful.

Dacee June stepped back into the room and partially closed the window.

"Mrs. Fortune, I see you up there. I need to talk to you."

She leaned her head forward. "It's the middle of the night, and there is no Mrs. Fortune up here."

"I saw you standing at the window. I need to talk to you, ma'am."

Where have I heard this voice? "My name is not Mrs. Fortune." *He is obviously not from around here, or he would know that.* "So just who, exactly, do you need to talk to?"

"I need to talk to a purdy lady who works at the hardware and sold me a carbine around noon today."

She laced her fingers together under her chin. "Mr. Justice?" *What on earth is he doing down there? Where did I lay that pistol?*

"Yes, ma'am."

She cleared her throat and took one step toward the window. "I'm the one who sold you the gun. My name used to be Fortune. I'm Mrs. Toluca now." She still couldn't see the man in the shadows below the window.

"Mrs. Toluca, I need to talk to you. It's important."

"I believe the sheriff is looking for you." She rubbed her fingers across her chapped lips.

"What for?"

"There seems to be a raft of rumors about you, Mr. Justice."

"Mrs. Toluca, if you promise not to believe all the rumors you hear about me, I promise not to believe all the ones I hear about Dacee June Fortune."

She flung open the window. "I beg your pardon!" She could barely make out a tall man with a wide-brimmed felt hat.

"No offense, ma'am." He tipped his hat, but she could not see his face. "I'm just saying that not everything told about me is true."

She brushed her hair back over her ears. "I know for a fact you swindled me out of five guns today, and if my brothers and I hadn't taken them back at gunpoint, you would still have them." *Why on earth do I care what my hair looks like?*

"I reckon you're right. Do you suppose we could visit just a spell a little closer? I don't want to shout and wake up the neighbors."

"I can hear just fine. Besides, there aren't any neighbors. This is a business district."

"Yes, ma'am. I heard your daddy was sick. I didn't want us to wake him."

She rubbed along the long sleeve of her dress and could feel the hair on her arm tingle. "What are you suggesting?"

"Maybe you could come downstairs and then at least we could holler through a lower window. I saw you were still dressed so I figured it wouldn't imposition you much."

He was watching me through the window? He knows what I am wearing? I must keep the windows closed. She watched the steady breathing of the old man in the bed. "I will be down in a minute."

"Thank you, ma'am."

Dacee June tucked the covers around her father and plucked her .32 caliber pocket pistol off the dresser. A lone electric bulb illuminated the top of the stairs as she entered the darkened shadows of the silent hardware store.

Lord, I can't believe I am doing this. I don't know why I am doing this. The man is a notorious outlaw. A vicious man. I should telephone the sheriff, except he's probably down in the Badlands tonight arresting drunks and I'd merely wake poor Emily. I could call Sammy. But I sent him home to get some sleep. Of course he didn't obey me. He is more tired than I.

This is insane.

An outlaw shouts through the window and expects a lady to come down in the middle of the night and talk to him? Who does he think he is?

Who does he think I am?

Maybe it's a dream.

Dacee June scurried over to the dormant potbellied stove and grabbed the back of an oak chair and dragged its squeaking legs clear across the store to the locked double doors at the front of the building. She pushed the chair where it faced the tall oak doors and sat down, her revolver in her right hand.

"Are you still there, Mr. Justice?" she asked.

"Yes, ma'am. Are you going to open the door?"

"No, I am not."

"Are you going to check the lever on that carbine?"

"I do not have a carbine."

"Maybe you'll just cock the hammer on the pistol."

With her right thumb, Dacee June yanked back the hammer on the revolver.

"Small caliber?"

"It's a .32 Whitneyville rimfire. But I believe it will dispatch a man at this range, don't you, Mr. Justice?"

"Yes, ma'am. I reckon it will. And if you don't mind, I think I'll just stay out on the sidewalk."

"I believe that is a judicious decision." She leaned back in the chair yet kept the brass-framed revolver pointed at the doors. "What do you want, Mr. Justice?"

"I want to apologize for takin' your guns." From the position of his voice, she knew he had either sat down or squatted to the left side of the doorway.

"I can have you arrested for that."

151

"Yes, ma'am, I know that. Could you let me speak my peace first? Then you can call the sheriff. Last I saw of him he was down at the Piedmont stoppin' a knife fight."

"In that case, go ahead and apologize."

"Mrs. Fortune . . ."

"I told you, I'm Mrs. Toluca."

"Can I just call you Dacee June?"

"No, you may not."

"Mrs. Toluca, I was a very desperate man. I needed six guns, and you know how little money I had."

"You needed guns to go bushwack some miners?"

"It's a very long story, Mrs. Toluca. But the truth of the matter is, what I did was very wrong. I apologize."

"That is a good start, Mr. Justice. In the name of Christian charity, I will accept your apology."

"Thank you."

"You're welcome."

"Now, I'd like to buy those five guns."

Dacee June leaned forward in the chair. "What?"

"I have the money now. I'd like to buy the five guns. You'll have to sell them as used, and I'll pay full price for them. I believe it was $24 each, plus money for the bullets. That should be $129.50."

She glanced around in the darkened room as if to find moral support. "You want me to sell you the guns? I can't believe your audacity."

"Mrs. Toluca, I'm trying to make things up to you. And the best thing I could think of was legitimately to purchase the guns."

"You have $129.50?"

"Yes, ma'am."

"I hear Chop Lin's in China Town was robbed tonight. You don't happen to know anything about that, do you?"

"No, ma'am, I was in Hill City today."

"That's strange. Your friends were out trying to kill innocent miners today."

"Mrs. Toluca, there were no innocent miners out there. There were eight hired gunfighters."

She rubbed her small, upturned nose with her fingertips. "I was there. But you are right; they were not miners."

"My friends told me all about this wild lady. I surmised it was you."

"Are you saying you did not put mine and my husband's lives in jeopardy out there?"

"I was not there, of course. But I can tell you our intention was not that anyone get hurt. Especially you, your husband, and your brothers."

"I find it difficult to believe that a man buys—or should I say—steals five guns and has no intention of hurting anyone."

"Mrs. Toluca, like I said, it's a long story."

She sat back in the chair and stretched her legs out in front of her. "I have time."

"Are you joshin' me? Do you really want to know?"

Although the chair was stationary, she began to rock back and forth. "I am curious to know how you will justify stealing five guns."

"There's no justification for that. I apologized. I am ready to pay you cash dollars for the guns."

"And I think the suggestion that I sell you the guns is ludicrous. Mr. Justice . . . je serai le gage d'aucun homme."

"No, ma'am, I don't reckon a gal like you would ever be any man's pawn. I'm not tryin' to get you to do anythin' you don't want to do."

Mr. Justice, you are a mysterious outlaw. "You speak French?"

"Yes, but I would rather you didn't ask me how I learned."

"OK. That's fair enough." *There is a story here even more interesting than one by Mr. Anatole France.* "One story at a time."

"Mrs. Toluca, three months ago I was in prison."

A smile broke across her face, and she glanced over her shoulder to see if anyone was watching. "Somehow that doesn't surprise me."

There was laughter in his reply. "Nor will you be surprised when I claim to be innocent."

She leaned forward, her elbows on the wooden arms of the chair. "Don't all prisoners say that?"

"Not all." His reply sounded pensive. "But the truth is, I was in the Montana State Prison at Deer Lodge. A Mr. Albert Sween was a friend of the warden. Or at least let his money buy a friendship. Sween was brewin' some big deal to open up a gold mining district in Northern British Columbia. Do you know Sween?"

"I've never met him, but I understand he recently purchased the Broken Boulder from the Raxton sisters. They were good friends."

"Yeah, that's him. Anyway, the prison was crowded, and Sween talked the warden into lettin' me and seven others finish servin' our time by drivin' his cattle up into British Columbia to this minin' district of his."

"He owned a mine? Or mining district?"

"The whole district. He sold off claims at a very steep price. Anyway, they needed beef, and he wanted cheap cowboys."

"You didn't get paid?"

"We were promised one hundred cash dollars and freedom when we delivered the bovines."

"What would keep you from ridin' off once you got out on the open range?" she questioned.

"Those hired guns that you saw out at the Broken Boulder."

"Those men guarded you?"

"Yep."

"Did they shackle you at night?"

"Yes, ma'am."

"That's horrible. It sounds like slave labor. Why did you agree to it?"

"You ever been in prison, ma'am?"

"Of course not," she snapped.

She heard him chuckle. "No, I mean to visit. Just to look around."

"I did mission work at a woman's prison in Chicago when I was in college."

"We wanted to get outside and figured it couldn't be any worse than what we had. I suppose we hoped there might be a way to break free."

"But there wasn't?"

"No, ma'am, we were hobbled to the stirrups in the day and shackled at night. But we were out under the stars on horses and well fed. We had no complaints. At first."

"So you drove the cattle north?"

"Eleven weeks on the trail. A little snow. Lots of rain. But we got them there."

"And you got your one hundred dollars and freedom?"

"No. Sween had some official from Ottawa meet us and say we were considered prisoners and would be arrested and deported back to Deer Lodge unless we remained under Sween's control."

"Which must have been disappointing."

"That's an understatement. A couple of the boys would have killed him with bare hands if it weren't for the shackles."

"So then what happened?"

"Sween said it was no problem. We'd just ride back down to the states, cross the line, then he'd give us the money and set us free. In the meantime he had eight freight wagonloads of ore he wanted us to drive down for him."

"That sounds like predetermined slave labor."

"Yep. But he promised us another one hundred cash dollars each."

"And when you reached the border?" Dacee June plucked a linen handkerchief from her sleeve and patted her neck dry.

"We drove them into Idaho in the middle of the night."

"He was avoiding a tariff no doubt."

"We were just happy to get to the states. But he said it would be safest if we drove on to Montana. Near Missoula we realized he was takin' us right back to prison at Deer Lodge. No freedom, no money, nothing."

"I suppose that did not sit well."

"We were shackled to the wagons, so there wasn't much we could do. Benny and Cape tried to take off on foot but were gunned down in the backs still shackled."

"Murdered?"

"By Albert Sween himself. I think he would have shot us all, but some of his men restrained him. Of course, the official record says they were prisoners shot while attempting to escape. Sween claimed their escape attempt forfeited the money and parole for the rest of us. So he piled us in a wagon and personally took us back to Deer Lodge. We were jammed in the dark cells in the middle of the night."

"How did you ever get out of there?"

"With the help of a lady friend who visited me, I snuck a letter out to the newspaper in Helena about the warden making a profit from slave labor. But no one believed it until the governor's wife investigated. I knew her back in Miles City."

"You have a number of lady friends."

"Yes, ma'am, I reckon I do."

"So what happened?"

"About three weeks ago, an investigation was to be launched at the state prison in Deer Lodge. Suddenly, all six of us were released and put on a train with a one-way ticket to New Orleans."

"To get you out of the way?"

"But as soon as we got to Omaha, we hopped off the train and started workin' our way back west. When we got to Sidney, Nebraska, we read in a newspaper that Albert Sween had bought a mine near Deadwood, so we headed north. We figured to sell the horses in town and buy some guns and storm over to his mine."

"But the Broken Boulder is too far to walk to," she said.

"That's what we learned. So I came in to buy one gun. That was my intention. But those new '94 carbines are so smooth and with that .30 caliber bullet. I knew I needed to get one for each of us."

"So you stole my guns?"

"Yes, ma'am, I did."

"Then you headed out to the Broken Boulder?"

"Yep, but when we got up the road to Central City and asked directions to the mine, we found out that Sween had just been through on his way to Hill City but the others were still out there. The boys thought I ought to pursue Sween because he was the one who had the money and shot Benny and Cape. They were to pin the others down while I settled up with Sween."

"Did you intend to kill them all or just Sween?"

"We intended to get our $200 each and . . ."

"And?" she pressed.

"Well . . . vengeance est le plus doux quand il est rapide," he argued.

"Yes, but vengeance belongs to the Lord."

"Ma'am, that's a mighty fine sayin' for the righteous. Me and the boys figure the Lord don't really care what happens to us."

"That's not true."

"What is true is that the boys rode out to the Broken Boulder and got in a gunfight, which you busted up."

"And what about you? Did you catch Sween?"

"Nope. By the time I reached Hill City, he was on the train to Rapid City. I didn't want to abandon the boys, since they didn't have a penny or scrap of food to their names. We pooled our money for that one carbine I bought. So I stopped the pursuit. That's when my luck changed and I ran across Trena."

"Another lady friend?"

"Yes, ma'am. She was still packin' around my ol' Visalia saddle. So I sold it at the mercantile for two hundred dollars and headed back this way. I met up with the boys just outside of Lead. I took 'em some groceries and they're camped up there now. I slipped into town, bought myself supper at Beano Billy's, and waited to buy those guns of yours."

"So that you can go kill more men?"

"I've never killed anyone who wasn't trying to kill me. We just want our two hundred dollars each. It's ours. We earned it."

"Whatever happened to the wagonloads of ore you drove into Montana?"

"I don't know. And I don't care. We heard Sween was linin' up another prison crew to go up for more wagons when they shut the whole thing down at Deer Lodge."

"Mr. Justice, you are a paradox. I have never heard more violent, gruesome stories than the ones I've heard about you. Cold-blooded murders, savage vengeance, deadly holdups."

"Not to mention the ones about me burnin' down orphanages and ravagin' a dozen young schoolteachers," he suggested.

"I . . . I . . . I didn't hear about those," she stammered.

His laugh revealed more emotion than humor. "They are all lies."

"How can there be so many lies? I don't hear stories like that about anyone except . . ."

"Except Indians?"

"Yes, but I never believe half of what I hear."

"But you believe it about me?"

"Perhaps I have been hasty. Yet how do such stories circulate?"

"My reputation started with the railroad wars. I had the nerve to change sides. That riled some people, and exaggerations flew. I guess it just snowballed after that."

"Why did you change sides?"

"I figured out I was on the wrong side."

"But they are such horrible stories. How is that possible?"

"I reckon all you need is a big liar and a bunch of folks who want to believe a lie."

"And the big liar would be?"

"Right now, it's Albert Sween. He surely don't want me back around here. So if he paints a bad enough portrait, someone drunk will shoot me in the back, and they don't have to worry about what I might say."

Dacee June eased the hammer down on her revolver and shoved it back into her skirt pocket. "Why didn't he just have his men shoot you up in Canada?"

"I've often thought about that. I guess he thought he could keep the system working. Besides, the warden in Deer Lodge would have to explain sooner or later what was happening to his prisoners."

"Mr. Justice, you should go to the authorities."

"The U.S. authorities? The Canadian authorities? The Montana authorities? They all think they need to arrest me."

"Do they?"

"I don't reckon so. I don't remember."

"You don't remember your crimes?" she challenged.

"No, ma'am. Do you remember all your sins?"

Lord, you certainly couldn't be using such a man to prick my conscience, could you? "You are quite right, Mr. Justice. I do not remember all my sins, and some probably should have been punished by law. But vengeance is only followed by more violence. Perhaps there are times just to ride away and forget the past."

"Mrs. Toluca, is your daddy Brazos Fortune?"

"Yes. Do you know him?"

"No, but ever'one in the Dakotas, Wyomin', and Montana has heard of him. His stories are more legion than mine."

"Your point being?"

"Did your daddy ever ride away when he was robbed and cheated?"

The air in the hardware store felt heavy, stale. "No, he never did."

"Then I reckon he knows how I feel."

She brushed down her skirt and folded her hands in her lap. "Yes, I suppose he does."

His voice was soft yet insistent. "Will you sell me those guns now?"

"I don't think so," she replied.

"Why not?"

"I don't know why you were in prison in the first place."

She heard him approach the locked door. "What does that have to do with it?"

"That's what I'd like to know." Dacee June's hand slipped into her dress pocket and fingered the cherrywood pistol grip.

"I told you I was innocent," he barked.

"Of what?"

His voice softened. "Manslaughter."

"With a gun?" she asked.

"Yes."

"Did you shoot a man?"

"Yes."

"Then why do you say you were innocent?"

"Because he shot at me three times before I shot back."

"Were there witnesses?"

"Yeah, one."

"And what did he say?"

"*She* said I shot the man in a fit of rage."

"Were you in a rage?"

"Of course I was. Havin' a man shoot at me three times tends to do that."

"Did she testify that he shot at you first?"

"No."

"Why not?"

"That's a long story that I'd rather not get into."

"It seems to me, Mr. Justice, that you have many long stories."

"I reckon you're right." His voice came from lower. She guessed he was seated on the sidewalk again. "I never had anyone want to listen to them before."

"Have you ever been married?" she pressed.

"What kind of question is that?"

"What's wrong with it? It seems quite logical to me," she insisted.

"Married women don't usually ask me if I'm married."

Her hand covered her mouth. *What is this man thinking?* "Mr. Justice, I assure you that I only asked that to see why it is you've never had anyone to listen to you before. Everyone needs someone to confide in."

"Well . . ." he drawled. "I do talk to my horse a lot."

Dacee June burst into laughter. "Thank you, Mr. Justice, for relaxing the tension of the conversation."

"It was gettin' a little tight, wasn't it?"

"I believe so."

"I have to be honest, Mrs. Toluca. I ain't talked to a gal through a door like his for more than two sentences before in my whole life."

"I presume you usually just say, 'It's me, darlin',' and she opens right up."

She could hear him chuckle.

"Thanks, darlin', I needed a laugh too."

"I'm glad I can help you out that way."

"You can help me out one other way."

"Oh?"

"You could sell me the guns."

"Mr. Justice, it seems to me to be morally wrong to sell guns that will most assuredly cause a gunfight in which some men will die."

"Do you think any of the guns sold at the hardware have ever killed someone?"

"I'm sure they have. But if I had known that ahead of time, I wouldn't have sold them either. Besides, you can go somewhere else and buy guns."

"I'd have to go to Rapid City to get new smokeless .30 caliber '94s; you know that. Or I could wait until tomorrow and pay some bummer five bucks to come in here and buy the guns for me."

She tugged on the sweaty collar of her dress. "Please don't."

"Then, Dacee June, please sell me the guns."

"Mr. Justice, you are a very persuasive man. Yet all my friends have told me how violent and treacherous you are. The sheriff was convinced of your villainy. The only dealings I've had with you have been when you stole five guns and when your pals shot at me and my brothers. So exactly why should I trust you?" *Did he just call me Dacee June?*

"For one reason, because we've talked through the door for thirty minutes and we shared some laughs. I've told you things that I've never told anyone else. And besides, you know in your heart that I'm tellin' you the truth."

"I beg your pardon," she gasped. *You are an incredibly presumptive man!*

"Dacee June, since you were about ten you've been the type of gal who could look in a boy's eyes and listen to him talk for two minutes and know for sure if he was talkin' straight or not. Isn't that true?"

You do not know me that well.

"Isn't that true?" he repeated.

"Wade, I cannot see your eyes."

"Then open the door."

Did I call him Wade? My word, what am I doing? "I do not like the direction that this conversation is going. Perhaps you should leave now," she stammered.

162

"Do you know why you want me to leave?"

Yes, I do, and I am not about to tell you that. Lord, I need to leave this conversation. "You are starting to annoy me."

"No. You want me to leave because I do not conform to your preconceived image of me. A relationship is easier when the principles are defined in black and white. To find out Wade Justice isn't so easily defined is disarming, isn't it, Dacee June?"

"Wade, we do not have a relationship."

"Sure we do."

"Listen to me, we do not have a relationship. We have merely chatted."

"Dacee June, merely chatting is when you stand in the meat market and some lady you have never seen before or since asks you, 'How does the lamb look today?' and you tell her, 'It's a little dark and old' and by the time you get home, you will forget whether her eyes were blue or brown or even if she asked about lamb or ham."

"What is your point?"

"Twenty years from now you'll be sitting in a dark room, waiting for something, and you'll remember sitting in that wooden chair by the door in the hardware store with your hands on that .32 revolver. And you will smell the dust, the tin, and the leather. You'll hear my gravely voice rumble around and remember words that we've spoken and a little smile will crack across your lips and you'll say, 'I wonder what ever happened to Wade Justice?'"

Dacee June leaped to her feet and hollered at the closed door. "That is very presumptuous of you. Just what makes you so confident that you can predict what will be in my mind in the future?"

"Because, Dacee June Fortune Toluca, twenty years from now, if the Lord is that gracious to me, I'll be sitting out by some campfire in the dark and listenin' to the wind and the wolves and it will grow real quiet and I'll hear the lilt in your voice and feel the emotion you pack into every word. And I'll remember your disarming giggle, and I'll ponder, 'Whatever happened to Dacee June?'"

She slapped her hand to her chest. Her heart raced. *Lord, this isn't right!* She gulped a deep mouthful of air and felt the perspiration pop out on her forehead.

"That's a nasty cough," he said.

"I am not coughing," she stammered.

"No, I meant your daddy . . . that's a nasty cough."

Daddy? Oh, my word, Daddy!

Dacee June circled the chair and sprinted toward the stairs. She heard a deep rattling cough explode from the upstairs apartment.

I should have been by his side! What am I doing! Lord, I am so weak. I can't believe I gave that man two minutes, let alone an hour!

She burst into the room. Brazos hunched on the side of the bed and clutched the bedpost with his right hand, his chest with his left. The cough sent chills down Dacee June's back.

"Daddy, what are you doing? You can't sit up!" She raced to his side. "Let me put you back in bed."

With eyes still closed, he violently shook his head and continued to cough. Fluid rattled in his lungs.

Dacee June sat next to him and held his shoulders. His fresh nightshirt was wringing wet with sweat. She grabbed a towel off the bed. "Daddy, if you insist on coughing, go ahead and cough it all out. Cough it up, Daddy. Get that bad stuff out of your lungs. I'm here, Daddy. Your Dacee June is here."

She wiped his mouth and chin after every cough. Finally, he stopped coughing and collapsed on her shoulder.

A voice filtered up from the street. "Is everything all right, Dacee June?"

"Wade, I must ask a favor of you."

"Do you want me to get a doc?"

"Yes, please hurry. Dr. Kendrickson is on Sherman Avenue, right next to the bank. If you ring the electric buzzer, he will come down from his apartment above the office."

"I'll go fetch him."

Boots tapped a fading cadence on the concrete sidewalk.

"Oh, Daddy, I'm sorry I wasn't here. There was a man at the door, and I went to see what he wanted. Oh, Daddy . . ." She rocked him back and forth. "Do you want to lie down now?"

He gasped for air but shook his head.

"OK, Daddy. We'll sit right here. You and me. Just like the old days. Remember when we were living up here in the apartment in the old building? When one of those Dakota lightning storms hit, we huddled on the edge of my bed. You'd rock me back and forth and tell me that the clouds were just jockeying to see who would be the bell mare?

"And then someone would pound on the door and need to buy coal oil or another lantern, or miner's candles, or a rat-tail file at 3 A.M. and you and I would go downstairs. While you were findin' what they needed, I'd toss another stick of wood in the fire and boil the water and make us a thick cup of Brazilian chocolate. Then you'd bundle me up in a quilt and we'd scrunch down by the fire until the thunder stopped. Then you'd let me sleep in the big chair. When I woke up, Yapper Jim would be talking, and the rest of your Texas Camp hovered around the stove. Oh, Daddy, how I wished those days would never end."

She brushed his gray hair back off his forehead and wiped off his mouth again. "Do you want to lie down now?"

This time she could barely see his head shake "no."

"OK, Daddy, you stay in my arms at least until the doctor comes. But I'll have to lay you down so I can go unlock the door for him. I'm sure Mr. Justice went to find him."

Why am I sure he will go get a doctor? Do I know him that well? Why should he bother?

She wadded the towel and patted the perspiration off his face and neck.

He's right, Lord. I do judge a man by his eyes and his voice. And I know that he will go get the doctor. I don't know why you allowed that man in my life tonight. I am very disturbed with you for doing that. Yet he was there to run for the doctor.

Dacee June held her father in her arms as he slept.

"Daddy, I love you very much. You know that. You've always known that. And I got to have you for thirty-one years. Mama just had you for twenty-six, so I know I cannot complain. Mama will be so happy to see her Henry."

Under other conditions Dacee June would have leapt to her feet when she heard the downstairs front door swing open followed by a crash and a shout.

This time she just kept seated on the edge of the bed, rocking the old man in her arms back and forth. Boot heels banged on the steps as someone raced up the wooden stairs.

She didn't bother looking back over her shoulder.

"Sammy, I'm glad you came."

"Is he gone, Lil' Sis?" The voice was out of breath, shaken.

"No, not yet. He had a horrible coughing spell, but he coughed some wretched black phlegm out of his lungs and went back to sleep, as long as I hold him up."

Sam Fortune squatted down on his haunches in front of Dacee June and Brazos in the dim light of the apartment. He wore boots, duckings, and hat, but no shirt.

And no gun.

"The doc's on his way," Sam reported.

Dacee June noticed an old knife scar on her brother's muscled shoulder. "Did you break the door down? I heard a crash."

"No, I had my key." He reached down and rubbed his shin. "But some fool left a chair right square in front of the door. I like to broke a leg trippin' over it."

She covered her mouth with her hand. "Oh . . . dear . . . I, eh . . ."

Sam stood and stepped to her side. "Is there anything I can get you, Lil' Sis?"

Dacee June nodded at the headboard. "Could you stack some pillows and that comforter against the headboard so we can sit Daddy up against it?"

He hurried to the other side of the bed.

"Sammy, how did you know to come down here?"

He fussed with several pillows. "The phone call."

"What phone call?" she asked.

"The guy you asked to phone me said to hurry, Daddy was having a bad spell and that you needed me and he was goin' to fetch the doctor. Who was that?"

Why did he call Sammy? I didn't ask him to do that. "He just happened to be on the sidewalk in front of the store when I needed help, and I hollered at him from the window."

"I owe someone a mighty big thanks. Could you see who it was in the dark?"

"I, eh, couldn't really see what he looked like." She started to scoot her father back against the headboard of the bed. As she did, she heard the tap of boot heels coming up the stairs.

"Maybe that's the doc," Sam said. "Let me help you with him."

She didn't look at the door. "It's Todd," she mumbled.

Sam glanced back. "He's OK, big brother, just another of those gasping spells when he coughs up half his lungs."

Todd wore his suit pants, rumpled long-sleeve white shirt, and no hat. "How does he keep it up?"

"His Dacee June was with him," Sammy reported. "Did you get a phone call too?"

"Yes. I didn't recognize the voice. Who was that?"

"That's the strange part. Lil' Sis just called to someone out on the street," Sam reported.

"I didn't ask him to call either of you, just the doctor. I didn't have time to think."

This time the boot heels echoed with military precision.

Dacee June glanced at Sam, then Todd.

"That's Bobby," Sam said. "He's hiked to a military beat since he was four years old."

Robert Fortune pushed through the door wearing suit and tie, with crisp, wide-brimmed hat. "How's Daddy?"

"Sleeping now," Dacee June said. "It was a bad spell."

"You got a phone call too?" Todd said.

"Who was that?" Robert asked.

"Lil' Sis's guardian angel," Sam reported.

Todd patted Brazos on the shoulder. "Did you get the doc?"

Sam stood next to his older brother. "He's on his way."

Robert reached across the bed and handed Todd a short white envelope. "This was under your door, big brother."

Todd looked into the envelope and pulled out some bills and three coins. "Must be on someone's account, but there's no note or name."

He turned the envelope over and glanced at the name. "This is for you, Lil' Sis."

"Me?"

"It says 'Mrs. Toluca' on the envelope. But there is nothing in it except money."

She stared at the green bills in Todd's hands. "How much money?"

"Looks like one hundred and twenty-nine dollars and seventy-five cents," he replied.

The guns. Justice gave me the money for the five guns!

"What's this about, Lil' Sis?" Todd pressed.

"I'm not sure. Like you said, it's probably on account." She glanced toward the window. "I think I'll go down and wait for the doctor."

"We'll watch Daddy," Robert assured her.

Dacee June scurried down the stairs. The dim light from the top of the stairs made the hardware store a maze of shadows. She scrambled over to the glass gun case and began counting carbines.

His voice exploded behind her. "They are all there!"

She spun around but could not see his face. He stood next to the dormant woodstove.

"Wade?"

"I didn't take any of them, Dacee June," he replied.

"I can see that."

"The doc's on his way."

She brushed her unruly hair back. "I can't thank you enough."

"Ever'one has a daddy, Dacee June, even despicable outlaws."

She took another step closer, but his face remained in the shadows. "But you went beyond the call of duty when you telephoned my brothers. Where did you locate a telephone?"

"In the lobby of the Merchant's Hotel," he said. "Here comes the doc." A long arm pointed across the store.

"Yes, thank you again, Mr. Justice."

"You're welcome, Mrs. Toluca."

She started to the front door.

"Dacee June?" he called out.

She turned back. "Yes, Wade?"

"Can I have those carbines now?"

"No, of course not." She felt her neck stiffen. "Just because you . . ."

"Mrs. Toluca?" Doc Kendrickson called out. "Are you over there?"

"Doctor, thank you for coming!"

"What choice did I have?" The gray-haired man looked up through thick glasses. "I was told if I didn't get my sweet . . . well, eh . . . if I didn't get over here in five minutes, I'd be hog-tied and slung over his shoulder."

"Daddy had a horrible coughing spell. I need you to check his lungs. The boys are up there with him." She took the doctor by the arm and led him to the foot of the stairs, then paused.

"You go on, Dr. Kendrickson. I'll be right up."

169

The short balding man with the beige linen suit shuffled up the steps, black leather bag in tow.

Dacee June took one step toward the corner of the store with the potbellied stove. "Wade, I changed my mind. You may have those carbines."

"Thank you, Dacee June. Do you want to come count them out for me?"

"That's not necessary, Mr. Justice. I trust you."

"And those, Mrs. Toluca, are the kindest words I've heard in years."

CHAPTER SEVEN

Thick gray smoke from the burnt eggs in the cast-iron frying pan blinked Dacee June's eyes open. She jerked the skillet off the stove and scraped the eggs with a circular motion. She glanced around at the empty kitchen.

This is not good. I went to sleep trying to cook breakfast. I think I need to sleep for about two weeks. I'm not taking very good care of my family.

"Mama, where are my lavender socks?" Elita called out from the front room.

"Those are for Sunday."

"I want to wear them today!" came the whine.

"Wear white ones today."

Jehane appeared barefoot at the doorway. Her brown bangs flopped down over her eyes. "She wants to wear them because

Uncle Sammy said they were very pretty and made her look mature."

"Oh, he did, did he?" *Sam Fortune, has there ever been a female of any age that didn't jump at your every word?*

"Mama, what's mature?" Jehane stuck her fingers in her ears and puffed her cheeks out.

"It's something an eight-year-old need not worry about."

Jehane reached under her thin cotton nightshirt and scratched her side. "Mama, can I wear the red dress?"

Dacee June scraped the brown and yellow eggs into a shallow bowl, then stared at the empty basket. "Yes, that would be fine." *I guess we'll have to eat burnt eggs. I don't have time to go to the store for more.*

Elita appeared at the door, six inches taller than Jehane. "She can't wear the red dress, Mother, I'm wearing the red dress."

Dacee June wiped her hands on the flour-sack tea towel. "I thought you said you're wearing lavender socks."

The eight-year-old folded her arms across her chest. "You said I can't wear the lavender socks, so I'm wearing the red dress."

Dacee June added a stick of firewood to the stove.

Jehane stood on her tiptoes. "No you aren't. I asked first." She punctuated the statement by sticking out her tongue.

A younger voice filtered in from the front room. "Mommy, I think I made a mess on the couch."

Dacee June slammed the firebox door on the stove. "What do you mean, you think you made a mess on the couch?" she called out.

The young voice was near panic. "I really, really made a mess on the couch."

Dacee June laid strips of bacon across the sizzling frying pan. "Elita, check out your little sister. My hands are sticky."

"Oh, that's very foul!" She heard her oldest daughter gasp.

"Try to clean it up. I have to finish these eggs," Dacee June called out.

"Me?" Elita whined. "I don't want to touch that stuff."

"I'm cooking bacon." Dacee June wiped her sticky fingertips on her checkered apron.

"Mama, the telephone's ringing," Jehane reported.

"I can hear it ring."

Elita came to the doorway. "Do you want me to answer it?"

"No, I want you to take Ninete into the pantry and wash her up."

Elita rolled her eyes. "But Mother, I'm getting dressed!"

The shorter girl tugged on her mother's apron. "The phone is still ringing, Mama."

"I can hear it, Jehane!" Dacee June shouted.

The girl jumped back. "Are you mad at me, Mama?"

"Baby, I'm tired and busy. I'm sorry." She ran her hand along the girl's wild dark brown hair. "Let the phone ring. They'll call back."

"What if Uncle Todd is calling about Grandpa Brazos?" Jehane asked.

"OK, you watch the bacon. I'll answer the telephone."

"Me? Elita is the one who helps cook."

"Big Sis' is busy with Lil' Sis. So I need your help, darlin'. If it starts looking cooked, come get me."

Jahane's eyes grew wide. "What do you mean 'cooked'?"

"You'll know."

Dacee June purposely didn't look at the sofa as she scurried through the front room to the entry hall. The putrid smell was rancid and familiar.

"Yes?"

"Dacee June, you were slow getting to the phone."

"Carty, is it Daddy?"

"No, it's the guns."

"You called me about guns?"

"Joey said those carbines are missing again. I called the sheriff. Todd said maybe someone slipped in the store last night during all the commotion with Daddy Brazos."

Elita staggered into the entry hall carrying a stark naked sister. "Mama, what do you want Ninete to wear?"

The girl squirmed to the floor. "I can dress myself!"

Dacee June dropped the receiver to her side. "Let her pick out a dress."

The naked six-year-old scampered up the stairs with her older sister trudging behind.

"Dacee June?"

She lifted the black receiver back to her ear.

"What about those guns?"

"No one stole them, Carty. I sold them."

"You what?"

Panty-clad Ninete appeared at the top of the stairs. "Mama, Elita says I can't wear my yellow dress."

Again the telephone dropped to her side. "You have to save that one for Sunday."

"But I want to wear it," Ninete sniffed.

"Dacee June?" Carty called out.

"Just a minute, honey . . ." She waved her hand at the girls at the top of the stairs. "Ninete, wear the brown dress."

"But you said I can pick one out," the sandy-blonde-headed six-year-old whined.

"That's the one you picked out," Dacee June snapped. "Now go on and get dressed."

"When did you sell the carbines?"

Dacee June rubbed her temples. "Last night. The man who went to get the doctor paid cash dollars for guns. There's $129.50 in an envelope in the cash box. Todd knows that. I gave it to him last night."

"One-hundred-twenty-nine fifty for five guns? Did you overcharge him?"

"The extra is for cartridges. Carty, I'll fill in the receipts when I come down."

"Mama, what's that smoke?" Elita called out from the top of the stairs.

Dacee June glanced into the smoky front room and shouted, "Jehane, is the bacon burning?"

"Yes!"

"What was the name of the man who bought those guns?" Carty demanded.

"Why didn't you tell me?" Dacee June yelled.

"Tell you what?" Carty replied.

"I don't like bacon," Jehane cried.

"Carty, I sold the guns. The money is all there. Now I have vomit to clean up, bacon to redeem, and three grumpy girls to take care of . . . no, four grumpy girls, including me. So unless you are coming home to cook and clean, I'm going to hang up."

"Who bought the guns?" he shouted.

"Mother! Why can't I wear the red dress?" Elita pleaded.

"Carty, I don't have time for this!"

"Mommy, I think the bacon caught on fire!" Jehane screamed.

"You sold guns in the middle of the night to a stranger?"

"Carty, this is absurd. Good-bye. I'll talk to you later."

Dacee June hung up the telephone receiver and raced back to the kitchen.

Lord, did I just hang up on my husband? This is not good.

Dacee June grabbed the smoking skillet of bacon and darted out the back door to the steep hillside behind their house.

She didn't know if it was the thick smoke.

Or the lack of sleep.

Or her children.

Or her husband.

But she started to bawl.

She jammed the skillet on a log round, wiped her eyes with a clean spot on her apron, and trudged back into the house.

Lord, this is silly. I don't have time to cry. I've used up my quota. Now it's time to get something done.

Why is it I never remember my mother getting this hassled?

She paused at the back door.

Why is it I have such a hard time remembering my mother at all?

☞ ☞ ☞

Dacee June surveyed the girls. Elita was picture-perfect in a light blue dress. Jehane giggled and tugged at her red collar. Ninete had a damp spot on her yellow skirt where strawberry preserves had recently been washed off.

"Alright, girls, come on, I'll walk you down," Dacee June announced.

"Can we walk with Camilla?" Elita asked.

"I'm going to the hardware to see Grandpa Brazos. You can walk that far with me."

"Please, Mama," Elita insisted, "we want to walk with Camilla and Nettie."

"And Hank and Stuart and Casey?"

"Uh, Mama," Jehane mumbled, "maybe Stuart and Casey can walk with you."

"Tell your cousins to stop by the hardware. You can finish walking with them."

Elita bit her lip. "Mama, I don't . . ."

One glance from Dacee June silenced her.

The two oldest daughters scampered up to the front porch of the house next door. Dacee June held Ninete's hand as they descended the Williams Street stairs to Shine Street.

Halfway down, they paused.

"Mama, I'm sorry I throwed up on the sofa, and I'm sorry I spilled jam on my dress. And I'm sorry I made you mad."

Dacee June leaned over and kissed her youngest daughter's forehead. "Baby, you don't need to apologize for anything. Mama's so tired this morning that she's very, very grouchy. Is your tummy feeling better?"

"Yes, but I didn't eat any of the bacon. It tasted like charcoal."

"I don't think anyone ate it."

"Elita did, but she said it was icky."

The two continued their descent of the Williams Street stairs. The little girl's eyes widened as she surveyed the back side of Main Street. "Mama, I think it's too lovely a day to be grouchy."

Dacee June gazed up at the Dakota sun reflecting off white rocks above Mount Moriah Cemetery straight across the gulch from where they stood. The blue skies set off the cliffs and the scattered green ponderosa on the hillside. No breeze blew, yet the air felt summer cool.

Dacee June studied her immediate surroundings.

The back side of the Main Street buildings looked old and battered. A fine dust hovered above the street. Garbage from the alley behind the Chicago Cafe left a rank stench. A large rat darted behind the greasy barrels half full of stagnant water. Horse manure littered the alley, which was no more than two weedy ruts in places.

Dacee June continued the trek. "You're right, baby. This is as nice a day as we have in Deadwood, South Dakota."

Ninete laced her fingers into her mother's. "It's the Fourth of July, you know."

Dacee June squeezed the little hand. "Yes, I know that."

"Do you think any buildings will catch fire this year?"

"I certainly hope not. Why did you ask?"

"Hank says every year a building burns down on the Fourth of July. He and some of his friends are betting on which one burns down."

Images of the fires of 1879 and 1894 filtered across Dacee June's mind. For a moment she could feel the flames. "That doesn't sound like a very good game."

"He bet twenty-five cents that the Star-Light Club would be the first to burn."

Dacee June stared down at her daughter's round eyes. "Hank told you that?"

"No, but Nettie heard him talking to Jimmy Trooper, and she told Elita, and I heard Elita tell Jehane."

The Fortune grapevine strikes again. "I'm going to pray that no buildings burn down."

Ninete rubbed her chin. "Then who would win the money?"

"No one."

The six-year-old let out a deep, animated sigh. "That would be quite boring."

"But wouldn't it be nice to enjoy a quiet, peaceful evening?"

"The play won't be boring."

"I imagine it won't."

"The twins are going to serve the punch and cake."

"I'm looking forward to the play. But I'm not sure the cake will be edible."

"The frosting is very tasty."

"So I hear. I have a feeling its remains were what I scrubbed off the couch," Dacee June said. "Don't you eat any today during practice."

She and Ninete waited at the corner of Main and Shine Streets for Elita and Jehane.

"Dacee June!" The deep male voice commanded attention.

She turned to see a gray-haired man with a brown leather vest and a gun strapped to his hip cross the street. His tie hung loose around the stiff collar of his white shirt.

"Good morning, Sheriff. I trust your evening wasn't too bad last night."

"This town likes to celebrate the Fourth of July. Tonight will be worse, of course." He tipped his wide-brimmed, beaver-felt hat. "Hello, Miss Nettie."

She looked down at the toes of her scruffy brown shoes. "I'm Ninete. Nettie's my cousin."

"Sorry about that. All you Fortune girls are so purdy a fella gets quite confused."

Ninete looked up and giggled. "I'm a Toluca girl."

He pointed a rough, calloused finger at her. "Yes, I did know that much. But you are all one family."

"My Grandpa is Brazos Fortune," Ninete bragged. "We're goin' to see him."

"You tell him hello for me, darlin'. There ain't a finer man who ever lived in these dreary Black Hills." He cleared his throat and lowered his voice. "Dacee June, did you know that Wade Justice is back in town?"

She glanced down the street at two men in dark suits who loitered in front of Beano Billy's. "I heard something to that effect."

"Rumor has it that he and five others are all with carbines. I reckon he found someplace else to steal the guns."

Dacee June brushed her hair back over her ears with her fingertips. "I suppose he could have purchased them."

"I heard a stage got held up over at Sundance, Wyoming, last night. Four people killed and purtneer two thousand dollars stolen. Must have been Justice and that bunch."

A string of firecrackers cracked from several blocks south. A chorus of dog barks and yelps accompanied it.

She studied the tanned-leather-looking creases on the sheriff's face. "It's fifty or sixty miles to Sundance. When was the stage held up?"

"If they relayed horses at Spearfish, they could have ridden all night to get there and back. I suppose the stage company will offer a reward."

"Where did you hear this report?"

The sheriff gazed south along Main Street. "Beano Billy said an old boy on a swayback mule showed up this mornin' who claims to have talked with a tinker who was the first one who came upon the stage over near Sundance."

"Then he rode all night to get here?"

"I reckon. I ain't never heard of anyone as vicious as that Wade Justice."

"And I've never heard of anyone riding a swayback mule from Sundance, Wyoming, to Deadwood in a single night. And I've surely never heard more stories told about Wade Justice than anyone since Colonel Custer and Wild Bill Hickok."

The sheriff nodded. "That's right. I figure if only half the stories is true, he ought to be arrested on sight."

She took hold of the sheriff's arm. "But what if none of the stories are true?"

He patted her hand. "What are you sayin', Dacee June?"

She laced her fingers together and raised her index fingers to her lips. "If Justice is as dangerous as you say, then don't call him out for something that might not be true."

His hand slipped to his walnut-gripped revolver. "Men like that have to be stopped."

"Killers and outlaws have to be stopped. But go after him for something you can prove. It's not worth putting your life on the line for a rumor, Sheriff. I don't want you shot just to find out that he hadn't really committed the crime."

"You don't think he deserves to be shot on sight?"

She watched the sheriff's thumb rub the hammer of the Colt revolver. "I suppose I don't think anyone deserves to be shot on sight."

"I reckon that's why we won't ever have a lady sheriff," he mumbled.

"Not in Dakota. I hear there are a few in Wyoming," she replied.

"We ain't that desperate." He turned and stepped toward the middle of the street. "Give my regards to your daddy. And tell your brothers that Justice is on the prowl and he's armed to the teeth."

☞ ☞ ☞

When all four entered the hardware store, Elita and Jehane stopped in the front aisle.

"Come on, girls, we'll go up and see Grandpa Brazos," Dacee June said.

"Mama, maybe we'd better wait by the door in case Camilla and Nettie come by," Elita suggested.

"We have a few minutes. Come on."

"Do we have to?" Jehane whined.

Dacee June put her hand on her daughter's shoulder. "What did you say?"

Jehane burst into tears. "Mama, you know I love Grandpa Brazos with all my heart, but he's so shrivelled and sick. It breaks my heart, Mama. Please don't make me do it."

She ran her hands through her daughter's long hair.

"I know, darlin', I know. The night Mama died, I hid under my bed. And I've felt guilty ever since."

"Please, Mama," Jehane implored.

"How about you, Elita?"

Her oldest daughter's eyes widened. "Maybe I should stay with Jehane."

"And you?" she asked the six-year-old.

"I want to go with you, Mama," Ninete insisted.

"OK, you girls stay here. Lil' Sis and I will go see grandpa."

Todd barged out from the storeroom about the time she reached the bottom of the stairs. "Lil' Sis, I hear you didn't get much sleep."

"Where'd you hear that?"

"Carty said you were a little grumpy this mornin'."

She frowned and shook her head. "Yes, that's a nice way of putting it. I was a pill, and you do know what kind of pill I can be."

"Hi, Uncle Todd," Ninete interrupted.

Todd squatted down in front of the girl. "Hi, Ninete, darlin'. That's a pretty yellow dress."

"You can hardly see I spilled jam on it."

"Why, no, I didn't even notice."

"Are you coming to see the play tonight?"

"I'll be in the front row." Todd patted the girl's cheek, then stood.

"How's Daddy?" Dacee June said.

"He's sleeping without coughing."

"Who's up there with him?"

"It's my turn, but I had to inventory a freight load. How about you checkin' on him?"

"We were just headin' up there."

"Did you know Justice and that crew hit town?" Todd said.

"The sheriff told me."

"I heard he shot a sheepherder out at Bear Butte and stole his carbine."

"The sheriff seems to think Justice was in Wyoming last night."

"Either way, something needs to be done. I was thinking of contacting Fort Mead. Maybe have a patrol come up for the parade and stick around overnight."

"You mean in 1895, Deadwood can't take care of itself?"

When Todd stiffened his back, he looked even taller than six-feet-two. "Dacee June, this man's a vicious outlaw. And we might be the target."

"I don't have time to worry, Todd. We've got a big day of celebrating."

"You act pretty calm, girl."

"Perhaps it's the Lord's peace, or perhaps I'm just too tired. Anyway, me and Ninete are going to see Grandpa."

"Say, that money in the envelope last night, was it for the carbines?"

"Yes."

"So, you were able to sell the stolen guns as new?"

"Yes."

"I think I'll telegraph New Haven for another case of the '94s. I didn't know they would sell so well."

☞ ☞ ☞

Morning sunlight broke into the second-story window of Fortune & Son Hardware. The dust hanging in the air gave it a golden hue. The old man in the bed was on his right side, covered with just a white cotton sheet. One arm flopped down over the edge of the bed. His eyes were closed.

Dacee June could hear labored breathing as he slept.

Ninete ran to the side of the bed. "Hi, Grandpa Brazos! It's the Fourth of July. Isn't it a wonderful day? I'm goin' to be in a play that Amber wrote. It's called Queen of the Black Hills, and it's all about Mama. Isn't that grand?"

"I think Grandpa's asleep, honey."

"Yes, but he hears my voice. I just know he does." The six-year-old peeked down at the sleeping old man. "Guess what, Grandpa? Daddy said if there was enough ice left in the cellar, we will have ice cream tonight! Oh, the cake! Did I tell you about the most wonderful cake in the world?"

Dacee June watched the animated child rock up on her toes as she spoke. *Oh, Daddy, if you could see her eyes sparkle and her little pink lips form each word, you would laugh and grin like the old days.*

"We have an elephant cake! It's the biggest cake in the entire world. It's shaped like an elephant, sort of, and the frosting is gray and it is very tasty even if it is a little gritty. And after the play and the cake, there will be more fireworks, and the band will play, and Mother has invited a very special guest to sing . . . the best singer in all the Black Hills . . . and then we will have some more fireworks, and a building will burn down, and then some more cake, and more ice cream and then I will throw up!"

Lord, she will never know his strength of character. And he will never see her run and giggle and ride fast ponies.

"Elita says I'm very good at throwing up, perhaps even the best in all of Deadwood, but I don't want to brag or nothin'."

She reached down and lifted Brazos's limp arm in her hand and stroked it. "Grandpa, are you dreaming of Grandma Sarah Ruth? Mama says when you sleep you dream of Grandma Sarah Ruth. I try to dream of Grandma, but the dreams are always black. I wish I could have seen my grandma."

Dacee June walked to the window and stared out at the rising Dakota sun. She wiped the tears from the corner of her eyes.

Ninete tucked Brazos's arm alongside him on the mattress. "I've seen pictures of Grandma. She was very, very pretty. Uncle Sammy says that all Fortune women are very, very pretty. He says it's a law that we have to be pretty, but I think he's just funnin' me. I think I'm pretty, but Elita says I sort of look plain. Do you think I look plain, Grandpa?"

Ninete held her skirt out and twirled around.

"I think I'm pleasant and pretty, but Jehane says it's not good to brag. I don't think I'm bragging, but maybe I am. I'm not beautiful like Amber. Si je ressemblais elle, jene me vanterais pas. Je pas dois."

Ninete leaned close to the sleeping man's face. "Mama, does Grandpa know French?"

"No, he doesn't, darlin'."

"Grandpa, I said, 'If I looked like her . . . Amber . . . I would not brag, I would not have to.' Did you know that Mama is teaching us French? Some day Elita is going to go to France. She said if I am very, very good that I can go with her. Jehane doesn't want to go to France."

A young girl's voice wafted up the stairs. "Mama, Camilla is here!"

"Time to go with your sisters, Baby."

"I have to go, Grandpa. I hope you have a pleasant day. I will come see you later and bring you some cake with lots of gray icing. Mother calls me Baby, but I'm six and one-third years old. Did you ever call Mama your baby? She is your baby, isn't she?"

Dacee June led her to the top of the stairs.

"It's nice being the baby in the family, isn't it, Mama?"

"Yes, I believe you are right about that. Now, be nice today and mind Amber."

"I will, Mama." Ninete got halfway down the stairs, then turned around. "Mama, did Grandpa Brazos ever call you his baby?"

"Yes, he did."

"Even when you were big like me?"

"Yes, he did."

"Did you like it when he called you Baby?"

"Yes, I did, darlin'. Now go on, your sisters are waiting on the sidewalk."

"I like it when you call me Baby," Ninete said.

"I'm glad, because I don't think I could ever stop calling you my baby."

Dacee June watched her youngest sprint to the front door, then she returned to the old man in the bed.

"Daddy, that little French-speaking girl adores her Grandpa Brazos." *Oh, what I'd give to have him call me his baby girl, just one more time.*

Robert and Jamie Sue strolled into the room.

"Mornin', Lil' Sis."

"Mornin', Bobby, Jamie Sue. How are things in Ingleside today?"

"Nothing but excitement about the rescue ride of the Fortune trio," Jamie Sue replied. "You and your brothers are the talk of the town."

"It's a tradition," Dacee June said. "What would the Black Hills be without a new Fortune family story?"

"Little Frank is upset that he missed it all," Robert reported.

"With that heart-stopping shy grin of his, I imagine he will have plenty of excitement in his life," Dacee June offered.

"Is Daddy sleeping all right?" Robert probed.

"No coughing that I know of."

"You go on, Lil' Sis. The children are at play practice. I don't have to go back to work for a couple of days. So let Jamie Sue and me stay with Daddy. Carty says you need some rest."

"Oh, he said that?"

"He said you were . . ." Robert glanced at his wife. "What was his word?"

"Cantankerous," Jamie Sue grinned.

"Yes, I just can't seem to sleep much lately. And Bobby knows how I get when I get too tired."

"Did I ever tell you about the time Lil' Sis . . ."

"Don't you start on me, Bobby Fortune!"

He folded his arms and surveyed his sister. ". . . took off all her clothes . . ."

"Bobby!" she shouted.

" . . . and went to sleep on the front pew at the church in Brownsville?"

"Really?" Jamie Sue covered her mouth. "How old was she?"

"Four or five, I believe."

"I did not do that. The boys made that story up just to watch me blush. Daddy said I never did it!"

"That's 'cause Mama hustled down from the choir and made you dress in the baptistry before they finished taking the offering."

Dacee June marched across the room. "It's all a lie, Jamie Sue."

"Don't worry, honey, your secret is safe with me. I won't tell a soul," Jamie Sue assured her. "Except Abby and Rebekah."

"Oh, thanks."

Robert walked his sister to the window. "Lil' Sis, did you hear that those bushwhackers from the mine are in town this mornin'?"

"The sheriff said something about it."

"And they are armed again."

"So are most other men down in the lower end of town."

"That's true enough. Some say they will be comin' after you, me, and Todd."

Dacee June shook her head. "I don't think so."

"Oh? You have some inside knowledge?"

"Just a guess. I think they have some purpose for showing up here and the purpose isn't to harass us. So I figure they'll go about that business, whatever it might be."

"Did you hear what Justice did last night?" Robert asked.

"Which version? The one about the stage in Sundance? Or the one about the sheepherder on Bear Butte?"

"What? He was there too?"

"What did you hear?"

"Justice boarded the train in Hill City and rode into Rapid City and held up Montgomery's Jewelry Store. He nabbed a lady clerk and the money. The woman and Justice have not been seen since."

Dacee June felt her mouth drop open as she shook her head. "Where did you hear that one?"

"The night telegraphers spread the story up and down the line, and Johnson at the depot picked it up when he came on shift this morning."

"Bobby, do you think a man could kidnap a woman in Rapid City, kill a sheepherder on Black Butte, and rob a stagecoach in Sundance, Wyoming, all in the same night?"

"That's absurd."

"Is the sheriff going to arrest Justice for the Rapid City crime?"

"He said he had to wait for a telegram from the sheriff down there."

"It seems strange the crime hasn't been reported to neighboring towns yet."

"It's the Fourth of July. I suppose everyone is busy." Robert began to whisper. "I don't want to alarm Jamie Sue, but I think you'd better be packin' your pistol today. One thing I do know for sure, that gang at the mine is totin' carbines this mornin'. And they were not happy when we disarmed them and chased them off. Sammy saw a couple of 'em that fit the description camped along Whitewood Creek. Do you have your gun?"

"No."

"Maybe Todd has an extra one here at the store."

"Perhaps I should wear my buckskin dress, strap on a double holster, and tote Daddy's Sharps carbine like the old days."

"Are you mockin' me, Lil' Sis?"

"Bobby, I'm so tired I could fall over and sleep on the floor. I just can't get worked up about possible gunmen."

"Maybe you need to sneak home and take a nap."

"I couldn't agree with you more."

☛ ☛ ☛

Carty met her at the bottom of the stairs. "You hung up on me."

She slipped her arm around his waist. "I'm sorry, honey, everything got so hectic at home. I felt you were interrogating me."

"I just wanted to know who you sold those carbines to."

"I told you, the man who went to get the doctor for Daddy." She laid her head on his chest. *He is the strongest thin man I have ever known.*

He circled his hands around her waist. "Some carbines showed up in the hands of the Justice gang. I was worried they might be ours."

"They aren't ours anymore. I sold the guns for cash money. They belong to someone else." She stepped back and picked a piece of navy blue string from his long-sleeved white shirt.

"But did you sell them to one of Justice's men?"

"No, I didn't sell them to one of Justice's men."

"Maybe he sent some stooge to buy them for him."

"I didn't sell the guns to a stooge."

Sam Fortune strolled into the store, and Carty pulled straight back.

"I reckon you heard they were armed and in town looking for us?" Sam reported.

"Who's looking for us?" Carty pressed.

"Skeeter said Al Parker told him Justice came to town last night lookin' for a fight."

"If he came to town last night, how could he be in Sundance, Bear Butte, and Rapid City at the same time?" Dacee June inquired.

"What are you talkin' about, Lil' Sis?"

"Seems to be a raft of crimes Justice purportedly instigated all over the region all during the same evening."

"One thing's for sure, they are all armed again with Winchester '94s," Sammy reported. "I spied two of them myself. Where did he lay his hands on them this time?"

"I sold them to him," Dacee June blurted out.

"You what?" Carty gasped. "You said you sold them to the man who went for the doc."

"I did. It was Wade Justice who went for the doc."

"And called me?" Sammy asked.

189

"Yes. And called Todd and Bobby."

"Why did you do it, Dacee June?" Carty growled. "He tried to kill you out at the mine."

"He didn't try to kill any of us, Carty. He wasn't even there."

"You know what I mean," he snapped. "I can't believe you did that!" Carty moaned.

"Lil' Sis, what's gotten into you?" Sam quizzed.

"I can't believe you two are upset. Someone wanted to pay for the guns. We have guns for sale. It was a cash sale this time. The money is in the box."

"But you saw what they were tryin' to do at the mine," Carty complained.

"I didn't think those mine guards were all that respectable look-ing. How do I know which side is right?"

"You are talkin' crazy," Carty mumbled.

"I am not talking crazy. Did the two of you ever stop and won-der why in the world such wild rumors are being told about Wade Justice? They can't possibly all be true. So why is this being done?"

"Sounds like Justice is quite the salesman," Sam said.

"You let him sweet-talk you, didn't you?" Carty groused.

Dacee June folded her arms across her chest. "What are you implying?"

"He told you lies and you believed him. You believed some sweet-talkin' outlaw."

"Carty Toluca, I . . . I can't believe you said that. I deeply resent that remark."

"Did he flirt with you?" Carty pressed.

She searched the room for someone to rescue her. "I . . . I can't believe this!"

Carty grabbed her arm. "You didn't answer me!"

She yanked her arm back. "I don't know if I'm more humiliated, insulted, or just angry. I'm going home."

Carty turned to Sam and lifted his arms. "I can't believe she sold him the carbines!"

"And I can't believe you have become so vicious with your suspicions," she said.

He followed her to the door. "I didn't say I was suspicious."

"You most certainly implied it. Didn't he, Sammy?"

"Don't you drag me into this. All I know is you sold Justice carbines, he's armed his men, and half the town expects a gunfight out of them. Most reckon he will be shootin' at a Fortune or a Toluca."

"I think everyone is getting so jumpy that someone innocent is going to get shot and that this town is about to blow up like a spark in a box of China rockets."

"Mrs. Toluca," Carty grabbed her shoulder, "perhaps we should go into the storeroom and talk this out in private."

She pulled away. "Mr. Toluca, I'm going home and take a nap. There is nothing to discuss." She stomped to the front door of the hardware store. "There are many things I need to worry about on this day. Wade Justice is not one of them."

"Dacee June!" Carty called out.

She neither slowed down nor glanced back.

☞ ☞ ☞

Even with the windows open in the front and back of the house, the living room was stuffy. Dacee June loosened the high collar of her dress and fanned herself with a folding Chinese fan. She laid back on the worn, slick velvet couch and laid a damp tea towel over her eyes.

Her head throbbed. Her eyes burned in her sockets. Her temples swelled. Pressure in her ears and neck hurt so bad she could hardly turn from one side to the other.

Lord, things are spinning out of control. I'm saying things and doing things that I would never do if I were rested. It's hard to be holy when my body and soul hurt so bad.

I was merely being fair to Wade Justice. It's not a sin to be fair. I did not flirt. I did not fall for some slick lines. And I absolutely did not lust after that man.

Of course, no one said I did, so I don't know why I feel a need to explain myself. I need to back up and take these last two days all over again.

Oh, Jesus, we should get a dress rehearsal for each day, so when the real thing comes, we know how to do it right.

Maybe that's what life is.

Just a dress rehearsal for heaven.

Sounds like something Daddy would say.

Her thoughts drifted to the tired old man in the bedroom apartment above the hardware store. She saw herself sitting on the edge of the bed, rubbing his back. In her mind she borrowed a pillow and laid it across the foot of his bed.

"Are you goin' to sleep all day?"

The gravelly old voice sounded like it drifted down from the heavens. Dacee June sat straight up and fanned herself.

"You took a little nap, girl."

"I'm so tired."

"It only gets worse, darlin'. The older you get, the more tired you are."

"If age were measured in alertness, I'd be ready for the rocking chair," she replied.

"Slow down, take care of yourself, darlin'."

"I know. I know. I'll do it."

"When?"

"After the Fourth, and . . . you know . . . after . . ."

"After I'm gone?"

192

"I need to take care of you until then. I'm your girl. I'm your only girl. The Lord took Patricia and Veronica. Then he took Mama. So it's my job to take care of you."

"And it's your job to turn loose of me. I'll be OK."

"I know. But will I be OK, Daddy?"

"Darlin', you are Dacee June Fortune Toluca. Even the gates of Hades can't stand against you. The Lord will see to that."

"Are you goin' to leave me now?"

"Very soon, darlin'. Are you OK?"

"I'm OK. I feel better. You go on."

"Not without a hug."

The man's arms engulfed her and squeezed so tight she could barely breath.

"Baby, I'll be waitin' for you."

"I know, Daddy . . . I know."

Once or twice a year there comes a gust of wind, a gentle breeze, so fresh . . . so pure . . . so peaceful . . . so real that a person remembers it for months. When Dacee June opened her eyes and sat up, such a breeze drifted through the front room.

For several minutes she sat and took deep gulps. Each one seemed to bring strength to her mind, her body, and her spirit.

She had just fastened the top buttons on her dress when she heard an excited shout drift across Williams Street.

"Mama! Mama! Come quick!"

She scampered to the front door and flung it open. The bright noonday sun blinded her. "Elita, what's the matter? Is it Grandpa Brazos?"

Her oldest daughter stood in the middle of the street shading her eyes with her hand. "Guess who is coming to the play tonight?"

"Who?"

"The governor of South Dakota!" Elita shouted.

"What?"

"The governor came to town after all, and a senator, and a judge, and some other men with silk top hats."

"They are in Deadwood?"

"Yes, isn't it exciting? Uncle Todd asked them to come to the pageant at the church, and they said they would."

"I thought the governor couldn't make it. Why are they here?"

Elita held out her arms and did a slow twirl in the street. "I guess they heard about our pageant."

Dacee June walked down the steps toward her daughter. "I think there might be a little more to it than that. Is the play practice all done?"

"Yes, and Aunt Jamie Sue invited all of us over to her house for lunch. Can we go?" Elita quizzed.

"That's very nice. Of course you can. I'll walk back with you."

"To Aunt Jamie Sue's house?"

"No, to the hardware. I need to talk to Daddy."

"Do I have to wait for you?"

"No, you can go on. I need to wash my face. But don't run down the stairs," Dacee June cautioned.

"Can you believe it, the governor of South Dakota! I wonder if he likes elephant cake?"

☞ ☞ ☞

By the time Dacee June got down to Main Street, the Dakota sun hovered straight above. There was no breeze at the bottom of the gulch, and the bright sunlight bored through her dark green dress. She tried to stay in the shade.

"Dacee June!"

She shielded her eyes. *I can't believe I came downtown without wearing a hat.* "Skeeter? How are you today?"

"Did you hear about them men in town?"

"The governor and the others?"

194

"The governor of what?"

"Of South Dakota."

"Oh, him. Yeah, I heard about that. I meant them other men, the gunfighters."

"Wade Justice's gang?"

"Are they still in town?" Skeeter gasped. "I ain't seen none of them since last night. 'Course, I ain't been lookin', neither."

"That was a rumor I heard this morning."

"Ol' Jack Smilie said that his brother heard Justice robbed the Texas Pacific of $100,000 last January. Do you reckon that's true?"

"That was the Hughes gang down in Texas. I believe Mr. Justice was in a Montana prison last January," she replied.

"Are you sure? Ol' Man Tompkins said he got a letter from his nephew who claimed Wade Justice killed three marshals and wounded two more in the Indian Nation right before Christmas."

She watched a black leather surrey roll up Main Street carrying six men in silk top hats. "I believe that was Tom Smith last July."

"How come you know so much, Dacee June?"

She looked at the tall man's unshaven face. "I read the *Police Gazette*, Skeeter, don't you?"

"Uh, no ma'am. I ain't much of a reader, if you get my drift."

She took his arm and walked him out to the edge of the concrete sidewalk. "Now, just exactly who are the men you say are in town?"

"They are tough-lookin' gunslingers. They are packin' pistols and rifles. Why would you need so many guns in Deadwood?"

"How many are there?"

"I only seen four, but Beano Billy says there are eight of them."

"They work for Albert Sween. We met them at the Broken Boulder yesterday. They are mine guards or something."

"Don't know nothin' about that. They ain't minin' men, that's for sure. They are second-story men; that's what they are."

"What do you mean?"

"You walk down lower Main Street, and there's one of 'em peeking out of nearly ever' two-story buildin'."

"What do they want?"

"I was hopin' you'd know."

"A good view of the parade, perhaps."

"Shoot, a man can get a good view most anywhere in town. No need to camp out in them buildings with guns."

"I'll ask the sheriff. Perhaps he knows what is goin' on. Did you enjoy your fried fish for breakfast?"

He tipped his hat. "Yes, ma'am, I guess I smell like trout."

"There are worse smells."

"If you find out anything juicy about them second-story men, you'll let me know, won't you?"

"I'll do that, Skeeter."

☞ ☞ ☞

When she got to the hardware store, Sam Fortune stood in the shade of the building talking to the sheriff. "You heard about our special guests?" he asked her.

"Elita ran all the way up the steps to tell me the governor and senator are in town."

"Yep," the sheriff reported. "And a dozen men from back east."

"Why?" she pressed.

"Bankers and the like, I hear. They are probably wantin' to invest," the sheriff reported.

"What is there left to invest in?"

The sheriff pulled off his hat and fanned his face. "They surely aren't tellin' us."

"I heard the governor and the senator are going to be in the parade," Sam reported.

"That's nice," Dacee June said.

"It's horrible," the sheriff reported. "I'm tryin' to talk them out of it."

"Why?" she questioned.

"Rumor has it that Justice is here in town to assassinate the governor."

"Where did you hear that?"

"Chun Lee heard two old Chinamen talk about it."

"That's a serious accusation," she said.

"He's a serious outlaw. You heard about him holdin' a whole schoolhouse full of children for ransom down in Scott's Bluff, didn't you?" the sheriff said.

"If I hear one more Wade Justice whopper, I'll scream. To hear tell, he makes the false prophet and the beast look like a barn mouse. Now, why are there men with guns parked in balconies along Main Street?"

"Albert Sween came through for us," the Sheriff reported.

"Oh?" she pressed.

"He let us deputize his men and station them along the parade route."

"Why on earth would you deputize sleazy gunslingers?"

"To protect the governor and senator . . . and all of us . . . from the likes of Wade Justice."

"And who will protect us from Sween's men?" she challenged.

"What are you saying, Dacee June? You were out at the Broken Boulder. You saw what that Justice gang is like," the sheriff challenged.

"And I saw what Sween's men are like. Sammy, do you trust Sween's men?"

"I wouldn't want them to sneak around behind me," Sam acknowledged.

"Sheriff, do you have one warrant from any authority for the arrest of Wade Justice?"

"No, ma'am. Not yet."

"Then why have you condemned him and posted saddle-tramp gunfighters in our stores? I certainly wouldn't allow a one of them in our building."

Sam raised his gray eyebrows. "Uh, a little late for that, Sis."

"What?"

"Todd let the sheriff station one up in Daddy's room to use that window," Sam reported.

She glanced at the window above the front door of the hardware. "I can't believe this!"

"Are you goin' to pitch a fit?"

"No, I'm not. I've pitched my quota for today. I'm going up to see Daddy."

"We'll weather this thing, Lil' Sis," Sam said.

"What's his name?"

"Who?"

Dacee June tugged on a dangling, gold earring. "The man in Daddy's room."

"Theron," Sam replied.

☞ ☞ ☞

Three men stood in front of the counter at the back of the store. Another was in a wheelchair by the potbellied stove that had long since grown cold.

She walked straight up to the man behind the counter and threw her arms around his neck, then kissed him on the lips.

"Dacee June, what are you . . ." Carty blushed and tugged at his collar as he addressed the two customers. "Eh, this is my wife."

"I love you, Carty Toluca. I'm sorry for being so grumpy this morning," she purred, then turned to the startled men. "I was quite the pill, I fear. So I'm just going to have to make it up to my husband. Don't you think so?"

"I reckon if my wife greeted me like that, I'd figure I was in the wrong house!" one man drawled.

She waltzed over to the man dozing in the wheelchair. "Quiet Jim, how's my second favorite Texan in the world?"

He blinked his eyes open and patted her hand. "I'm kind of melancholy today, darlin'. How's your favorite ol' Texan?"

"I'm going up to see. He didn't have a very good night." She bent over and kissed his hand. "I thought we were going to lose him."

"I know, darlin'. I couldn't sleep." He took her hand and brushed a dry, chapped lip across it. "Today's the day, isn't it?"

She bit her lips shut and nodded her head. Her voice was soft when she spoke. "I believe you're right. Funny how we know that, isn't it?"

"I dreamt he showed up and told me it was today," Quiet Jim reported.

"Daddy's been busy. He was in my dream as well."

The old man stared at the black potbellied stove. "Fourth of July is a good day to go."

"You're right, Quiet Jim. Would you like to go up and sit with him for a while?"

"I believe I would."

She scooted back over to the counter where Carty and the customers still stood. "Carty, whenever you and Joey and Todd get a chance, tote Quiet Jim up the stairs. He wants to sit with Daddy."

Carty walked her to the stairs. "Are you all right, darlin'?"

"Yes. And I'm sorry I embarrassed you."

"Darlin', having you kiss me has never embarrassed me."

"You turned quite red."

"I was a bit . . . flustered, not embarrassed."

"Good. Because you're stuck with me for a long, long time."

☞ ☞ ☞

The man by the window wore dirty duckings, a leather vest, and a faded blue cotton shirt. He wore a gun at his hip, and held a lever action carbine at his side. He smelled of garlic, whiskey, and sweat.

A cigar crammed between his lips smoked the room.

"Howdy, ma'am. You're that spitfire that was out at the Broken Boulder Mine."

"Yes, I am. And I hear your name is Theron."

"Yep."

She scooted up beside him and stared out the window. "Are you protecting the parade?"

"Yep."

"It doesn't begin for three hours. It must be rather boring just waiting up here."

"Yes, ma'am. You don't happen to have a spot of rye whiskey, do you?" he asked.

"I'm afraid this is a dry household."

"Yeah, that's what I figured. Don't matter, it'll soon be all over."

She continued to stare out the window and not look at the man. "What will be over?"

He pointed out the window. "Sure do have a nice view from here. A man can see way down the street."

She scooted up a little closer to the man. "My that's a nice-looking gun. It's a Winchester '92, but looks a little small for a carbine."

Theron yanked the cigar out of his mouth and held the gun up. "Ain't it a beaut? Not many of them around quite like it. It's a '92 saddle ring Trapper with a special order eighteen-inch barrel."

"That is rare. I didn't even know they made one that length."

"That's cause there ain't another one just like it. I took it—I mean I bought it—from an ol' boy in Mexico who had it special-ordered. The factory told him it was the only one they made."

She chewed her lip. "May I take a look at it?"

"Sure." He handed her the carbine, took a long drag on the cigar, and blew smoke across the room. "Ain't it swell?"

She held it with one hand on the receiver. "It has nice balance. What caliber is it?"

"That's the good part. It's a .44/40, just like my Peacemaker."

Dacee June held it to her shoulder and pointed it out the window at the blue sky. "And nice balance. It comes up easy to the shoulder."

"And it don't kick near as much as them new smokeless .30 WCF."

She cocked the lever.

"Careful, ma'am, it's loaded."

"I should hope so."

She swung around and pointed the short carbine at the man's chest. "And now, Theron, it's time for you to leave."

"What?" He glared as he stepped back and raised his hands.

"I do not want you in my father's room. You will have to leave the hardware store."

"I ain't leavin'. Mr. Sween stationed me here."

"I thought you'd probably say that. That's why I'm the one holding the carbine. You are leaving."

"No long-skirted lady ever tossed me out of a room."

"There is always a first time, then. Don't feel bad. It isn't personal. I'd toss Albert Sween out of the room if he were here. I will have no cigar-smoking assassins in my father's room."

"I can put out the cigar," he replied.

"I think you missed the point." She jammed the gun barrel into his midsection. "Out the door, Mr. Theron."

"You ain't kickin' me out of here. I don't chase easy."

She jammed the barrel in his stomach again. "Do you bleed easy?" He backed toward the door.

"But the men downstairs said I could stay up here," he griped.

"They were wrong. Now go on. I assure you I do know how to pull a trigger."

"That's my saddle-ring Trapper."

"I intend to give it back to you, but not right now."

They reached the door just as Todd and Carty carried Quiet Jim in his wheelchair to the top of the stairs.

"Dacee June, what's goin' on!" Carty exclaimed.

"She sweet-talked me out of my carbine and turned it on me," Theron whined.

"Lil' Sis, I told Mr. Sween he could put a man up here," Todd said.

"Daddy doesn't need a whiskied, cigar-smoking bushwhacker in his room, Todd."

Todd stared at Theron. "I told him not to smoke."

"I must have forgot."

"Bushwhacker?" Carty thundered. "But they are supposed to protect the governor."

"Look at him," she said. "Is this the kind of man you would hire to protect anyone at all?"

Quiet Jim surveyed the man from head to foot. "She's right, boys. Me and the Texas Camp have faced too many of this type. Give me a carbine, and I'll scout the window."

"But he's a cripple. He cain't protect no one," Theron growled.

Todd stiffened. "Mister, you just lost me with that comment. Quiet Jim has put his life on the line for this family on more than one occasion. There's no debate now. Get out of the store."

"Albert Sween ain't goin' to like this," the man fumed.

Dacee June shoved the barrel in the man's midsection again. "Is that supposed to mean something to us?"

"You'd better not cross Albert Sween!" the man threatened as he stumbled down the stairs.

"Oh? What will happen?" she pressed. "Will he shackle us and shoot us in the back?"

The man stopped and spun around. "What do you mean by that?"

"What do you think I mean? You weren't up here to protect the governor. You were going to shoot some men who know enough to get Albert Sween and the rest of you tossed in prison."

"Who told you that?"

"What difference does it make?"

"It's a bold-faced lie!"

"Here's something that is true. We don't want any of Sween's men in this building."

Thelma Speaker stood to attention in the ready-mixed paint aisle as Dacee June marched the man past her. "My word, dear, what are you doing?"

"Just cleaning out the riffraff, Mrs. Speaker."

"Finished with Christian charity, I presume?"

"I haven't shot him yet."

"Dear me, he does look rather scruffy."

"You have no idea what you're doin'," the man snarled. "You got a cripple and a dead man upstairs, and you're goin' up against Albert Sween."

Dacee June aimed the cocked gun at the man's head. "No one is dead upstairs!"

"Oh, dear." Thelma Speaker followed them to the door. "That was a rather injudicious statement you made. I'm afraid she will shoot you now for sure."

Dacee June barrel-jabbed him to the door.

"I haven't done anything!" he whined.

"You should make him go outside, Dacee June. Remember the last time?" Mrs. Speaker said.

"What happened last time?" the man snapped.

"Oh, in the telephone office. It took weeks to get the red stains out of the wall and floor. It was quite unseemly," Thelma replied.

"I don't believe this!" the man muttered.

Thelma Speaker rested her fingertips on her cheeks. "You know, I believe that is just what that other man said . . . rest his soul."

CHAPTER EIGHT

Dacee June spun around to face Todd and Carty. "What are you two grinning about?" She shoved the carbine into her brother's hand.

He held the gun by the receiver and rocked back on his heels. His sandy-blond-and-gray mustache and goatee framed his oval mouth. "We were just commenting on how good it was to see Lil' Sis toss someone out on their ear again."

"Oh, is that so?"

Carty rubbed the tension from the back of her neck. "Darlin', it's been a while since you trained a gun at some no-account drifter."

She patted Carty's rough, calloused hand. "I think you two are exaggerating a little. I merely asked him to leave."

"Mrs. Speaker?" Carty stepped over to where the older woman stood holding her black leather purse in front of her. "What is your opinion? Did Dacee June just toss that ol' boy out on his ear under threat of sure and certain death?"

"Oh, yes, of course." Thelma Speaker's wide smile revealed just a hint of a smirk. "Our Dacee June is very, very good at it, I might add."

Dacee June puffed to try to blow her bangs back out of her eyes. "Putting it that way doesn't sound very ladylike."

Mrs. Speaker scooted over and laced her arm into Dacee June's. "But, dear, I meant it as a compliment. From the time you were little, all you ever wanted to be was identical to your daddy. You are a beautiful wife and mother, Dacee June Toluca, but your heart still rides the range with the Texas Camp."

Dacee June grinned. "It's rather daunting to be in a town where so many people know me that well." *I don't believe I've felt this good in a long while, which makes me feel rather guilty, Lord. Is the only time I feel alive when I have a gun in my hand threatening some man?*

Mrs. Speaker's gloved finger picked a piece of lint from Dacee June's sleeve. "You have not exactly lived a sheltered, hidden life."

Dacee June stared out the tall, open double doors of the hardware store at a rumbling, empty freight wagon. "I have the past few months." She turned back toward the others. "But that's over today."

"Exactly what is going to happen today, dear?" Mrs. Speaker queried. "Perhaps I should put on my comfortable shoes."

"To start with," Dacee June pointed at the Winchester '92 Trapper in Todd's hands, "I presume a Mr. Albert Sween will come collect that."

Todd examined the gun. "I reckon he won't be too happy."

Dacee June strolled down the aisle of wooden barrels filled with horseshoes. "This is just not a good time for Mr. Albert Sween. He has no idea how unhappy he's going to be before the day is out."

Carty trailed after her. "What are you talkin' about?"

"This is going to be a momentous day," she blurted out. *Lord, it is as if I've awakened from a long sleep.*

Carty plucked up a pitchfork hanging from a nail on a post, turned the tines away from the aisle, then rehung it. "Darlin', how do you know what's goin' to happen today?"

"You'll see," she said, then whisked over to the back counter where her brother stashed the carbine. "Todd, do you think you can locate the governor and those other silk top hats? I have some business to take care of, then I need to talk to them."

He pulled a gold watch from his vest pocket. "Talk to them about what?"

"There are some things they should know about Mr. Albert Sween," she insisted.

"Do you know Sween?" Carty asked.

"I've never met him in my life."

"Dacee June, you aren't makin' any sense," Carty replied. Two men, covered in dirt from head to foot, entered the front door, and he went to wait on them.

Todd pointed across the street. "They all are huddled at the Merchant's Hotel with a gaggle of mining engineers, lawyers, and a raft of papers."

"What mine are they going to buy?" she asked.

"I don't know. They won't talk about it. They have some deal cooking up. It's all a big hushed-up secret," Todd explained.

"I wonder what the governor and senator have to do with it?"

"Potential investors, I suppose," Todd suggested. "Everyone wants to own a gold mine, even politicians."

"Is Albert Sween with them?"

"I believe so."

"Would they be talking about the Broken Boulder?"

"Stranger things have happened in the mining business."

"I need to talk to the governor without Albert Sween around."

"I can't just barge into that meeting and say that my Lil' Sis wants to talk privately with everyone but Sween," Todd cautioned. "You want to tell me what this is all about?"

She paused a minute. She could hear Carty explain a pneumatic drill to the two men covered in dirt. "Sween's men aren't up there in the second stories to protect the governor. They are up there to shoot Wade Justice," she whispered.

Todd looped his thumbs in his vest pockets. "He does seem to give them cause."

"They don't want to shoot him for crimes he committed, Todd. They want to shoot him for witnessing crimes they committed."

"What are you talking about?"

"I just need to arrange a meeting with the governor, Todd. Will you do it for me, or do I just barge into that room myself?"

"I'll see what I can do."

Carty strolled back toward them, brushing his hands off in front of him.

"Carty, the girls are at Bobby and Jamie Sue's. If they show up here and I'm not around, get them washed up for the parade," she instructed.

"Where are you going?"

"Down to the Badlands."

"Dacee June!" Carty protested.

"Now, darlin', you trust me down there, don't you?" she purred.

"Yes, I trust you. It's all those red-eyed bummers and drifters that I don't trust."

"Now, Big Brother, what would Daddy say if he knew there was goin' to be a gunfight by evening?"

"A gunfight? Good heavens, Lil' Sis. What are you instigating?"

"You didn't answer my question."

"What would Daddy say about a gunfight tonight? He'd probably say, 'Let's go get 'em right now.'"

"That's what I'm doing."

She turned to the stairs.

"I thought you were goin' down to the Badlands," Todd said.

"I am. I need to go upstairs and say good-bye to Daddy."

"Good-bye?"

"Yes. And call Bobby and Sam. Tell them Quiet Jim and I think this is Daddy's last day."

☛ ☛ ☛

When Dacee June reached the bedroom apartment, Quiet Jim Trooper had rolled his wheelchair to the window. He watched the street below and kept an eye on the old man in the bed.

"Darlin', what's all this about with men stationed at every tall building?" Quiet Jim asked.

"I believe Albert Sween is going to pull something, and he wants to get rid of Wade Justice and the others."

"Why? It's Justice that is the outlaw, so I hear."

"I'm not sure why." She strolled behind the wheelchair and rubbed Quiet Jim's back and shoulders. "Wade Justice is not the evil man everyone says he is."

"Have you talked to him, Dacee June?"

She continued to rub his thin, bony shoulders. "Yes, and I have to talk to him again."

"Why, darlin'?"

"What do you mean, why?"

"If Sween or Justice or any other hombre is goin' to stir something up, why not just hunker down and let it pass? It's not your fight."

Dacee June circled around to the front of the wheelchair. "I can't believe you're saying that."

Quiet Jim's voice was barely audible. "I want to hear it from you."

"I'm Brazos Fortune's daughter and a part of the legendary Texas Camp. It's in my blood to oppose evil. God have mercy on my soul if I didn't do something."

The man's narrow, wrinkled face brightened. "Now, that's my girl. I haven't heard anyone say that in years. You need me to help you?"

"Yes, I do. I need you to stay by Daddy's side. I've got a lot to do, and I can't be here. I hope Columbia will understand."

Quiet Jim spoke with steady resolve. "Columbia is, as you know, the most understandin' woman God ever created." He looked over at Brazos. "Are you going to be here when he goes to glory?"

"I might not. The timing is up to the Lord. Daddy always told me, 'Dacee June, I want Quiet Jim to sing me into heaven with "Amazing Grace".' Can I count on you?"

"For you, darlin'." He took a deep sigh and brushed his eyes.

She kissed Quiet Jim's forehead. "The Texas Camp will always live on in our hearts."

"I didn't think so when this day began. I thought it would die with that old man in the bed. But when I saw you boot out that bummer, I knew it was alive. That ol' boy didn't know what hit him."

"I guess I've been saving it up."

Dacee June scooted over to the bed. She lifted her father's head, fluffed his pillow, brushed down his long, drooping mustache, and kissed his dry, chapped lips.

She held his limp hands and stared at his slightly moving chest. *It seems so long between breaths. One just like this will be his last.*

"Daddy, I don't know how dreams work, but we had a nice visit in mine. I think it's time for me to say good-bye. You know how many tears I have already shed in this room over the past months. I am not crying now because in just a little while your life will be so very wonderful beyond belief. You will be with Mama and the girls . . . and our precious Lord Jesus. And I'm not crying because I just don't have time. You see, there's trouble in town. And the sheriff doesn't know what to do about it, but I do. Evil has to be stopped. It needs to be stopped right now, right here. That's what you always taught me. So, I'm going to borrow your Sharps carbine and go take care of things. Now, don't worry about me. You taught me well.

"What's the worst thing that could happen to me? That I end up shot and walk into heaven with you hand in hand?

"Now, Daddy, what Fortune was ever afraid of heaven? I'm going now. You were the best daddy for me in the whole world. There has never been a girl who was luckier than me. It is a blessing I can never repay but only pass on to others.

"Quiet Jim is here. He's going to sing you to glory.

"Bye, Daddy, you will always be in my heart and on my mind. Listen for the Lord. He'll be calling soon. Can't you almost hear him? 'Well done, Henry Fortune. Very well done, indeed!'"

She hugged the man in the wheelchair tight. Neither said a word.

She walked out the door of the upstairs apartment.

And didn't look back.

☛ ☛ ☛

Dacee June cradled the Sharps carbine as she strolled toward the young clerk. "Joey, give me three .50 caliber cartridges for this carbine."

"You goin' huntin' today?"

"You might say that."

Carty walked her to the door. "Would you like me to go down there with you?"

"I need to do it by myself. I need you to be with the children."

"This is crazy, Dacee June. I don't even know what's goin' on, except my wife is packin' a Sharps carbine and strollin' through the Badlands."

"It's helpin' me with Daddy, Carty. I just can't sit there and watch him die any more. I don't want to talk about it, because it might not be anything. But I need to keep active. I really need to do this by myself. I have to do what Daddy would do. I don't know how to explain it any other way. Please." She slipped her free arm around his waist.

His voice was low, almost childlike. "Will you stay here if I ask you to?"

She laid her head on his shoulder, and they stared out at the street. "Why did you say that?"

"I've just been wonderin' lately. What would you do if I wanted you to do something different from what you wanted?"

She watched two boys pull a wagon with a big dog riding in it across the street. *Lord, my life has been a tear-stained blur for six months. I've been useless to my family, my husband. And this morning you cleared it all up. Now I can breathe deep and see clearly. Why, why did you let Carty say that?*

"Dacee June?" Carty pressed.

She shoved the Sharps carbine at her husband. "I won't go down there if you don't want me to. You're my man, Carty Toluca. If you want me to go home and knit doilies, I'll knit doilies. You're the only one on the face of the earth that I'd listen to on a day like today."

"If your Daddy woke up, you'd listen to him." Carty stroked her hair back over her ear.

"No. Not today. I said good-bye to him, Carty. You're stuck with me now. You can't go runnin' to Daddy for advice. You have to figure me out on your own."

"I like that." He brushed her hair to her back and kissed her on the neck. "I like bein' stuck with you, Dacee June."

"So do I. Do you want me to go home?"

He shoved the carbine back at her. "No, I want you to go do that thing that the Lord burns your bones to do. I just needed to know you'd stay if I asked you to."

"Carty, I am obsessive and possessive. I don't know if I can ever be different. I believe you are the most patient man on earth."

"I believe you're right about that. I'll get the kids ready for the parade. What shall I tell them their mother is doing?"

"Tell them I have some business to take care of for the Texas Camp."

"Will they understand that?"

"They will some day."

☛ ☛ ☛

Rutt Mangin's tie flagged over his left shoulder and his gray vest was unbuttoned when Dacee June approached Lizzie's. He held a short, double-barreled shotgun in one hand. It looked like a miniature next to his bulky frame.

"Dacee June, when did you start packin' a Sharps carbine?"

She laughed. "A girl needs her jewelry, Rutt."

"Most of 'em down here are a little more discreet with their weapons."

She cocked her head and batted her eyes at the big bouncer. "Do you think I'll scare all the boys off?"

Rutt Mangin roared with laughter. People across the street stopped and stared. "I reckon you will, Dacee June. And I reckon that's exactly what you want to do. You goin' to be in the parade?"

"Yes, but I have a few things to take care of first." She watched a crowded coach from Sturgis roll up the street.

A short, bald man staggered out of Lizzie's. He glanced at Dacee June and her gun, then twirled around and went back inside.

Rutt winked at Dacee June. "I take it your purpose includes that carbine?"

"I've got some bushwhackers to keep an eye on."

"Which bunch? The ones with Justice or the ones with that railroad man, Sween?"

"Rutt, you're about the only one in town that seems to understand there are two sides to this."

"My main concern is to make sure Lizzie and the girls ain't hurt." He folded his massive arms. "What's goin' on, Dacee June?"

"I'm not sure, but the two sides were shootin' it out at the Broken Boulder Mine yesterday. It looks like they brought their fight to town."

"Which side are we on?"

A smile broke across her face. "We?"

"Dacee June, I don't intend to be in the sights of that .50 caliber bullet of yours."

"You might be surprised if I told you."

"I'd guess you're sidin' with Wade Justice, if you are forced to choose."

She shaded the bright sun with her hand. "Why did you say that? You've heard all the rumors about him." *I should have worn my hat! What would mother think?*

"Standin' in front of Lizzie's allows me to hear all sorts of rumors and stories. I don't count them for much. Say, did you ever hear about the time I single-handed tipped over an entire stagecoach full of whiskey drummers?"

Dacee June's eyes widened. "You did?"

"Of course I didn't. No man can do that. But I heard two boys swear last night that they saw me do it in Yankton. Rumors don't pay the rent or pull a trigger. You're sidin' with Justice. I'm right, ain't I?"

She nodded her head. "But I don't understand how you knew that for sure. My family thinks I'm crazy."

"I've seen some of Justice's men. They are dangerous, violent men. The ones I saw will look you in the eye and shoot you if you get in their way. But that's better than Sween's. That type will sneak up and shoot you in the back when you're on your way to the privy. I never could side with that type."

The little bald-headed man once more staggered out and stood between them.

"That's the way I size it up," Dacee June said, ignoring the intruder. "And I'm just sure there's going to be shooting today."

213

Rutt Mangin rubbed his square chin. "And someone standin' and watchin' will take a bullet."

The man yanked up his trousers and scurried back inside.

She looked down at the boardwalk. "I need to talk to Wade Justice before anything happens."

Rutt scratched the back of his neck. "I heard you and your brothers got your guns back."

"Yes."

"Rumor has it Justice got 'em all carbines today."

Dacee June licked her lips. They felt rough and dry. "Yes, I sold them to him."

Rutt Mangin bellowed.

She heard several dogs bark, and she watched Mangin's brown eyes. "What's so funny?"

"What other gal in these United States would ride out to the Broken Boulder and retrieve her stolen guns, then turn around and sell them to the same fella that stole them when he came up with the money?"

"It was the right thing to do. Rutt, I have to talk to Justice. Do you know where he is?"

"Nope. Seen some of his men on Whitewood Crick this mornin', but they ain't there now. They've been lyin' low. Meanwhile, the rest of the town is goin' on like it's just a Fourth of July picnic." Rutt strolled to the corner of the windowless building, and Dacee June walked beside him. "One gang is sneakin' in the two-story windows, and the other is hid out. They are both mad enough to kill each other, and no one knows why. They ought to go out in the woods and shoot it out."

"I suppose that's what they were tryin' to do yesterday when we took their guns away and chased them off."

Mangin loosed the top button on his white shirt. His neck was as big as Dacee June's waist. "What if I can get to Justice? What message do you want me to tell him?"

"Tell him to meet me."

"Where?"

"Down at the mill ground, before the parade starts."

"There'll be a crowd congregatin' to start the parade."

"It might be easier to talk to him in a crowd," she said.

"Dacee June, do you know what you're doing?"

"What difference does that make?"

"True enough," he snorted. "Just make sure you tell me who I ought to shoot."

"Don't you jump in front of a bullet, Rutt Mangin," she cautioned. "You have to sing at the program tonight, remember?"

"Yes, ma'am. Are you sure them good folks won't chase me off?"

"Are you kidding? With me totin' a Sharps, how can they object? I'll shoot the first one that tries to sneak out the door!"

He took her arm and led her back to the front of Lizzie's. "Dacee June, darlin', there ain't no other gal like you in all the Black Hills."

She fussed at straightening his tie. "I'll bet you're glad of that."

"Yes, ma'am, I reckon I am."

☞ ☞ ☞

Dacee June hiked back up Main Street, the carbine looped in her right arm. The sidewalks were already crowded with people waiting for the parade.

Many of the faces were familiar to Dacee June.

Some were not.

"Look, Mama, is that Annie Oakley?"

She turned to see a woman in a green and black wool suit, her hair pulled back so tight her eyes slanted. Next to her a young girl about twelve wore an identical dress.

Dacee June paused. "I'm not Annie Oakley, but I did see her and Buffalo Bill over in Nebraska once."

The girl stared at her with mouth wide open. "Then what are you doin' with that gun?"

215

"Why, darlin'," Dacee June drawled, "I'm looking for a man."

The girl glanced up at her mother and held her breath.

The mother patted her on the head. "That's the way they do it out here on the frontier."

The young girl rolled her eyes in anguish. "But mother, I don't even know how to shoot a gun! How will I ever find a boy?"

Dacee June trudged through the crowd to Shine Street. She heard someone shout. She waited as the sheriff puffed over to her.

"You goin' bear huntin' with your daddy's Sharps?" he asked.

"Oh, this little gun?" She glanced up at the second-story window at the bank. "I'm just making sure I don't get bushwhacked."

He waved a paper in front of her. "Do you know what I have in my hand?"

"What is it?"

His right hand rested on his holstered revolver. "An arrest warrant."

Her boots pinched her feet, and she shifted her weight. "For Wade Justice?"

"No, for Dacee June Toluca."

She grabbed the piece of paper out of his hand. "What?"

"Albert Sween and a man name Theron filed a complaint. Theron said you threatened to shoot him and stole his carbine."

"It was a Trapper, not a carbine." She shoved the paper back into the sheriff's hand.

"You took it?"

"Yes, it's at the store. I told him to send Sween by to pick it up. So they really filed an arrest warrant?"

"Yep. I told them I'd serve it if I had time. Maybe next week things will calm down, and I'll serve it then. What's goin' on, Dacee June?"

"Sheriff, Sween's men are a bunch of drifting gunfighters. I asked Theron to leave the hardware store because he was camped out in Daddy's room. I guess he didn't think I was serious."

"That's what I figured. Can I retrieve his gun?"

"Certainly."

The sheriff rubbed the stubble of a three-day beard. "Have you seen Justice?"

"No," she said. "But I'm looking for him."

The sheriff tried to hide his grin with his wide, calloused hand.

"Are you laughing at me?"

"I'm just tired, Dacee June. Ain't slept much in several nights. I was just thinkin' it was funny for a purdy married gal to be stalkin' the streets of Deadwood with a big-bore carbine lookin' for justice."

"Sounds like one of Hawthorne Miller's 'Stuart Brannon' dime novels, doesn't it?"

He pointed at the carbine. "Do you intend to shoot Wade Justice?"

"No. I need to talk to him."

They stepped to the edge of the sidewalk to allow a wide woman with a tiny dog on a leash to pass by.

"Wade Justice is a dangerous man." The sheriff's voice died out as he watched the large woman waddle on down the sidewalk. "That's the strongest perfume I ever smelled in my life."

"It was the dog that was perfumed."

"Sounds like a waste of perfume."

"Depends on the dog."

The smile dropped off the sheriff's face. "Do you know how many men Justice has faced down at the point of a gun?"

Dacee June glanced up the street to see a man in a checkered suit enter the hardware. "Sheriff, out of all the men in Deadwood right now, who do you suppose has faced down the most men?"

The sheriff gazed up and down the crowded street. "I don't reckon I know everyone that's come to town for the celebration. So I'd have to say either your daddy or your brother Sam."

"Would you call them dangerous men?"

"Nope."

"Sheriff, the dangerous ones are the back-shooters, or those hiding in upstairs windows. What if I told you I know six witnesses that say Albert Sween killed two men by shooting them in the back even though they were unarmed and shackled."

The sheriff's voice grew quiet. "I'd have a tough time believin' that. Sween is as big a man as Harriman or Hearst. I'd like to talk to the witnesses before I drew any conclusions."

"Before the day's through, perhaps we can."

Suddenly, it seemed like everyone on Main Street stopped talking and stared up the gulch toward Lead.

"They shut down the stamp mills," the sheriff murmured.

"It's either Christmas, Easter, or the Fourth of July."

☞ ☞ ☞

Todd was waiting for Dacee June at the hardware store. "Lil' Sis, the governor and senator are tied up on some kind of deal with the Broken Boulder."

"The Broken Boulder? Is that what they are after? Sween's trying to sell them a played-out mine?"

"Apparently. They did say I could bring you over for an introduction."

"Were they signing any papers?"

"I have no idea. I think they are waitin' for some of the New York men to get back from the mine site."

"Good."

"You think there's a catch to the mine?"

"The Raxton sisters said it was played out and sold it for salvage. So how does Sween show up and know immediately that it's rich enough to need eastern backers?"

Todd shrugged. "You know how it is. Some engineer comes up with a new process, and old mines take on new life."

"Maybe."

"People go crazy over gold mines. It's been that way for twenty years in these hills."

"But you wouldn't think it would go on forever."

"Dacee June, a hundred years from now some old boy will have a get-gold-quick scheme and find a hundred eastern suckers to invest in it. Greed never changes."

She stared around the store. "Where's Carty?"

"He went to the church to help clean up the girls for the parade."

"Were they dirty?"

"Your baby had gray frosting all over her face."

Dacee June marched over to the young clerk. "Joey, go to the Montana Livery and get our big wagon, then park it at the church. Amber has banners to mount on the side about the program tonight, and we're taking the cake out for a ride in the parade."

"No foolin'?"

"Yes, it should be quite an attraction." She buzzed over to the gun case. "Todd, I'm taking two holsters, two bullet belts, these two Colt .44s, and a couple boxes of cartridges."

"To go to see the governor?"

"No, they are part of my parade costume."

"You're not dressin' up like a railroad engine this year, are you?"

"No!" She paused at the foot of the stairs. "How's Daddy?"

"I haven't checked in an hour or so," Todd reported. "But Sam and Bobby came over for a while after I called them."

She tilted her head. "Have you heard Quiet Jim singing?"

"No."

"Then Daddy's OK."

☛ ☛ ☛

The governor and the others kept on their silk top hats with their long black dress coats, even though the day was very warm. Several men stood around a large oak table covered with maps and charts as Todd strolled into the ballroom at the Merchant's Hotel, Dacee June on his arm.

They stood beside the table until one of the men looked up.

"I'm sorry," the short man said. "I thought you were hotel staff. This meeting is private."

"The governor invited us over," Todd replied.

A tall, bearded man stepped back from the maps and graphs. "Yes, yes, I most certainly did." He walked over to Dacee June and held out his hand. "You must be Todd's little sister. How nice to meet you."

"We've met before, Governor," Dacee June replied. "At Pierre, and again at Yankton."

"Please accept my apology." He held his top hat in his hand. "I should never forget one of the Fortunes of the Black Hills."

"I'm married. My name is Toluca now," she informed him.

"You don't say? Congratulations. Sorry I missed the wedding. Legislative business being what it is, I have little time for myself."

"I've been married for ten years," she declared.

"What? My, you don't look a day over twenty."

Governor, it is not an election year. You do not need to campaign so hard. "Thank you for the generous compliment. I need to talk to you in private for a moment." Dacee June surveyed the other men, trying to discern which one was Albert Sween.

"I do wish my wife was here. You would have enjoyed visiting with her."

Dacee June bit her lip. *Are you telling me I have no business talking to anyone but women?* "I'm sure I would. But what I have to discuss is for you, governor."

The governor glanced back over his shoulder. "We're quite busy here at the moment."

"Yes, I'm sure you are. As for me, I just have the care of my dying father, my husband, and three daughters. I have all the time in the world. However, this will just take a second of your time and might save someone's life."

The governor looked at her brother. "I say, Todd, what is all this about?"

Todd Fortune glanced at Dacee June and winked. "Governor, it would be a grave mistake for you or anyone to try and dodge around Lil' Sis. You've got to deal with her face-to-face, just like the rest of us."

"I need to talk to both of you in private, right now," she reasserted.

The governor stepped back over to the group of men. He mumbled a few words then returned.

"I'll get back to you a little later. The timing on this matter is absolutely critical." He backed toward the table.

Dacee June grabbed his coat sleeve. "I assure you, what I need to tell you is even more critical."

He glared down at her hand on his arm. "Perhaps you can speak to my secretary, Mr. Singletary."

"This cannot wait." She dropped her hand to her side.

"My word," the governor mumbled, "this is precisely why we needed a private meeting." He started to return to the table.

"Mister Governor," Todd called out loud enough that everyone at the map table stopped talking and turned to stare. Two men who sat near the door leapt to their feet and yanked out their pistols. "Mr. Governor, I don't know how things work in Pierre, but in the Black Hills no gentleman turns his back on a lady while she is speaking to him."

He spun back around, removed his hat, and bowed. "My apologies, Mrs. Toluca. Your brother is quite right. Now, please excuse me. I simply must take care of this business."

Dacee June sidled up close to the governor. "Don't sign any papers with Sween on the Broken Boulder!" she whispered.

"What? What do you know?"

"I know Sween is a cheat and perhaps a murderer, and he is trying to pass off on you a worthless mine," she said.

The governor began to laugh. "Oh? So that's what this is all about?"

"Why are you mocking me?"

"I didn't mean it personally. I can understand the dilemma you faced. You knew the mine was unproductive and wanted to protect us. I should have expected that concern from a child of Brazos Fortune. Rest assured, Mrs. Toluca, we would not be interested in the mine were if not for a new vein that Sween's engineers discovered quite by accident. There are tons and tons of samples. Quite impressive. And we are quite aware of the past."

Dacee June folded her arms and glared at the governor. She leaned close and whispered. "Are you aware that Albert Sween personally shot and killed two shackled, unarmed prisoners near Deer Lodge, Montana? Or that he bypassed import tariffs by bringing eight freight wagons of Canadian pay dirt across the line? Are you also aware that he has hired gunmen in most every second-story window in order to ambush certain parties during this parade who might be able to testify against Sween?"

The governor tugged at his sweaty white shirt collar. "Good heavens, is this part of the famous Black Hills drama?"

She dropped her arms to her side, but left her fingers clenched tight. "Do you think I'm making this up?"

"Mrs. Toluca," he murmured, "do you know who Albert Sween is?"

Dacee June glanced down at the polished wooden floor. "No, I don't. Which one is he?"

"I'd introduce you, but he stepped out for a moment on other business. I have known him for some time. He is hard driving, even ruthless, like all the wealthy men I know. But he is not the type to murder and swindle. If I didn't know better, I would say you are jealous of his great success. The wealthy always come under attack."

"And some who are wealthy become quite desperate to maintain that wealth. Greed is never very rational, is it, Governor?"

"I really must attend to this matter. We only have a short time to make big decisions," the governor insisted.

"Are you ignoring me?" she snapped.

He motioned back at the men at the table. "I have important things to do."

Todd took a step straight toward the governor. "I think you ought to listen to Lil' Sis."

"Mr. Fortune, I have great respect for your family. You know that. But this idea about Albert Sween is preposterous."

"Why?" Todd challenged. "Has my sister ever lied to you before?"

"I hardly know her."

"Then why do you discount her words?"

"I don't discount them. I merely don't have time for them. There is a very small period of time to accept a very lucrative offer. I will not be governor forever, and I need to plan my future."

"What's the hurry?" Dacee June quizzed.

"When we arrived here, we found out that outside pressure has come to bear on Sween and he has to have a signed agreement in forty-eight hours."

"If I arrange a meeting, would you talk to some men who witnessed Sween's crimes?"

"As you must have heard, the rumor is that Wade Justice is lying in wait to ambush me. I don't intend on staying in Deadwood long. If you bring the witnesses to the capital, perhaps by then I could . . ."

"Bring them to the capital? They could be dead by nightfall."

"Yes, well . . . there is no way I can break away from this now."

"Governor, someone has to do something today. There is a very good chance someone will get shot. I sincerely hope one of them is not you!"

Dacee June spun on her heels and stomped out the door.

Todd hurried along behind her.

"That went well, Lil' Sis."

"Yes, didn't it? You've always said I'm as diplomatic as Daddy."

☞ ☞ ☞

After a hurried trek up the stairs to the house to change clothes, Dacee June scurried to the church at the base of McGovern Hill. The hardware's big freight wagon was parked in the shade by the back door. Sprawled inside was the massive gray cake. Twelve Fortune and Toluca cousins mingled with five Trooper kids.

Carty greeted her. "You wearin' the buckskin dress?"

Dacee June glanced down at the fringed buckskin. "Yes, it's been years, hasn't it?"

He pushed his hat back to reveal a receding hairline. "Why are you wearing it? You told me you hated it."

"Because it's a holiday parade. I'm celebrating days gone by, *and* . . ."

"And?"

"And the fact I can wear a dress that was made for me sixteen years ago. Not too many women can do that."

"And holsters across your chest?" Carty reached over and fingered one of the bullets in the belt.

"I'm doing it for the Texas Camp. I'm going to carry Daddy's carbine too."

"Not much left of the Texas Camp," he said.

"And that's why I'm doing it. Besides, we have a lot of Eastern visitors. We need to put on a show. You never know when an extra gun is needed in Deadwood."

"You're talkin' like it was '75 instead of '95."

She adjusted the bullet belts. "In a gold-mine town, greed never changes."

Elita ran up to her side, "Mother, you aren't going to wear that, are you?"

Dacee June ran her fingers across her oldest daughter's cheek. "As a matter of fact, I am."

Elita's blue eyes confirmed her anguish. "Oh, Mother, how could you?"

"You can sit at the back of the wagon and pretend like you belong to Aunt Rebekah," Dacee June suggested.

Ninete scooted and held her hand. "Can I get a dress like yours, Mama?"

Dacee June ran her arm across the little girl's shoulder. "When you are old enough, maybe I'll give you this one."

"Can I have the pistols too?"

"No, Baby, maybe not the pistols. They belong to the store. Now, come on, kids, load up. We don't want to be late for the parade." She turned to her nephew, "Little Frank, I believe you are driving this rig."

"I am? But I was goin' to ride in the back with . . ."

Dacee June glanced to the back of the wagon where Fern and Sarah Trooper were in some kind of argument.

"On second thought," he said as he pushed his hat back, "I think I'll drive."

Dacee June climbed up into the wagon seat next to Little Frank. She surveyed the group. "Who are we missing?"

Eight-year-old Garrett Fortune pulled his flop hat over his forehead and looked at his scuffy boots. "Amber is still getting her costume on."

"Look," Jehane hollered, "here she comes."

Amber waltzed out of the back door of the church wearing a fringed buckskin dress.

"She looks just like you, Mama!" Elita cried out.

"Darlin', I never in my life looked as pretty as Amber."

Amber's straight white teeth glistened in her soft, easy smile. "Aunt Dacee June! Thanks for wearing the buckskin! I was afraid you wouldn't want to wear it."

"I didn't know you wanted me to, honey," Dacee June said. "I just thought of it this morning."

"But I told Little Frank to tell you." She glared at her cousin.

"Oh, yeah," he blushed. "I got plum distracted."

"This is going to be the best Fourth of July parade and pageant ever!" Amber climbed up on the wagon next to Dacee June.

"I do believe it will end up being one of the most memorable ones," Dacee June said.

☞ ☞ ☞

Lower Main Street swarmed with rigs, horses, kids, and decorated wagons. The Fortune wagon lined up behind the buggy that had been decorated by the Hyde Brothers Creamery and Judge Bennett's surrey.

"Mama, I have to go potty," Ninete announced.

"No you don't."

The six-year-old's round blue eyes widened. "I don't?"

"Not until after the parade, darlin'," Dacee June insisted.

"I think the icing is melting a little more," Patricia called out from the back of the wagon.

"It would last longer if you kept your finger out of it," Veronica said.

Dacee June stood to survey the assembly grounds.

"Are you lookin' for someone, Aunt Dacee June?" Little Frank asked.

"Yes."

Ninete tugged at her mother's dress. "Mama, I really have to go potty."

Little Frank pointed toward a half-collapsed log cabin by Whitewood Creek. "There's an old privy behind the Iowa boys' place."

"Mother, she can't go over there. The parade will start soon," Elita insisted.

"Some things will not wait. Come on, Little Sis, we'll hurry."

Dacee June sat Ninete to the ground, then took her hand as they trotted toward the dilapidated cabin. The privy was ten feet behind the shack. Its faded gray boards revealed cracks an inch wide.

Ninete clutched her mother's skirt. "Mama, do I have to use that?"

Dacee June opened the door. "It's the best we can do, baby."

Ninete hid behind her mother's skirt. "But it stinks in there."

Dacee June shoved the girl toward the open door. "Of course it does. It's an outhouse."

"But what if someone sees me?"

"There's no one around for a hundred yards."

The deep male voice rolled out of the ruins of the one-room log cabin. "Mrs. Toluca!"

Dacee June jumped.

Ninete screamed.

"Are you lookin' for me?"

"Mama, who is it?"

"Is that you, Mr. Justice?" Dacee June called out.

"Yes, ma'am. But I'd appreciate it if you went about your business and didn't look my way. I'd rather spot Sween's men before they spot me."

"Mama, I don't have to go. I can wait," Ninete insisted.

"Go ahead. I'll close the door."

"You wanted to see me?" Justice probed.

"Yes. Sween has men posted in most every two-story building. I think he's looking for any excuse to shoot you and your partners, then say you were threatening the governor."

"I want to find the governor for sure. And tell him what I know about Albert Sween. I was hopin' he would be in the parade."

"He's decided to skip it. He heard that Wade Justice was lying in wait for him."

"That's absurd. Why would I shoot the governor?"

"Over some court case in Pierre."

"I've never been to Pierre."

"Mama, I really, really, really don't have to go," Ninete insisted.

Dacee June held the sagging wooden door open and kept her back toward the cabin and Wade Justice. "Would you be willing to testify to the governor about what you saw Sween do?"

"As long as I have assurance that I wouldn't be arrested."

"Mama, please don't make me go in there!" Ninete sobbed.

"Baby, hurry up, we have to get back to the parade." Dacee June took a step back. "Mr. Justice, what could they arrest you for?"

His voice rolled about an octave lower than the sound of Whitewood Creek. "Never underestimate Albert Sween's power. He took over the Cooper and Ashley mine up in Canada by shooting Cooper and hiring men to testify it was Ashley who killed him. There are some men who can't be stopped unless they are dead."

Ninete clutched her mother's leg. "Mama, I can't go in there!" she sobbed.

"OK, Baby, but you have to hold it in until the parade is over." Dacee June glanced over her shoulder. "The governor and others are convinced they will make a pile of money with the Broken Boulder Mine. They aren't wanting to talk about anything until they sign those papers."

"I don't care about a gold mine," Justice said. "And I don't care how much money they lose. I want two hundred dollars for me and each one of my friends. That's what's owed us. And I want Sween to be accountable for the murder of two unarmed, shackled men."

Ninete pointed back up to the road. "Mama, the parade is about to start."

"I'll get you that safe meeting with the governor, but you have to come with us now, Mr. Justice." Dacee June slammed the outhouse door and strolled over to the shack. There was a sudden crack and a bang behind them. Both of them twirled around. The left side of the outhouse sank, then popped, then collapsed, and the privy toppled down the hill.

"Mama!" Ninete squealed. "What if I had been in there!"

"Baby, there are some thoughts too ugly to even think about." She turned back to the cabin. "Wade, are you coming with us?"

"You just said they are lyin' in wait to ambush me."

"But they won't be looking for you on the children's parade float."

"I think I'm better off out here."

"My prediction is, if you don't let me help you, by the end of this day you will either be murdered or be a murderer."

"Those aren't very good choices."

"Then ride with us on the parade float. I'll keep you out of sight and see that you get to talk to the governor."

"I don't aim to hide behind some woman's skirt."

"My word, how noble can a dead man be? Besides, you won't be hiding behind my skirt. You'll be behind Ninete's skirt."

"Who's Ninete?"

"That's me!" Ninete squealed. "And I don't have a very big skirt."

Dacee June hiked around the cabin to where the man hunched down among the collapsed logs. "Yes, give me your carbine and carry Ninete back to the wagon."

"This is crazy," he muttered.

"This is Deadwood," she replied.

Dacee June carried the Winchester '94 carbine over her shoulder as they hiked back to the parade. Wade Justice toted Ninete in his arms.

"Hurry, Mama," Elita called. "It's time to start."

"Who's carrying Ninete?" Little Frank blurted out.

"This is my friend, Mr. Wade Justice."

"You captured Wade Justice?" Little Frank blurted out.

"Shh . . . don't make a scene of it. I didn't capture him. He's a friend, and we are going to let him ride on our wagon."

"Aunt Dacee June," Amber gushed, "this is so exciting!"

Justice sat Ninete up on the wagon.

"It's likely to get more exciting," Dacee June added. She waved the carbine like a pointer. "Now, Wade, you get up there and sit on the floorboard with your back to the seat. Pull that canvas tarp up to your chin and keep your hat down. Ninete, if you stand on one side of him and Jehane on the other, no one will even know he's there. When we get to the Merchant's Hotel, we'll figure a way to scoot Mr. Justice in to talk to the governor."

"I won't go inside a building where they can trap me," he retorted as he crawled into the wagon.

"Well, I'll think of something." She handed him the gun. "Now, sit on this and don't fire it, or you'll jeopardize the children."

Dacee June plopped down between Little Frank and Amber, then plucked up the Sharps carbine.

Little Frank glanced at her, then over at Amber. "You two look like bandit queens."

"That's next year's pageant!" Amber shouted. "The Bandit Queens of the Black Hills!" She clapped her hands. "I love it!" She leaned over. "Aunt Dacee June, is that man really *the* Wade Justice?"

"Yes, he is," Dacee June whispered back.

"But he looks so . . . so . . . so normal."

"Yes, he does."

"He even looks a little better than normal, don't you think?" Amber whispered.

Dacee June studied Amber's wide eyes. "I hadn't noticed."

A canon fired from the courthouse steps at the upper part of town signaled the parade to begin. A chorus of shouts was raised all the way down to the old mill where the parade assembled. The Dakota Plains Drum Corp led off, followed by the veterans of the Grand Army of the Republic. After them came the mayor's carriage and the veterans of the Confederacy. Dacee June was not sure if all the men in either group could actually march the entire way up the gulch. Most teetered on canes. Some had crutches. The wagon crept out into the dirt street.

They rolled along and waved at the crowd for about a block, then stopped.

"What happened?" Justice grumbled.

"Everything comes to a standstill in front of Wang Fo's. He gives everyone in the parade a sweet," Amber reported.

"But it's a two-story building," Justice said.

"Little Frank, can you hold this team from bolting?" Dacee June asked.

"I reckon," he replied.

"Amber, you and me are going to do some promotion for the pageant. Crawl down, honey."

While all the children waved at Wang Fo and his big family, Dacee June turned her back to the crowd.

"Amber, glance briefly up at the second-story window of Fo's Oriental Mercantile. What do you see?"

"A man in a brown hat leaning out a window."

"Does he have a rifle?"

"Yes."

"Is it pointed at the parade?"

"Yes, it is."

"Does the window slide up and down, or swing out?"

"Up and down."

Still facing the wagon, Dacee June cocked the massive hammer of the Sharps .50 caliber single shot. She looked up at the children in the wagon. "Kids, I'm going to do a stunt. As soon as I fire this gun, you all cheer and clap, like it's part of the play."

"Good grief, Aunt Dacee June. You aren't goin' to shoot the man, are you?" Little Frank gasped.

"Trust me, dear. I just want to make a point."

Dacee June spun around and fired the Sharps. A chip of brick flew above the window. At the same moment the blast sounded, the slide window dropped down on the man. His rifle tumbled out the window. He cursed and pulled back inside.

Amber cheered and clapped. The children and the crowd followed her lead. When the noise finally died down, Amber who shouted, "This was just a preview. Don't forget, tonight at the church, a patriotic pageant all about our very own Dacee June, Queen of the Black Hills!"

"Dacee June, is everyone invited?" a man called out.

"Yes, Slackjaw, but you cannot bring your pig!"

"Dacee June's havin' a party at the church, and we're all invited!" a big woman hollered.

Dacee June climbed back into the wagon as it began to jolt along.

"Aunt Dacee June, I can't believe you did that," Little Frank moaned.

"This is so exciting!" Amber called out. "Real life is better than the pageant."

"You don't intend on shooting that carbine at every second-story man, do you?" Wade Justice asked.

"Only the ones that really deserve it," she replied.

CHAPTER NINE

The parade lunged forward, then yanked to a halt every fifty feet as the pace of the aged marching veterans began to slow. A warm Dakota wind blew in their faces. The buckskin dress stretched some in the heat, and Dacee June began to sweat. The noise of the crowd rolled north in waves. They stopped in front of a new brick two-story building where a fire had raged the year before.

The crowd cheered. The Fortune kids waved small American flags back.

Gray frosting melted under the July sun.

Dacee June hopped off the wagon. "Come on, Amber, we have more work to do!"

"Mama, are you going to do more shooting?" Jehane held her fingers in her ears.

"I hope not." She grabbed the Sharps carbine, then she and Amber strolled over to the crowd at the wooden boardwalk.

"Look," a young barefoot boy in sagging coveralls shouted, "there's Dacee June Fortune and her daughter!"

Dacee June glanced at Amber and rolled her eyes. *Daughter? She's barely ten years younger than I am! We could be sisters! And no one in Deadwood will ever learn to call me Toluca.*

Amber's green eyes flashed, and she waved her hands in enthusiasm. "We're havin' a special patriotic pageant at the church tonight! It's going to be a history, and it's called Queen of the Black Hills. Everyone is invited!"

Dacee June paced in front of the sidewalk-lined horde. "And right now, I need all of you to help me!" she shouted. "I need you to be part of a skit. I want you all to turn and look up above the awning to the open bay window in Mr. Parker's new store. Scoot out here in the street if you need to."

Two dozen people, mostly children, surrounded them.

Dacee June wrapped her arms around their shoulders. "Now let's all wave to the man with the rifle in his hand and wearing the tobacco-stained leather vest. Let's say, 'Hello, Mr. Ambush-man!'"

The man held his position and glared down at them.

"Come on, say it with me," Dacee June coached.

Like an antiphonal hymn with a well-rehearsed choir, the crowd shouted in unison, "Hello, Mr. Ambush-man!"

The unshaven man ducked back inside the building and slammed the window shut.

The wagon lurched forward as Dacee June and Amber climbed back in.

"This is like doing a play out in the street!" Amber giggled. "I love it."

"But we are making up the script as we go along," Dacee June added.

"Mama, I really, really have to go potty," Ninete whined.

"Yes, I imagine you do. When we get up to Aunt Abby's shop, you can run in there."

When they pulled up in front of the Gem Theater, Dacee June spun around to the kids in the back of the wagon.

"Come on, everyone, stand up, except you, Mr. Justice." She put her hand on the man's hat which peeked up from the green canvas tarp. "You stay down."

The children stood, circling the cake.

"I want everyone to look over at the balcony of the Gem and raise both hands straight up. Raise them high, like it was a stagecoach holdup."

"Just like scene 3!" Amber hollered.

"You have a stagecoach hold-up in the play?"

"Sure. That's when my father got killed, and you, Aunt Rebekah, and mother captured that outlaw gang."

"Oh, yes, *that* stagecoach holdup. I didn't exactly remember it that way."

"I adapted it a fudge," Amber admitted.

"Yes, you did." Dacee looked at the wagonload of kids. "OK, everyone raise your hands!"

A lady with waist-length black hair leaned against the entrance of the Gem. "What are you doin', Dacee June?" she yelled. "Prayin' for us?"

"Stella, I always pray for you, you know that. But, we're raisin' our hands because the man up there in the balcony has a gun pointed at us." Dacee June folded her hands under her chin. "Don't shoot, mister, we surrender!" she hollered. Then she stuck her hands straight up in the air.

"Oh, pppllllllllllleeeeaaaasssseeee don't shoot us!" Amber drawled.

A chorus of melodramatic pleas filtered up from the children in the wagon. Fern Trooper faked a faint and managed to collapse in Little Frank's strong arms.

Stella led the whole crowd as they surged out to stare at the man in the balcony with the rifle.

He shied back into the building.

The crowd roared.

The wagon pitched forward.

Stuart Fortune stumbled back, jammed his hand into the trunk of the giant cake, and wound up with frosting clear to his elbow.

By the time they reached Fortune & Son Hardware, Dacee June had threatened, embarrassed, and tormented eight of Albert Sween's men. Each had retreated from his position.

And Ninete had gone potty at Abby's Dress Shop.

"There's Daddy and the boys!" Jehane shouted as her short dark bangs bounced on her forehead.

Carty, Todd, Sam, and Robert reclined on a bench at the hardware. Dacee June spied Quiet Jim in the upstairs window. Even in the noise of the crowd, she cupped her hand around her ear as if to listen to him.

Quiet Jim shook his head.

Dacee June blew him a kiss.

The crowds surged around the wagon.

"You got another skit, Dacee June?" someone yelled.

"The parade's over!" she called out.

"Encore!" several yelled.

"What are we goin' to do now, Aunt Dacee June?" Amber said.

Dacee June surveyed the crowd. "Keep down Mr. Justice," she cautioned. "They are pressing closer to the wagon."

"They want another skit, Mama," Elita said. "Are there any more rascals to chase out of the second story?"

Dacee June laughed. "I think we did a good job of clearing them out."

"Maybe too good a job." Wade Justice kept down against the bulkhead of the wagon. "Dacee June, there is one thing that bothers me about your heroics."

"You are wondering where all those gunmen went to once I chased them off their perches?"

"An unseen enemy is much more dangerous than a seen one."

"Oh, don't worry. I can see them. They are all out here in this crowd."

"I'd better grab my carbine and try to make a break for it."

"You will do no such thing! I'll just bring the governor to you."

"Do it quick, cause I'm meltin' under this tarp."

"Little Frank," she said, "go into the ballroom of the Merchant's Hotel and tell the governor he's needed out here by himself."

"Me? Talk to the governor? He won't listen to me."

"Tell him you're Frank Fortune and your Grandpa is Brazos Fortune, and that your family just gathered a big crowd for him to speak to, and if he wants any chance of carrying the Black Hills in the next election, he'd better get out here. Tell the others they can stay inside."

"I can't tell him that. I'll just tell him Aunt Dacee June wants him to come out and give a speech."

"Whatever works."

She stood up and raised her hands to quiet the crowd. "Everyone! We are going to have a little encore, if you promise to come to the patriotic pageant at the church tonight. In just a minute we will have a special preview of our program tonight. Amber will lead the children in a song."

Amber spun around, her mouth open. "I will?"

"Children, stand up on the edge of the wagon and make a big circle . . ." Dacee June coached. "Now, Amber go ahead and lead them."

"What are we going to sing?" Amber said.

"How about your special version of the Dreary Black Hills?"

"You mean, with my words?" Amber giggled.

"Do it, honey. All the kids know it."

Amber Fortune propped her hands against the strong shoulders of Quintin Trooper. The crowd grew silent as she and the younger children began to sing.

Some in the crowd danced in the street.

Before the song was over, Little Frank stood beside the wagon and tugged at Dacee June's skirt. "Here's the governor. But I couldn't get him by himself. When I said I was Frank Fortune, he hustled right out. I can't believe it."

"What did I tell you? You are one of the Fortunes of the Black Hills!" Dacee June climbed down and hiked to where the governor shook hands with some in the crowd. "Mrs. Toluca, let me introduce you to Mr. Albert Sween." He pointed to the shorter, clean-shaven man who stood next to him.

She stared at the man's small, narrow gray eyes. "So, this is the man who swore out a warrant for my arrest?"

"He what?" the governor said.

Sween backed into the crowd. "It was a mistake. It's all taken care of now. I've dropped the charges," he mumbled.

Dacee June took the politician's arm. "Governor, you'll need to get up on the wagon and sit, so you'll be ready to speak."

"As I told you, Mrs. Fortune, I didn't really plan on a speech."

"Oh, come on, Governor, this is a wonderful opportunity to shore up your support. What an image. You will not be surrounded by politicians for once, but flag-waving children. It would make a wonderful reelection campaign poster, don't you think?"

The governor glanced over at Sween. "She's right about that."

"You get out in that crowd, and you'll be an easy target," Sween warned.

"I'm sure he'll be safe," Dacee June said. "Your men are scattered throughout the crowd, Mr. Sween. They are there for the governor's protection, aren't they?"

"Certainly!" Sween muttered.

The governor stared at the swelling horde. "My word, I don't think there are any ambushes in the Black Hills today."

With the children singing in the background, Dacee June took the governor's arm and tugged him toward the front of the wagon. "You have heard of the discontent of the miners," she whispered in his ear.

The white-haired governor stiffened his back. "Discontent? My heavens, I hadn't heard."

Dacee June turned to the man trailing them. "You'll need to wait here, Mr. Sween."

"Yes, I do need to make this speech alone."

"But you haven't signed the papers," Sween protested.

"Time enough later. Now it's time for a speech."

"At least let me stand beside you as a bodyguard," Sween shouted.

Dacee June stared at the man in the top hat. "Mr. Sween, I have two .44 pistols and a .50 caliber Sharps. I think the governor will be well protected."

"Having protection from one of the legendary Fortunes of the Black Hills, like Mrs. Toluca, is all the protection anyone needs." He patted her arm. "I do know your name, young lady."

As the children continued to sing in the background, the governor climbed up into the wagon.

Dacee June followed him, then studied the men in the crowd. *Lord, I've been working to do the right thing. How can I get things so messed up? Not only is Wade Justice in the line of fire, but so is every grandchild of Brazos Fortune. This isn't good, Lord. I really, really do need you to provide.*

She scooted over to the governor, who watched Amber Fortune. "Don't look back, Governor. But Wade Justice is the man under the tarp straight behind you in the wagon."

"My word, is he going to shoot me?"

"Not hardly. He wants to tell you a few things about Albert Sween. Smile and look out at the crowd but listen to him."

"What is the meaning of this?"

"Just listen to him, Governor."

As the governor hunkered down, Dacee June stood and joined in the singing. When they finished "The Dreary Black Hills," she had Amber lead them in "Shenandoah."

Toward the end of the song, she leaned over to the governor. "Did you hear enough?"

"My word, if that is true, Albert Sween should be arrested immediately."

"It's time for your speech," she reminded him.

When the song finished, Dacee June quieted the crowd. "And now here's the governor of the great state of South Dakota!" she announced.

When the governor stood, the children sat. Dacee June motioned for Amber to shield Justice on the west side, as she did the east.

Within seconds, the governor shouted out a spellbinder. Wade Justice leaned close to Dacee June. "Mrs. Toluca, you succeeded in gettin' me surrounded."

"And I got you a talk with the governor."

"That don't matter a whole lot if I'm dead. They aren't goin' to let me out of this wagon."

"I have a plan," she mumbled.

"Good, 'cause if they come after me, I'm goin' to grab this carbine and start shootin' back."

Dacee June pulled Amber over and whispered in her ear.

Soon the whispers spread to each member of the Fortune clan.

When the governor came to a rousing conclusion, Dacee June shoved Ninete to his side. "Wave your flag, darlin'!"

Ninete waved the flag.

The governor beamed.

The crowd cheered.

In the Badlands, someone shot off a China rocket.

Then all the Fortune and Trooper children jammed their fingers into the gooey frosting at the bottom of the cake and lifted it straight up about two feet.

"Free elephant cake tonight after the patriotic program!" Dacee June hollered. The children put the cake back down. Dacee June helped the governor off the wagon. "Keep Sween inside the Merchant's, and don't sign the papers," she told him.

"But what about Justice?" the governor asked.

"Just wait for me." *That's the story of mankind on this earth, isn't it, Lord? What about justice?* "I'll bring him over to confront Mr. Sween as soon as I lose his men."

Little Frank crawled back up on the wagon. "Where to now?"

"Drive the rig to the back of the church to unload the cake," Dacee June instructed.

"Looks like we didn't lose all the crowd." Little Frank nodded to four of Sween's men who trailed along fifty feet behind the wagon.

"What are they doing?" Amber asked.

"I suppose at least one of them spied someone under the tarp from the second story. They aim to find out who he is," Dacee June said.

"Mama, my hands are sticky," Jehane called out.

"Everyone's hands are sticky. We'll all wash up at the church, darlin'."

Little Frank pulled up close to the raised wooden backdoor steps of the church. "How are we goin' to get that cake downstairs? It's 175 pounds heavier now."

"We'll need help," she announced.

Sween's men stopped at the edge of the church property. The sticky-fingered children leaped off the wagon.

Dacee June leaned over to Amber. "Toss that tarp out to show we aren't hiding anyone under it." She hopped off the wagon and hiked straight at the men.

All four men carried rifles in their hands and stiffened as she approached, the bullet belts still across her chest, the Sharps carbine in her hand.

"Did you men need something?" she demanded.

"No ma'am, we're jist . . ." the tallest stammered.

"We're jist lookin' at that cake," one with a tobacco-stained vest added.

"Ain't never seen one like it before."

"I need your help," she announced.

"What? You shot at me down at the Chinaman's market and now you want me to help you?"

"Nonsense. I shot at the windowsill above your head."

"And you got the crowd laughing at me," he glared.

Dacee June flipped her head back to get her bangs off her forehead. "Some actors would have been thrilled with that acclaim."

"We ain't no actors," he said.

"You did very well. I appreciate your going along with the skit. It will help attendance at our pageant. You saw how enthusiastic the crowd was."

"You mean, it was all just play-acting?"

"Certainly. You don't think I'm really out to get you, do you?"

"Theron said you was a crazy woman."

"Nonsense. You boys are very good actors. Did you ever think about hooking up with Buffalo Bill Cody? He has a wonderful show."

The heavyset man scratched behind his ear. "I thought about it one time when I was in jail."

"You see? I knew it. Now, could I get you to help with the cake? It's very heavy, as you can imagine, and I need to take it downstairs at the church. You see what a mess the children made when they tried to lift it."

"We ain't cake-lifters," the tall one protested.

"Oh, you don't have to stick your fingers in it. Just grab that wooden stretcher under it and tote it down the stairs."

"We cain't stop our work to carry cake."

"Your work? I thought you worked at the Broken Boulder? Didn't I see you out there yesterday?"

"Yep."

"And my brothers and I disarmed and chased off those ambushers who were shooting at you?"

"I reckon you did. But you sent our guns down the bucket."

"That's because we didn't know who you were at the time. We were being cautious. But I would think you could help me carry a cake down the stairs," she said.

"Lady, you just humiliated us and turned the crowd against us, and now you want us to carry a cake?"

"That would be very nice of you."

"I can't believe this!" the fattest man moaned.

"Yes, it is a very unusual cake," she said.

"Unusual cake? It is you that is crazy. Theron is right. Come on, boys, let's go find Sween. There ain't nothin' here but a bunch of kids, a crazy woman, and a armadillo cake in that wagon." The four men plodded back down Main Street.

"Armadillo? It's an elephant cake," Dacee June mumbled.

She turned and hiked toward the others.

Patricia and Veronica sidled up next to her. "Aunt Dacee June, what did you say to those men to chase them off?"

"I asked them to come help us carry the cake downstairs."

A man's deep voice filtered up from under cake. "You did what?"

☞ ☞ ☞

After helping Wade Justice extricate himself from the hardware cloth cavern under the cake, Dacee June helped get the big cake, and the gunman, to the church basement.

"You said you had a plan to get me out of this jam," Justice grumbled as he wiped gray frosting off his boots.

"I got you out, didn't I?"

"I need to confront Sween face-to-face, you know that."

"I'll figure something. Just stay down here with the children until I come back for you."

"Where's my carbine?"

"It's under the steps by the back door. I'd rather you didn't have it in the church."

"I feel naked."

"I assure you, you aren't. There are at least eight armed men still out there who will shoot you on sight. Wade, I've worked very hard to keep you alive, so don't jeopardize that now."

"Do you think the governor believes me?"

"I think so."

"Men have gotten killed when they 'thought' something that turned out wrong."

"I don't intend this to be one of those times," she declared.

☛ ☛ ☛

When Dacee June reached the hardware store, Carty and her brothers sat on a long bench in the shade on the boardwalk. Each one ate a thin slice of watermelon.

"I can't believe this . . ." she mumbled.

"It's our annual Fourth of July watermelon seed-spittin' contest," Carty explained.

"Do you know what I just went through?"

"We saw them trail you," Sammy said. "We were just headin' down there when you turned them around."

"We figured if we stormed down there they would really think something was wrong," Robert said.

"Besides, you did tell me this was something you wanted to do on your own," Carty added.

"So you sat up here and spit seeds?"

"It seemed innocent at the time." Robert shot a seed halfway across Main Street.

"Was the man on the wagon Wade Justice?" Sammy asked.

"What man on the wagon?" Carty said. "I didn't see any man on the wagon. Did you, Bobby?"

"Yep. What did you do with him, Lil' Sis?" Robert asked.

"I smuggled him in the cake."

"In the cake?" Todd spat two seeds far out into the street.

"It's hollow, hardware cloth and plaster lathes. The cake is only about a foot thick. When the kids lifted it up, he slid underneath."

"I didn't see any man on the wagon," Carty muttered. "Why didn't I see him?"

"He's not still in the cake, is he?" Robert pressed.

"He's waiting for me to find a way to get him out of the church basement and over to the governor."

"You want us to transport him?" Sam asked.

"There would be gunfire for sure," Dacee June cautioned. "There must be another way."

Carty shot a seed halfway out into the middle of Main Street. "You'd have thought I would have seen a man riding on the wagon."

"I have to think of a way to get Sween away from the governor," she said.

"Why?" Sam challenged. "I don't think Sween is the threat. It's those eight gunmen. Take care of them, and you can march Justice right into that meetin'." He shot a seed that sailed right over the top of a man on a bay horse.

"Where's the sheriff? He said he'd keep an eye on Sween for me," Dacee June said.

"There was a shootin' right before the parade started."

"Who got shot?"

"Oakes," Todd replied.

"The cook at the Broken Boulder? Who shot him?"

"The only witnesses were a couple of Sween's men. They swore it was some of the Justice bunch. The sheriff and two deputies went out to their camp to arrest them," Robert said.

"Is the cook dead?"

"No, but he isn't in good shape."

"They said it was Justice who shot the cook," Carty added.

"Wade Justice didn't shoot anyone before the parade. He was with me."

Carty swallowed some seeds and pulp. "What do you mean he was with you?"

"Ninete and I found him next to the privy."

"What?" Carty exclaimed. This time a black seed sailed three-quarters of the way across the street.

"Boys, Sammy's right. I need to get Sween's men rounded up and out of the way before I can do anything else."

"You want us to sit on them until you get the deal with Sween figured out?" Sam quizzed.

"Yes."

"But we aren't supposed to shoot them?" Robert said.

"Heavens, no. Sween's the real villain. They are just mercenaries."

"I reckon," Robert said, "we could feed them all elephant cake. I do believe that would slow them down."

"I'm serious, Bobby."

"And I'm serious, Lil' Sis. The town is crowded with people and we got eight shootists roamin' the streets. It can't be done without firin' a shot."

"I think it can be done with three or four men and Lil' Sis," Sam reported.

Dacee June sidled up to Sam. "You have a plan?"

"I always have a plan, Sis."

"How long will it take?" she pressed.

"It depends on how fast it takes Dacee June Toluca to spread a rumor across the Dead Line."

"Give me five minutes and three contacts. After that, everyone in town will know in less than fifteen minutes."

"I suppose that means suspendin' the seed-spittin' contest," Todd declared.

Sam shoved his hat back. "Just temporarily."

"I believe I was winning," Carty bragged.

Dacee June grabbed Carty's piece of watermelon and ripped off a bite with her teeth. She ate the pulp and wiped her lips on her fingertips. With a wild flip of her head that caused her long hair to sail straight in front of her, she launched a seed entirely across Main Street.

"There, I won," she announced. "Let's hear Sammy's plan."

Carty stared at the street. "You never told me you could do that."

"You never asked."

☞ ☞ ☞

It took Dacee June ten minutes to tell Skeeter, Beano Billy, and Rutt Mangin that there was a rumor that Wade Justice was cornered in the Montana Livery. By the time she drove the rig back up Main Street she could see a couple of Albert Sween's men working their way through the crowd toward the back street livery. She parked the team by the water trough and scurried toward the door.

"What's Little Frank doing here?" she asked.

"He figured it was time to take his place," Robert said.

"I'm nineteen," he offered.

"What did your mother say?"

Robert shrugged. "Jamie Sue is busy with all the children. We didn't think we should bother her."

"Besides, Daddy gave him the Sharps. Remember?" Sam added. "And we figured any stand the Fortunes make should include that .50 caliber carbine."

"They are on their way," Dacee June reported.

"Then you better get out there and play your part, Lil' Sis," Sam instructed.

"Are you sure this is safe?" Carty pressed.

"It's just like ol' times," Todd replied.

"No," Sam said. "It will never be like ol' times unless we have that ol' man down here with us."

"He would love it," Robert said.

"I still don't see how this will work," Carty mumbled.

"No problem, as long as we don't get more than one or two at a time," Sam said. "That will be up to Lil' Sis."

Carty walked her to the door. "Darlin', this is crazy. The boys of Texas Camp of '76 are almost gone. We got law and order now."

"Carty, that's why we have to do it. This is the last day of the Texas Camp. And all of us know it."

"That's what Bobby said. I'm a Toluca, darlin'. Sometimes I just don't think like a Fortune."

She hugged his waist. "And you don't have to. Just be my Carty."

She left the men in the barn and hiked out to the team. Dacee June loosened the crossed bullet belts and tossed the holsters and guns in the front seat of the wagon. She watered the team of long-legged brown horses and was brushing them down when four of Sween's men rounded the corner, then halted when they spied her.

"What are you doin' here?" the heaviest of the men challenged. "I thought you was at the church."

"I have to put the team away. What are you doin' here?"

"We, eh, heard . . . this was . . . eh, we got business inside," the short one with a thick black mustache mumbled.

"Don't go in there," she cautioned.

One with a tobacco-stained vest pulled off his hat and ran his hand through his greasy hair. "What did you say?"

"My brother Sam has a man cornered in the back of the barn. He said not to let anyone in. Bullets could be flying at any minute, and he didn't want anyone hurt."

A sandy blond-headed man pulled out his revolver and spun the chamber. "He's got Justice cornered?"

"I'm not supposed to say what's going on. Only that if someone burst through that door, there's a real good chance a man could get shot."

"He ain't goin' to get our reward," the heavy man insisted.

"There's a reward?" she asked.

"It ain't for just anyone. We get Justice and we all get a $300 bonus. The one that shoots him gets an extra $500," the short man insisted.

"So we ain't waitin'," another declared.

"Do you really want to barge in on Sam Fortune with his gun cocked?" she said.

They stared at one another. "No, I reckon we don't, but we jist can't stay out here and wait for him to collect," the sandy blond replied.

She waved them closer. "Boys, let me tell you something. If you go through that hay window on the side, you could probably slip in unnoticed."

"Why are you doin' us a favor?" the shortest man sneered.

"Because you were good sports for the skit on Main Street, and I'm worried about Sammy. He might need some help. You've heard the rumors about Wade Justice, haven't you?"

"Heard 'em? Shoot, ma'am, we started most of them." The greasy-haired man jammed his hat back on.

"I don't think you should all go in at once. Justice would spot you before your eyes got adjusted. Too much commotion."

"Maybe we'll jist slip in one at a time," the heavy man declared.

"That's a good plan! But it really would be safer if you just stayed out here."

"We ain't goin' to lose out on that reward."

"Be careful, boys. This is too nice a day for anyone to get shot. And please don't shoot my brother. He's just tryin' to help capture that dangerous gunman."

Dacee June stayed by the water trough as the tallest man hunkered down and sprinted toward the window. He swung open the top-hinged door and slipped into the barn.

One at a time, Sammy. You should be able to handle that easy enough.

A hand stuck out the doorway and signaled for the next man.

Carty Toluca, that's you! I know that hand. Why didn't you let Sammy do that?

The second man trotted to the barn and crawled through.

Again a hand came out and signaled another.

Maybe this is Carty's initiation as well as Little Frank's. Keep them all safe, Lord.

It took less than two minutes for all four to disappear into the barn. Dacee June had just turned back to the wagon when two more of Sween's men circled the building.

One had a long, drooping mustache. "What are you doin' here?" he growled.

"Watering my team and saving lives."

"Saving lives?" the other asked.

"There's a gunfight going on in that barn. Don't get too close."

The one with the drooping mustache cocked his ear toward the huge barn. "I don't hear anything."

"You open that front door and with any luck you'll hear the shot that kills you," she insisted. "My brother, Sam, is in there. He's got a gang pinned down, and he said not to let anyone in."

"A gang? He has all of that Justice bunch in there?"

"He didn't want me to tell anyone about it."

"He's tryin' to get the reward for himself!"

"I don't think he knows anything about a reward. But he might could use your help. Just don't go bargin' into bullets. That won't help him a bit."

"Maybe you could call him and tell him we're comin' in."

"And let Justice know too? You boys would be sitting ducks. I wouldn't do that to you. I know. I'll use our secret code."

"Secret code?" the mustached one replied.

Dacee June stuck two fingers in her mouth and let loose with two eardrum-piercing whistles.

"That's a secret code?"

"You wait . . . look! He's waving you in." She pointed to the hand signaling them from the barn door. "Be careful, boys. And remember, it will take you a minute or two to get your eyes used to the dark. So those first few seconds inside are crucial."

"Thanks for your help, lady."

"Don't mention it."

She heard what sounded like dual axe handles crack moments after the two men entered the barn.

A tall, lanky man crept around the corner of the alley, and Dacee June flagged him closer.

"They are in the barn," she declared.

"Who's in the barn?"

"Your pals."

"All of them?"

"How many of them are there?" she asked.

"Eight, but Theron went over to tell Mr. Sween about Justice being cornered."

"There are six in the barn. They told me to send you right in."

He looked her up and down. "Just barge in?"

"Keep your head low, and you'll be safe. You better hurry before you miss out on the excitement."

He pulled off his hat and scratched his head. "Let me get this straight. That Wade Justice bunch, the Oklahoma legend Sam Fortune, and six of us gunslingers hired by ol' man Sween are ready for a shoot-out?"

"Yes. Doesn't it sound exciting?"

He shoved his black felt hat back on his head. "It sounds riskier than a lighted phosphorus match in a dynamite factory. I ain't goin' in there. A man could get killed."

"A very astute observation." *Why does this one have to be a thinking bushwhacker?* Dacee June cocked her head sideways and squinted her eyes. "Do you think they'll share the reward with you, even if you hunker out here and are afraid to go inside?"

"Did you know your nose wrinkles when you squint your eyes like that."

"What?" she stammered.

"It's kind of purdy, though."

"I . . . I . . . I . . ." *Is he flirting with me?*

"Besides, that reward ain't all that much. Say, are you married?" A dimpled grin broke across his unshaven, unbathed face.

"Yes, I am. I can see you get distracted easy. You must not want that reward because you have all the money you want." *I've got to get this man inside! This conversation is getting absurd.*

"I ain't got no money at all, but I got breath in these bones. I don't intend to squander that. Say, do you like to dance?"

"I told you I am married. So you aren't going into the barn?"

"But you jist look like a gal who could really cut a smooth path on the dance floor. And, no, ma'am, I have no intention of goin' in that barn. I'll wait right here in case someone tries to escape. That way you and me can keep visitin'. I saw you out at the mine, you know."

"Then you met my husband and brothers."

"I didn't actually meet them. But I seen them boot those Justice men off the mesa. You got one tough family. It's surprisin' with such a background that you turned out so sweet and purdy."

She froze in place. "What was that?"

He held his hand to his ear. "What?"

"I heard something in the barn. You'd better check it out."

He held his rifle to his chin and pointed the gun at the barn door. "I think I'll wait right here."

This is getting absurd. Mister, get in the barn! "Is that Theron's '92 Winchester Trapper?"

"Nope, this is my carbine. I cut the barrel down to nineteen inches."

"Why?"

"'Cause I dropped it in the creek and the water froze. The next time I shot it, the end of the barrel peeled back like a banana."

"Does it shoot straight still?"

"Not real straight, but I reckon at this distance I can hit a man."

"My husband repairs guns. He can rebore it so it shoots straight."

"Are you serious?"

"It all depends on what the bore is like. Let me see it," she said.

"What?"

"Take out the bullet and let me see the bore," she commanded.

He dropped the lever and pulled out the bullet, then handed her the gun.

Dacee June stuck her thumb in the chamber and her eye to the barrel as she let the daylight reflect off her thumbnail.

"What do you think?" he asked.

"I think you have yourself a headache," she declared.

"The bore's that bad, huh?"

"No, I'm afraid that's the least of your worries."

With two hands on the buttstock of the gun, Dacee June cracked the barrel across the man's forehead. He slumped motionless to the ground. *I do appreciate the compliments, mister, but I just couldn't wait any longer.*

She marched to the barn. "OK, boys, number seven is by the water trough. Come out and tote him inside."

Carty and Sammy stepped out into the light.

"You had to get in on the action, Lil' Sis?" Sam laughed.

"I couldn't get that one within ten feet of the barn."

"Come on, Carty, let's tote him in with the others. How about number eight?"

Dacee June walked with them back to the unconscious man. "Good ol' Theron went over to tell Sween the good news about trapping Justice. You think he'll head over here?"

Sam grabbed the down man's legs. "Wouldn't you if you were him?"

"Sammy, I find it inconceivable to imagine being someone like Theron."

"I don't," Sam mumbled. "He'll be here. When he shows up, send him in."

Dacee June hiked out to the street. Theron lumbered toward her.

"I'm glad to see you got your Trapper back," she greeted.

"No thanks to you," he growled.

"Your pals are all in the barn dreamin' of a big reward," she said. "I think you missed out on everything."

"What did you say?"

"On second thought, don't go into the barn. There's been a violent confrontation. Maybe it's all over now."

"I hope so," he mumbled, "'cause we got to get over to help Sween. Them rich boys are tryin' to back out of buyin' the mine."

Theron took off on a trot to the front of the barn. He didn't even look back when she put her fingers to her mouth and let loose with one shrill whistle.

There was a crack.

Then a thud.

Carty was the first to stroll out. "I'm not sure your daddy would have done it quite that way."

Little Frank shoved the big door open and trotted out. "You ought to see it, Aunt Dacee June. Eight men coldcocked and hog-tied. Uncle Todd and Daddy have 'em stacked like cordwood in a stall."

"Those two were always very neat," she said.

Sam sauntered out with a wide grin. "Does Parker's sorrel horse still bite?"

"I believe so," she replied.

"Those boys are in for a little nippin'. We packed them in the sorrel's stall," Sam said.

Robert marched out. "That was almost too easy. We decided the Fortune gang might be the meanest in the Dakotas."

"Mean?" Dacee June grinned. "The only mean thing you boys ever did was tie me in Wilson Creek wearin' nothing but my long johns."

Todd ambled out and closed the barn door.

Little Frank's chin dropped. "They did?"

"I believe she was six at the time and had just spent the afternoon shovin' mud in all our gun barrels," Sam replied.

"I didn't know better."

"Dacee June?" Todd challenged.

"OK, I did know better. But that was mean of you. If Mrs. Speaker and Mrs. Driver hadn't come along and rescued me, I could have taken the ague."

"In a shallow crick in August in Texas?" Robert challenged.

"It was mean."

Todd stared across the gulch at the Mount Moriah Cemetery. "Texas is a long time back."

"I don't suppose we can call ourselves the Texas Camp," Robert replied.

"Nope. Where to now, Lil' Sis?" Sam quizzed.

"I want to get Wade Justice at the church and take him over to the Merchant's Hotel to confront Albert Sween."

"How 'bout the five of us?" Sam asked.

Dacee June led them back out to Main Street. "Sween is expecting his posse to rescue him."

"That's what I was thinkin'," Sam said.

"The sun's getting low. This day's about over. I'll check on Daddy on the way to the church," Dacee June said.

"I'll see if the sheriff made it back," Todd said.

Little Frank slipped the Sharps carbine across his shoulders. "I can't wait to tell Mama what we did!"

Robert shook his head. "Now that, son, is somethin' you should save up and do next time I'm in Rapid City."

☞ ☞ ☞

"I don't see why I can't carry my carbine." Wade Justice took long strides beside Dacee June as they walked along the sidewalk of upper Main Street.

"If you go barging into that meeting packing a weapon, no one is going to believe your testimony. If the governor's men don't shoot you on sight, Sween will. Then he'll proclaim himself the hero who saved the governor's life."

"They aren't going to believe me anyway," Justice muttered.

"I believe you."

"Yeah, and I don't know why. I did lie and swindle you. I could be doin' it again."

"But you aren't. You were right, Wade Justice. I can size up a man in thirty seconds."

"And I pass the test?"

"Yes, so don't do anything to let me down."

"I'm not goin' to let them arrest me on something I didn't do."

"Why would anyone try that?"

"You don't know Albert Sween."

"True enough. But I won't let them arrest you."

"How do you intend on stoppin' them?"

"Can you really conceive of a man not backin' down when I point your carbine at them?" she challenged.

"No, I guess not. How's your daddy?"

"What?"

"Your daddy? I do care, you know."

She looked at the man's piercing brown eyes. "Daddy'll be in glory by the time the fireworks go off in Deadwood tonight."

"How do you know that?"

"The Lord laid it on my heart."

They waited at the corner while a hack trotted past them.

"You Fortunes are religious people, aren't you?" he said.

"We trust Jesus as our Lord and Savior, if that's what you mean."

"I reckon so. Never had much use for it myself."

Dacee June stopped in the middle of the street and turned toward Justice. "What in the world does that mean? I've heard that all my life, and it's the dumbest thing I've ever heard. You have no need for the Lord?"

Justice stepped back and surveyed the street. "Don't take it so personal."

"I'm not taking it personal. But let me understand. You do not need the sun to shine or the rain to fall? You don't need God to provide for the seeds to grow or your body to get nourishment? You don't need the strength to get up tomorrow? You don't need anyone to forgive you of your sins? You don't need to be loved, even when you don't deserve it? You don't need justice meted out against Albert Sween?"

Wade Justice chuckled.

"What are you laughin' at, Wade Justice?"

"You are quite the exhorter, Dacee June."

"Did it do any good?"

"I learned never to bring up a theological proposition when you are around."

"That's all?"

"Until today I charted my own course and never trusted anyone with my life. Now, this makes at least the third time in twenty-four hours that I've let myself do foolish things because of you. Why do you suppose that is?"

"Probably my charm and handsome features," she offered, then led him across the street.

He rubbed his unshaven chin. "No, that isn't it."

"Hah!" She turned and slugged his arm.

Justice started to laugh.

"Forgive me, Wade, that was much too familiar. I must learn to be friendly, not familiar."

They paused on the front steps of the Merchant's Hotel. This time his voice was so soft it was almost inaudible. "I've learned one thing today."

"Oh?"

"That Mr. Carty Toluca is a mighty lucky man."

"And I learned one thing today," she countered in a whisper.

"I have a feelin' I'm not goin' to like this."

"I learned that Wade Justice is a handsome, sweet-talkin' drifter whom I will probably have to shoot some day."

He was still laughing as they shoved open the ballroom door. Their boot heels on the hardwood floor caused all talking in the room to cease.

"My word, you captured the murderer!" Sween called out. "Splendid work, Mrs. Toluca!" He reached in his coat pocket.

"Governor, would you relieve Mr. Sween of his sneak gun?" Dacee June called out.

"What is the meaning of this!" Sween hollered. "I most certainly won't surrender my weapon."

Dacee June cocked the carbine and aimed it at Sween's head. "I think you will."

The governor took the small revolver.

"This is an outrage. Governor, I never suspected you of being a party to such trumped-up charges."

"Sween," Wade Justice shouted. "You defrauded the U.S. government and shot and killed two shackled prisoners. And who knows how you are trying to swindle the governor and these men. Nothing we do can be a bigger outrage than that."

"Surely you don't believe a convict?" Sween paced in front of the big table. "Everyone knows the dastardly crimes this man has committed."

"We all know the lies you've spread about him," Dacee June corrected.

"No court will ever take this man's word over that of Albert Sween!"

"I'm just a little confused about all this," the governor mumbled.

The doors swung open, and the sheriff strolled in. "I've got Justice's men over at the jail," he announced.

"Good work, sheriff," Sween hollered. "Here's the murderer himself. He must be imprisoned immediately as well."

"I didn't say I had them in jail. They are over there where they can give testimony to Judge Bennett concerning certain crimes of Albert Sween. They have quite an interesting story to tell."

"What? I'm being shanghaied! I refuse to let this happen. No camp of frontier dolts can stop Albert P. Sween!" He turned toward the back door of the ballroom. "Men!" he shouted. "Come in here!"

259

The door swung open, and five armed men marched in. Four had handguns drawn; the fifth packed a .50 caliber Sharps carbine.

"Who are these men?" Sween called out.

Dacee June stepped up next to the governor. "The brown-eyed man with the square jaw and no hat is my husband, Carty Toluca. I believe you might know my brothers, Todd, Sam, and Robert. And the handsome young man with the dimpled grin and big-bore carbine is my nephew, Little Frank."

"But what happened to my men?" Sween shrieked.

"They are resting at the livery stable," Carty replied.

"I believe some of them might also want to talk to Judge Bennett as well," Dacee June said. "I'm sure they don't want to be tried for two murders that Albert Sween committed."

"Well, this certainly ruins the sale of the gold mine. I have no intentions of selling it to people who cast such aspersion on my character! This is a scandal!" Sween fumed.

"I've got a question about your mine, Mr. Sween," Carty announced. "Why are you hauling ore from down at Spearfish Canyon clear up to the mine?"

"I don't know what you are talking about!"

"Quint and I rode the oar carts down to Spearfish Canyon and back up again. The oar was being hauled up to the mine. That tram was built to haul ore out of the mine. So, why are you putting dirt back into that mine?"

Sween prowled around the table. "That's absurd. This is a conspiracy!"

"I was thinkin' the same thing," the sheriff replied.

"Are you goin' to arrest someone or not!" Sween shouted.

"I reckon I will. Mr. Sween, you are under arrest for attempted fraud, conspiracy, and suspicion of murder."

"I've got San Francisco attorneys who will have your job for this!" Sween shouted.

"They can have my job tomorrow. Actually, tonight would be best. I've been tryin' to get out of it for years!" the sheriff announced.

☞ ☞ ☞

The long line of armed men followed Dacee June out into the street and walked with her back to the church. Elita was the first to greet them. "Mama! Daddy! Guess what? Amber changed the play!"

Carty pulled out his pocket watch. "But the play is only two hours away."

"But we're goin' to have this wonderful new ending!"

Jehane ran up to the group. "There is going to be a parade on stage. We need the cake on stage at the finale."

Dacee June unfastened the top button at the neck of the buckskin dress. "That is the most worn-out cake ever baked."

Ninete skipped over to her mother. "Guess what the name of the play is now?"

"No more Queen of the Black Hills?" Dacee June probed.

"No!" Ninete replied. "It's going to be called, 'Last of the Texas Camp'!"

Dacee June hugged Ninete's shoulder. "I think that's a wonderful title!"

Amber scooted through the front door. "Come on, girls, we need to practice." She glanced over at the row of men. "Little Frank, quit playing and bring Grandpa Brazos's Sharps. You have to tell me what happened at the livery. Uncle Bobby, will you tell Aunt Jamie Sue we'll need some sandwiches and lemonade brought here since we have to work right through supper? Uncle Todd, tell Aunt Rebekah we'll need a long coat for Hank, after all. He's goin' to be the narrator. I just wrote a narrator's part."

"You've been busy." Dacee June prodded her girls toward the church steps.

Amber glanced over at Sam Fortune. "Daddy, you have to figure out how we can roll that cake out on the stage. I think there might be a dolly of some sort at the depot, and tell Mama that I will need her to sing 'Good-bye at the Door' after all. I'm sure her voice can hold out for that."

"I'll get the dolly," Sam replied. "But you talk to your Mama about singing. I'm no fool."

"Tell Mama I need to see her at the church. Aunt Dacee June, you can't wear your buckskin dress tonight. Your blue pleated dress with the white lace will be nice. And you might want to do a little something with your hair."

Amber swooped over and gathered up Ninete, Elita, and Jehane and sashayed back into the church. Little Frank trudged behind.

Dacee June glanced at her husband and her brothers. "Don't say it!"

A wide grin broke across Sam Fortune's face. "Don't say what?"

"I know what all of you are thinking!"

They walked five across back toward the hardware store, Dacee June in the middle.

"Lil' Sis seems a little touchy," Todd chided.

"Don't you start on me!" she countered.

"Probably just female problems . . ." Bobby added.

"Carty, they are picking on me!" she pouted.

"Darlin', you got to admit that Amber is turnin' out to be your twin sister."

"At least you didn't call her my daughter."

"I don't reckon I've ever seen two gals more alike that aren't twins," Robert added.

They all paused in front of the hardware store.

"To be honest, it felt good for all of us to tackle that Sween gang today," she said. "It's the first afternoon I haven't been consumed with Daddy in six months."

Robert put his arm across her shoulder. "Not one of the old timers was with us."

"Things are changin', boys," Todd said.

Sam jerked his narrow black tie off and jammed it in his vest pocket. "And what with Amber takin' the lead with social activities, we are all changing."

"Listen!" Dacee June called out.

All five stood still.

Dacee June locked her left hand into Carty's and her right hand into Bobby's.

It was a weak, halting, tenor's voice. "'Tis grace hath brought me safe thus far, and grace will lead me home."

"Finally," Sam sighed.

"He's at home now," Todd said.

Robert pulled off his hat and wiped his eyes. "With Mama."

Carty held her tight. "Are you all right, darlin'?"

Dacee June stared up at the open window, the taste of salty tears on her lips. "Sammy, you go get Dr. Kendrickson. He'll need to sign the death certificate. Todd, go get Mr. Rinaldi, the undertaker. Bobby, you and Carty will need to help Quiet Jim get home. I'll see that Daddy is decent, then I'll phone Rebekah, Abby, and Jamie Sue. We should all meet at the church and tell the children together."

She took a deep breath, then threw her shoulders back. "And sometime before that program tonight, I have to do something with my hair."

263

Look for the story of Brazos's grandson Frank in
Book Six
FORTUNES OF THE BLACK HILLS
The Next Roundup